Ron Ellis was at Liverpo
involved in the Merseyb
records from America for The Beatles, ran an entertainment agency and finally took to the stage himself as a DJ touring the country with his own disco roadshow. He was eventually appointed Promotions Manager for Warner Bros Records and made the New Wave charts with his own band and a song he himself had written. In 1992 the *Sun* acclaimed him as the man with the most jobs in Britain: eleven in total, including that of lecturer, librarian, sales manager, DJ, actor (he has appeared in *Coronation Street* and *Brookside*), journalist, landlord – and author!

Ron still lives on Merseyside with his wife and two daughters. He currently works on local radio and reports on Southport FC matches for the press.

EARS OF THE CITY is his first novel featuring DJ, and part-time Private Eye, Johnny Ace.

Also by Ron Ellis and available from Headline

Mean Streets

Ears of the City

Ron Ellis

First published in 1998
by HEADLINE BOOK PUBLISHING

First published in paperback in 1998
by HEADLINE BOOK PUBLISHING

10 9 8 7 6 5 4 3 2 1

ISBN 0 7472 5942 9

Printed and bound in Great Britain by
Clays Ltd, St Ives plc

HEADLINE BOOK PUBLISHING
A division of Hodder Headline PLC
338 Euston Road
London NW1 3BH

For Sue, Karen and Nikki.

Chapter One

Matt Scrufford's ears were posted to his father in a Jiffy bag. Not something that you'd want to open first thing in the morning over your Shredded Wheat. The rest of him turned up a few days later at the bottom of the Huskisson Dock.

I first read about it in the *Daily Post* whilst I was having breakfast at the ground-floor café in the Royal Liver Building. They call it The Diner. It's a handy place for me, just down the road from my flat in Waterloo Dock. I can be there quicker than burning my own toast.

Not many people know about the café but they do an excellent bacon sandwich and when you look through the tinted vaulted ceiling at the glass-sided offices shimmering into the sky, you'd swear you were in New York, not Liverpool.

Being below several storeys of offices, The Diner's clientele consists mainly of dark suits and their secretaries from the eight floors of offices above. Sitting there somedays in a double-breasted pinstripe, I feel like I'm in a staff canteen and should be selling insurance like everybody else.

The ears were the front-page headlines in the *Post*. I was curious. Scrufford wasn't a common name but I'd known a Mally Scrufford back in the sixties when we'd played together in a group called The Cruzads, hoping to be the next Beatles. He was the lead singer and the one all the girls fancied. Could he be any relation?

I read the article. The police were not releasing too

many details except the boy was nineteen, attended John Moores University and lived intermittently with his family in Woolton. No motive for the murder had yet been discovered.

The ears had arrived at the father's house last Saturday morning although the paper didn't say whether they had been accompanied by a ransom note, which I would have thought was the likeliest scenario.

But how would that explain the body turning up five days later? Had they called the police, who had botched the job? Had they refused to pay the ransom? Worse, had they paid it and the kidnappers reneged on the deal?

I walked across to the counter and took a second pot of tea back to my table near the fountain. A couple of office girls next to me were discussing their night out at the Multiplex. One of them had found *Striptease* a very boring film. 'Although there were fellas in the audience giving it plenty of mouth,' she said. 'Mind you, I don't know why, 'cause that Demi Moore's nothing special to look at.'

I'd seen it myself and I tended to agree with her as I'd fallen asleep halfway through. I often do that with slow films but I hadn't had a wet dream so it can't have been that sexy.

I poured another cup of tea and studied the *Post* report. I'd lost touch with Mally Scrufford after The Cruzads broke up in 1974.

It's a popular fallacy that every kid in Liverpool in 1962 who could hum a tune or play two chords on a guitar was offered a major recording contract. In reality, there were over three hundred groups playing around the city when the Merseybeat thing started and only a few dozen less left behind undiscovered when it was all over. The Cruzads were one of them.

For a few years afterwards we'd done the chicken-in-a-basket theatre club circuit, togged out in platform shoes and glitter, playing stuff like 'Yellow River' and

'Tiger Feet' to geriatric groupies with black crow's-feet and orange trouser suits.

Eventually, we realised we weren't going to make it as pop stars and called it a day. I became a DJ and started buying houses, Frankie and Oggi packed in show business and got 'real jobs' and Mally went on to do the clubs on his own, playing keyboards and singing. Not a bad living and more fun than working for British Gas.

I saw his name in the *Echo* from time to time, in the entertainments adverts, playing the dozens of social clubs around the city as Mal King. But that was nearly twenty years ago and Everton had had a good few managers since then. Our lives had gone in different directions and I'd never heard the name Scrufford since. Until now.

I checked my watch. It was nine thirty. I had a lunch date with Maria at one thirty which I wasn't looking forward to. Maria works in the local history archives at the Picton Library. I first met her a couple of months ago in the Everyman Bistro. We got chatting and I've taken her out a few times since. She's an intellectual sort of girl and I suppose you could say I like her for her mind although I'm not averse to her body either.

We've been for a couple of Indians, caught an Alan Bleasdale revival at the Playhouse and twice I've stayed the night at her flat out at Crosby. She's thirty-eight, divorced, with a son away at university in Reading. I thought the relationship was simmering along nicely with no pressures on either side, until last weekend she asked me to go to dinner at the end of the month with her sister and her husband in Formby.

When relatives start to creep into the picture I get warning bells, like I'm about to become somebody else's property. We didn't fix a definite date and it was left to hang but the odds were she'd mention it again. I like her company and I like her conversation but not exclusively and certainly not for ever.

I haven't told her about Hilary.

However, Maria was four hours away; enough time for me to drive out to Woolton to satisfy my curiosity.

I don't know what my motives were for even thinking about the trip. I'd not had the urge to get in touch with any of the band before. Perhaps I had time to kill. My radio show took up only an hour or so on weekday nights and the houses more or less ran themselves.

Who was I kidding? I'd had time on my hands before. No, it was the mystery that intrigued me. Where was the ransom? If there wasn't one, what could a nineteen-year-old student have done to warrant being murdered in such a fashion? And why send the ears?

It was the name, the chance it might be Mally, that gave me the excuse to play detective.

Woolton is about five miles south of the city centre. It used to be a country village and, before the war, John Lennon's uncle kept the local dairy. For a long time now, though, it's been a dormitory suburb for the moneyed classes.

It was at St Peter's Church fête in Woolton that Lennon, playing with The Quarrymen, first met Paul McCartney.

We played the same gig some years later but it did nothing for us although I remember Mally saying he preferred it to the usual dives we played, the rag-arse social clubs and the all-night shebeens round Upper Parliament Street that I liked best. But then I've always been attracted to sleaze. It wouldn't be too surprising, though, if Mally with his upmarket pretensions had ended up here.

The *Post* didn't give an address so I finished my tea and went out to a phone box by the Pier Head to call 192 for Directory Enquiries.

People say the new open phone boxes are an improvement on the old red ones which stank of urine and stale vomit. All I know is, you don't get directories in them any more and you can hardly carry on a conversation for the roar of the traffic.

'I'm looking for an M. Scrufford in Woolton, Liverpool.' I spelt out the name and waited. A computerised voice answered.

'I am sorry. The number you require is ex-directory.'

I needed the address more than the phone number but Directory Enquiries will never give you any information if they can avoid it. You have to be devious. I rang them back.

'I've just been told a number I want is ex-directory but I think they may have got the wrong person. The name is Scrufford, in Woolton, Liverpool.'

She checked. 'I only have one person of that name in Liverpool and it is ex-directory.'

'I'm sure he's in the book. Number 22 Greenfield Road?'

'No. This one's in Church Road.' She sounded relieved. 'There's nothing for Greenfield Road.'

'Oh, he must've moved. Thanks anyway.'

So, could this be Mally living in Church Road? I rang the library, told them I was from the council tax office and asked them to check the house number in the electoral register. No problem. They gave it me within seconds and confirmed a listing for a Malcolm Scrufford. It looked good.

The RAV4 was parked by Exchange Flags in the heart of the financial area. For some reason, since the meters were replaced by pay and display, I find it easier to get a parking space in town.

I used to have a Jaguar but I found it alienated a lot of folk. The 'society of envy', the anthropologists call it. People would raze their keys alongside the paintwork, presumably as a protest because they couldn't afford one.

An American guy was flogged for doing much the same thing in Singapore, and it seems everyone except our Government now knows how to stop vandals but, after more than enough resprays, I took the easy way out and swapped up the Jag for a Toyota RAV4.

I got the special edition Max model in jet black with CD player and air conditioning. It's just as conspicuousas the Jag, but people tend to smile at it as it passes them, the way they do at puppies. I'm told it also drives well across muddy mountains though I've not yet had cause to try it.

I put a David Allen Coe Hits album in the CD player, turned up the volume loud and eased the car into Water Street. The traffic round the Albert Dock was heavy and, with the usual crop of roadworks, the journey took me nearly half an hour.

Church Road is a tree-lined boulevard of detached Victorian villas. A promising area for double glazing salesmen. The Scrufford residence had a new conservatory built on the side and a new BMW parked in the drive. It certainly looked a good bet for a ransom.

I rang the doorbell, which chimed a few bars of '*Eine Kleine Nachtmusik*'. The lady who answered it was striking. She was tall, about five nine, spectacularly blonde, with laughing lilac eyes and a cleavage bursting from the scooped neckline of her black top that would have added a hundred pounds a week to the takings of any pub that hired her as a barmaid.

Although she was probably just the wrong side of thirty, I figured she'd still give Mally a good fifteen years.

'Er, I don't know if I've got the right house but I'm looking for a guy called Mally Scrufford.'

The big smile vanished. 'Are you another reporter because—'

'No, nothing like that. I knew Mally twenty years ago. We used to play in the same group. My name's Johnny Ace.'

'Johnny! I've heard Mal talk about you. And I've heard your radio show. You'd better come in.' She led me into a spacious oak-panelled hall where a small log gas fire burnt in a Victorian tiled fireplace beside the wide staircase.

'What was the name of your group again?'

'The Cruzads.'

'The Cruzads, of course. And you were the drummer, right? The crazy one.'

It's a well-known fact that in any band it's always the drummer who's the loony, just as in football teams it's the goalkeeper.

'I've given up the drums now.' I wasn't sure I'd given up being crazy though. After all, what was I doing here at all?

'Mal's in the lounge.' She lowered her voice. 'I take it you've heard about his son?' I nodded, picking up on the 'his'. This was evidently not Matt's mother. 'He's still stunned about it. Can hardly believe it's happened. I'm glad you've come, it might take his mind off things a bit. Look, you go in to him, I'll make a cup of tea.'

She opened the lounge door. 'Mal, you've got a visitor.'

The lounge had the same hallmarks of prosperity that favoured the exterior. A twenty-eight-inch Finlandia television with Nicam stereo and sound surround dominated the room, duly dwarfing the mountain of Technics hi-fi stacks with their accompanying hip-high speakers. A couple of large Impressionist prints, Monet's garden at Giverny, hung on the walls.

The man in the corner chair looked round. He had thick white hair, wore expensive tortoiseshell glasses, equally classy shoes, and the Pringle sweater was the genuine article, not a Stanley Market lookalike.

'Christ. You've done all right for yourself,' I said.

He stood up wearily. He looked startled for a minute then, 'Fuckin' hell, Johnny Ace! It must be twenty years. What the hell are you doing here?' He started to embrace me, then pulled away sharply. Close to, I could see the red rims under his eyes. 'Is this something to do with Matt?'

'I read it in the paper. There's not many Scruffords about so I tracked you down. I don't know . . . I thought, if it was you, I might be able to do something.'

It sounded pretty lame but he didn't take it the wrong way.

'Well, it's better than all those fucking reporters ringing up and banging at the door. "How does it feel to have your son cut up in pieces, Mr Scrufford?" "Oh, it's fucking marvellous, better than winning the football pools." I tell you, Johnny, I could strangle some of the bastards.' He stopped suddenly and looked at me. 'I'm sorry. Things are getting on top of me. Come and sit down.' Mally always had a high voice, that's why we did all the Roy Orbison and Gene Pitney hits, but now it was a pitch or two nearer to a whine.

He gestured me to a massive striped brocade settee that would not have been out of place in Blenheim Palace.

'There must be more money doing the clubs than I thought,' I said.

He lowered himself into the matching chair opposite and almost filled it. I figured he weighed in at around fifteen stone, probably two more than he needed.

'You're joking. I gave that up years ago. No, I'm into selling these days, working for a big American company publishing legal tomes for solicitors. I touched lucky. How many other ways could you leave school at fifteen with no qualifications and still earn 50K a year?'

I could think of a few – singing with the Beatles, for instance – but I was more interested in his life.

'And did you eventually marry . . . whatshername?' I struggled to recall the pale, flat-chested girl who often accompanied us on gigs back in the seventies.

'Maureen, you mean? Well, I did, but she's long gone. I'm on to my third one now, Marilyn she's called. Mal and Mal you see. One and Two.' It was obviously one of his buzz lines to get a quick laugh but in these circumstances it sounded out of place.

'And Matt?'

'He was Maureen's and mine. The only one as it turned out. Carol, my second, she and I had a daughter, Julie, but they're both living in London now. I don't see them at all. The parting was, shall we say, a trifle acrimonious. Carol married some Cockney oil-rigger and they moved to Hackney. Got a couple of kids of their own. I stayed here and married Mal.'

'Any kids?'

'We've got a two-year-old lad, Gary, and another on the way.'

'Did Matt live with you as well then?'

His voice broke. 'Matt stayed with us while he was up here at university but he lived with Maureen before then. She'd moved into her aunt's farm on the Isle of Man. I visit them quite often when I'm over in Douglas on business.' He stopped as if it was something he didn't want to talk about. 'But what about you, Johnny? Still in show business, eh?'

'Sort of. The show's a bit of a hobby, really,' I said. 'I'm more into property these days.'

'Not another Rachman?'

I don't suppose there's a landlord alive that hasn't been called that at some time or other. It still rankles with me but I no longer feel any need to justify myself and, anyway, this was no moment to argue. 'Something like that,' I agreed. 'Over the years, I've bought a few old houses and turned them into self-contained flats that I rent out.'

The need to explain further was saved when Marilyn came in with the teas. Mally jumped up to drag a large mahogany coffee table towards the settee while Mal Two laid down the tray and set about pouring the tea. She didn't look pregnant.

'It's not often we have famous people here,' she said.

It's funny how being on the radio impresses people. I get paid thirty pounds for doing the show, which is probably a lot less than Mally makes for selling one of his law guides. And I'm freelance, which means there's no job security and no pension.

On the other hand, I've got to admit there's a certain amount of power to the job. Apart from the fact that I get to play what records I like, and not what some producer chooses for me, the show goes out live so I can say what I want on air and frequently do. This hasn't endeared me to the station bosses, nor to some of the people I've upset publicly, but it's good for the ratings so I get to keep the slot.

'It's probably the worst time I could have come,' I apologised. They didn't seem to want to discuss Matt's death so I reckoned it was up to me to open the bowling. 'I read it in the *Post* this morning and I can hardly believe it. What exactly happened? Was he kidnapped or what?'

Mally groaned. 'Not as far as we know, he wasn't. That is, we had no ransom note or anything. All that happened is I got this envelope through the post with . . . with these ears in it. It was horrible.'

His wife broke in, 'But he didn't realise they were Matt's ears, not at first. It was only when I noticed Matt's gold earring that we knew. We were devastated.'

'And there was nothing else in the envelope?'

'Nothing,' said Mally. 'We went straight to the police, of course. Naturally we thought he'd been kidnapped though heaven knows why. We're not that rich.'

'Depends how poor they are,' I murmured. 'It's relative.'

'The police told us to expect a phone call, you know, further instructions, but none came. It was last Saturday that we got the envelope but it was Thursday, yesterday, that they found Matt's body.'

'How long had he been dead?'

'They weren't sure but they said it could have been up to five days. We heard from no one in that time.' His voice broke. 'They say his ears were cut off before he was dead.'

Chapter Two

There was a silence as we all constructed our own pictures of that scenario. I took a sip of tea but changed my mind about a Cadbury's chocolate finger.

'Why? That's what I ask myself, why?'

'There must be a reason,' I said. 'Had he upset some-body?'

'He was at university, for Christ's sake. People at university don't murder each other. It's not Toxteth.'

'Well, it is Toxteth, geographically speaking.' Many of the university buildings do stray into the Upper Parliament Street area. 'But I know what you mean. He wasn't involved with the drug scene or racial violence or anything like that?'

'Of course not.'

'As far as you know.' The sentence came out a little more sharply than I intended and they both looked up. Mally seemed as if he might jump up and lay one on me but his wife quickly intervened.

'Matt was a nice, quiet boy, Johnny. He has . . . had . . . a girlfriend at the uni and spent most of his time with her. They were engaged to be married.'

'Why didn't they live together?'

They exchanged glances. 'They did. That is to say, Sarah lived here with us. A flat would've taken most of their grants – you know how expensive they are in Liverpool?'

I did, more than most people. The fact is that virtually the only people who can afford flats nowadays are single mothers on housing benefit. What this is doing to the nation's balance sheet I don't like to think but I suppose it's less barbaric than keeping them in the workhouse or mental homes like they did in Victorian times.

'Where's Sarah now?'

'She's gone to her parents in Chiswick for the weekend. She's coming back for the funeral next Friday. We couldn't have it before then because of the post mortem.'

'When did you first realise he was missing?'

'He didn't go missing, not exactly. He left on Thursday afternoon for a weekend course in the Lakes. He was reading Geography and there's a field trip they have to go on to study glaciated landscapes.'

Marilyn added, 'And the envelope came two days later.'

'He never got to the centre,' explained Mally. 'They were the first people we rang, before the police, and he never checked in.'

'How would he have travelled to the Lakes?'

'Train. Student railcard.'

'Did anyone see him off?'

'No. Sarah had a tutorial, Mal and I were working. He was supposed to get the three thirty to Preston and change there.'

'So he probably never caught the train at all.'

'The postmark on the envelope was Liverpool,' said Mally, which seemed to confirm it.

'Which means he was accosted some time on Thursday and murdered within twenty-four hours.'

'That's what the police think, yes.'

I took a biscuit. The mystery was just as strange as it had first seemed in The Diner. There just didn't seem to be a motive.

'One thing,' I said. 'The paper didn't say how he died, only that he was found in the dock. Did he drown?' Not that it mattered much, I supposed.

'The death certificate said drowning but he was unconscious when he was dumped in the dock, probably from a blow on his head with a blunt instrument.' Mally shivered. 'I like to think the blow came before they cut his ears off as well.'

'Mal had to identify him,' said Marilyn. 'It was very upsetting for him.'

'What's happened to his mother in all this?' I asked. 'Has she not come over?'

'She's staying with her family in Bootle,' Mally explained. 'Er . . . she and Mal don't hit it off too well. Ex-wives and all that, you know what it's like?'

I could see Marilyn not being too keen on these visits to the Isle of Man. Especially if Maureen had no man with her out there. And Mally's track record with women didn't seem to have improved from his sixties days, judging by the number of wives he was getting through.

'What do the police say about it all?'

'Nothing, in a word. No clues, no leads, no reasons. They've interviewed kids at the university, Mal and me and Sarah and Maureen. They've been to all the places he visited in the week before he died and they've found nothing. Everything pointed to a kidnap, you see, but when that was ruled out they were as baffled as me and Mal.'

And me. I suppose I'd fancied solving the mystery myself but I realised now it was presumptuous of me to think I could find out anything the police couldn't. On the other hand, the police weren't doing too well themselves.

We talked for a while about other things. Mally hadn't seen Frankie and Oggi since the group broke up but he'd heard Oggi had moved to Australia. We remembered groups we'd played with in the early sixties, like Kingsize Taylor and the Dominoes, Faron's Flamingoes, and Rory Storm and the Hurricanes, that should have made it but didn't.

'I must be going,' I said, finally. 'I don't know what I can do for you but if you think of anything . . .' I gave Mally's wife a card. 'Don't forget, ring me if I can ever help.'

She still looked ravishing and I wished I'd met her at a different time and place.

'It's really nice of you to call,' she said. 'Please come again, won't you?'

Maybe I would.

It was gone eleven as I pulled away from the house but I figured I had time to pick up some rent from one of my Livingstone Drive flats on the way back into town. I drove through Mossley Hill into Smithdown Road and cut into Sefton Park.

The houses around Sefton Park are huge detached mansions, once owned by the rich shipping merchants when Liverpool was a major port. Now, apart from the odd hotel, restaurant or private school, they've been converted into flats and bedsits, which are let mainly to people from the universities.

I came off the perimeter road at Lark Lane. In the eighties, Lark Lane became a kind of miniature Greenwich Village with poetry and folk evenings held in the defunct police station and the old artisans' shops replaced by left-wing bookshops and businesses selling health foods, tarot cards, records, period fireplaces and the like. The recession has closed many of these but a few trendy restaurants are left and the area is still a Mecca for both college and media people in the city. Shop windows feature postcards advertising forthcoming events, accommodation to let, palms read, bands wanting musicians, musicians wanting bands and all kinds of esoteric items for sale.

Livingstone Drive is at the top end. John Lennon's half-sister lived there in the eighties and his Uncle Charlie still lives in a bedsit at the other side of the park, in similar poverty. His cat, Aigburth, died last summer, aged twenty-seven; must have been one of the oldest cats in existence. Charlie is seventy-eight himself. He's started doing gigs with a band now so, what with the trips to America where he's become a cult hero, he's not bothering to replace Aigburth.

You can't get far away from the Beatles in Liverpool.

My property is the middle of a Victorian terrace, four storeys if you count the basement. There are two flats on each floor, front and back, and in the top front flat lives Neville Mountbatten, known to his associates as Badger since he dyed silver stripes in his hair for a bet when he was sixteen.

His hair is now black as his skin and styled in long dreadlocks. He is believed to mix in dubious company yet holds a master's degree in English Literature. He's currently studying for a doctorate, writing a thesis on some eighteenth-century classical poet I've never heard of, called Matthew Prior.

He's pretty good on the Liverpool underworld too, though I doubt there's a degree course in that. Mind you, I'm told you can get a Ph.D. in folk music now so I guess anything's possible these days.

Badger's major problem is money. Despite reaching twenty-five without ever having had a job, he dresses in the height of fashion, drives a Porsche and has a bigger collection of CDs than Our Price. Strangely, however, he always seems to have trouble paying his way. Currently he owed me £150 rent and the latest cheque had just bounced.

I let myself in the front door and bounded up the stairs. Most of my excercise consists of running up and down the stairs of my various properties and I suppose it keeps me fit of sorts. Lifts are too expensive to install and strangers tend to pee down the shafts.

I knocked hard on the door and called. 'Badger. It's Johnny.'

Amazingly he was in and, even more amazingly, he answered the door. He wore a peach-coloured, double-breasted suit, yellow tie with a matching pocket handkerchief and a shirt that I'd have described as nigger brown if I wasn't so frightened of the anti-Enid Blyton brigade. In the parlance of old jazz slang, he was a cool dude.

'Hi, man.' He greeted me enthusiastically with a wide grin and firm handshake. 'Come on in. How ya doin'? Caught the show last week, man. Some nice rap you played.'

The large front lounge still had the high ceiling and original cornices. I always try to keep the Victorian character of the houses when I convert them. Forget the false ceilings and plasterboard. Shelves carrying books, videos, CDs and manuscripts covered most of the walls, hiding the dark green painted Anaglypta, and there were enough plants around to qualify the flat as a fernery. An Ice-T album played on the hi-fi.

I ignored the repartee. 'The cheque bounced, Badger. All one fifty of it.'

He looked genuinely surprised but I wasn't fooled. 'No? It can't have done. It must be the bank . . .'

'I'm prepared to do a deal.'

His face brightened. 'What can I get you, man? You want some stuff? I got contacts, you know.'

'I want some information, Badger, on a guy called Matt Scrufford. He was reading Geography at John Moores. I want anything you can get on him.'

'Wait a minute, ain't that the guy in the paper today? Fished up from the docks with his ears cut off?'

'The very same.'

'So what's your angle?'

What was my angle? I wondered myself. 'Son of a friend, Badger,' I said. 'I'll knock a ton off the debt if you come up with anything useful. The police have nothing.' Something was wrong here. Even if I did solve the case, who was paying me? Nobody had hired me.

I could see that amateur detecting could get to be an expensive business. Still, it beat train-spotting as a hobby and you didn't need to buy an anorak.

'The police round here are fucking useless, man. And bent. And fucking racially prejudiced.'

'Not too keen on women either, I believe. Very chauvanistic. We'll leave them out of it then, Badger, shall we?' I lowered my voice melodramatically. 'You work undercover and alone.'

'A ton, you say? Make it the one fifty I owe you.'

'A ton.' I tried to sound intimidating, lowering my voice to a Robert Mitchum croak. 'You can write me a cheque for the other fifty now and if this bounces I'll have that pretty suit made into curtains with you inside it.'

He only laughed. 'Nice one, man.' He wrote the cheque. 'Don't put it in till Thursday, right?'

'But it's only Friday today.'

'Hang cool. It'll get there. Now, about the sonny with the hearing problem; what are we looking for here?'

'Well, finding his killer might be nice, Badger, apprehended with full confession. Failing that, how about a few details of his chums, the crowd he knocked around with, any enemies, general stuff?'

'I thought this was a snatch job. They send the ears, the old man don't pay up, they cut their losses.'

'Didn't pan out like that. Nobody asked for a ransom.'

He pursed his lips and fiddled with his 24-carat-gold tie-pin. 'How about a ritual killing? Sons of Satan style, drinking his blood out of silver chalices, his eyeballs preserved in aspic, a sacrifice to the Devil?'

'Why not? Sounds par for the course these days. Check it out. I'll call back next week. Ring me if you get anything.'

I tidied some litter from the stairs on the way down. The tenant from the second floor back came out as I passed her door and took the opportunity to complain about the drains blocking. I told her to stop putting tampons down the toilet, which is what the problem is ninety per cent of the time.

It was twelve twenty-five when I headed for Park Lane into town. It's still pretty grim down the Dingle. The sixties tenement blocks are getting shabbier than the old terraced two up and downs they replaced and whole rows of shops have been boarded up, waiting for the demolition men.

On the corners, groups of youths in jeans and trainers hung around aimlessly. In the fifties they'd have been singing doo-wop like Dion and the Belmonts but now they just sold crack and glared menacingly at passing cars.

I took the Paradise Street route and parked in the multistorey by the Moat House, right in the city centre.

I was meeting Maria in Lucy in the Sky with Diamonds, a theme café in Cavern Walks, the city's belated attempt to cash in on its sixties heritage courtesy of the Royal Insurance, who put up the cash. They even rebuilt the Cavern. Nothing like the real Cavern, of course. We played there a few times in '62, a stinking hellhole with sweat dripping from the walls and a fierce heat that sucked the air from your lungs. It didn't matter what you played because the music was obliterated by deafening screams from teenage girls fuelled by prepubescent lust and Coca-Cola.

Like all the businesses in the Walks, LSD is privately owned, which means you get real food instead of that plastic chain-store junk, and the walls are full of pop music memorabilia including photos signed by various celebrities who've eaten there over the years.

Maria had already got a table when I arrived and was sipping a glass of mineral water. She looks a blue-stocking version of Cher with long dark hair and a sallow complexion that she attributes to her Egyptian ancestry.

I ordered a curried baked potato with garnish for myself and a tuna salad for Maria plus another bottle of mineral water with gas.

We made small talk. She was complaining of the staff shortages at work and I listened sympathetically. It seems that, in the nineties, everybody from firemen to bank clerks complains that their job is no fun any more. Makes me glad I don't have one. I don't count the show as a job.

Eventually I told her about Matt Scrufford. 'If it wasn't a kidnap,' she said, when I'd finished the story, 'could it have been a grudge killing? He could have got mixed up with some bad people and upset them somehow. And that could be why they sent the ears. As a warning to anyone else who tried it on with them.'

I couldn't really buy it. Matt was a university student not one of the Mob. Wasn't he? 'He'd have had to have done something pretty nasty,' I said. 'And, even if he had, wouldn't it have been simpler just to kill him?'

We got on to talk about revenge generally. Maria said women were better at it than men. She reminded me of straying husbands whose clothes had been cut up, cars set on fire and then there was Mr Bobbitt whose wife cut his dick off.

'Probably wasn't a woman did this then,' I said. 'Matt only lost his ears.'

We finished the meal amicably. I was relieved that no mention was made of the dinner party in Formby and promised to ring her over the weekend. I liked to keep my options open for Saturday night.

I walked back to the car park thinking about what Maria had said. It was feasible, I admitted to myself reluctantly. I didn't like to think of somebody with that much hatred in them.

I drove back to my flat. I've got this fourth-floor apartment in the old Waterloo Dock building overlooking the river. It's handy for town and there's a security guard on the car park, which is a major plus in Liverpool, but the main asset is the huge lounge which I need to accommodate my small recording studio, CD jukebox and the piano.

The piano is a white Steinway grand and it takes up half the room. I don't actually play that well but an hour at the keys is the best relaxation I know.

I went into the kitchen and set about making a pot of Darjeeling. I had a couple of hours to spare before I was due at the radio station. I took the tea and a piece of parkin to the table by the window and telephoned the police station.

As usual, the switchboard took an age to answer but eventually I got through and asked for the person in charge of the Matt Scrufford case. More waiting, then, 'DI Burroughs.'

I'd touched lucky. I'd known Jim Burroughs since school in Litherland and I'd done a few things with him on the show. The police are always anxious for a mouthpiece to the public and I'd helped him publicise a few cases so I thought he might just feel he owed me one.

As it happened, he wasn't able to tell me anything new. 'Why are you interested in this anyway, Johnny?' he asked curiously.

'Don't you remember Mally Scrufford? The father? Used to be our lead singer in The Cruzads.' Amazingly, Jim had once played bass for the Chocolate Lavatory but opted for the police as a more suitable career. I'd heard them a couple of times and knew he'd made the right decision.

'Christ, I do. It's him, is it? Bloody hell, Mally Scrufford! Used to be one for the women as I remember.'

'Still is, I think. He's on his third wife.'

'You still see him then, after all this time?'

I explained about my morning excursion. 'Don't you think there's something odd about this, Jim?'

'In what way?'

'No ransom note for starters.'

There was a silence, then: 'Do you fancy a jar tonight?' We arranged to meet in the Masquerade at eleven when he came off duty.

I sorted out the records for the show, took a shower and changed into jeans, a blue-check cotton shirt and a black-leather bomber jacket. We'd been having a bit of an Indian summer but it was late September and the nights got cold when the sun went down. As always, I walked across town to the radio station. I never take the car out at night any more on account of the drinking laws. Two designer ciders and you're over the limit.

The show runs from six to seven but I got there early to check the messages in my pigeonhole. There was the usual pile of mail to deal with, promo CDs, record requests and invitations to various events round town. I shoved them all into my holdall to deal with later and went into the studio.

The hour on air passed quickly. I played 'Love is All Around' – the Troggs' original version not the Wet Wet Wet copy – the Cramps' live version of 'Lonesome Town', with its reference to Rick Nelson's supposedly drug-assisted plane crash, plus my usual ragbag of dissimilar sounds including a rap record for Badger to remind him of his new employment.

I managed to bring in Matt Scrufford's name during my comments on current local news items and asked if anyone had seen him on that last Thursday to ring into the station. It was a long shot but worth a try.

It was seven thirty when I got away. I picked up an *Echo* from a vendor outside Lime Street Station and walked down to the Shangri-La in Victoria Street for a Chinese. The report of the Matt Scrufford case said nothing different from the morning *Daily Post* account except that the boy's mother lived in the Isle of Man and Mally had remarried. The police were still making enquiries but the story was already relegated to the inside pages.

Most of the back page was given over to Everton's slump in form. Whilst Liverpool were back on top of the Premiership, the Blues were three points off the bottom, hadn't won in eight games and had just been knocked out of the Coca-Cola Cup by lowly York City who had hardly won a match in their own division. Manager Joe Royle was reported to be puzzled whilst supporters were said to restless.

That was an understatement. I'd been an Everton supporter for thirty years and I was more than restless, I was livid.

I stretched my meal out with a pot of China tea and started to open my post. A couple of primary schools, one on the Wirral and one in West Derby, wanted me to open their autumn fairs. I never do public appearances. I prefer to keep a low profile. There was a new CD single from Madonna and a few record requests. I put aside the ones I wanted to play.

The last envelope was a small Jiffy bag postmarked Liverpool, probably carrying a demo cassette from some new band wanting airplay. But there was no cassette inside; indeed, it appeared to be empty. I opened the end wide and shook it.

Onto my lap fell ten clippings from somebody's fingernails.

I went cold. There was no note. I thought of the ears. Was there a connection?

Shaken, I put the clippings back in the Jiffy bag and stuffed it with all my letters back into the holdall. It was ten thirty. I paid the bill, took my mint imperial and set off for my night in clubland.

Chapter Three

The Masquerade Club occupies the ground floor of an old warehouse down by the docks just south of the city centre. The upper floors are deserted and overrun by rats so the owners leave a couple of cats inside during the week whilst the club is closed. This is one good reason for not arriving too early on a Friday night when the air fresheners have not had time to dissipate the odours of the resultant cat excretions and the cleaners haven't yet disposed of the leftover portions of chewed rodent.

Not that the clientele of the Masquerade are too bothered. The management's policy is to admit all the people who, for various reasons, have been denied access to the other clubs in town. Consequently, the place is full of social misfits of mixed race and indeterminate gender who are too grateful to be let in to care about the décor.

They are joined by a sprinkling of itinerant foreign seamen who, because of their ignorance of the language and the currency, pay extortionate admission prices at the door.

The owners are the McKale twins, brothers in their late forties, who grew up in the tough streets of Everton and are rumoured to have made their pile in protection, armed robbery, drug-running, prosititution and pornography.

They also happen to be friends of mine. I don't listen to rumours.

Tommy McKale was on the door and he greeted me warmly. 'All right, Johnny? Early tonight.' He's not a tall man, about five eight, but he's stocky, with powerful shoulders like you see on American wrestling shows on Sky. He was once a contender for Mr Universe and still lifts weights and trains regularly. Naturally, he owns a gym.

'Bit of business, Tommy.' He let me through with a nod to Dolly in the ticket booth. Regulars never paid at the Masquerade.

I ordered a Scrumpy Jack at the bar and looked across the cracked, glass-topped dance floor. A black disc jockey wearing a baseball hat and a luminous orange blouson was playing reggae records, and a few couples, who already looked half cut, were gyrating to the insidious beat.

The barman brought across the cider and poured it into a glass. 'You're early tonight.'

'Busy night ahead, Vince. Thought I'd get an early start.'

'You never played any Ivor Novello again this week, Johnny, very naughty of you.' He stood about six four with two days' stubble, a split lip and wore a pair of denim overalls over a bared chest, the broad straps covering his nipples. He didn't look like an Ivor Novello aficionado which shows you can't take things at face value although I suppose the gold ring in his left ear might have been a giveaway.

'I'll dig one out, Vince,' I promised. 'There's not too much call for Ivor these days.'

'The world's gone mad, dear. All this awful black music and jungle chanting.'

'You don't like rap then?'

'Oh, I don't mind rap but Noel did it so much better. Have you got "Who do you think you're fooling Mr Hitler?"'

I wasn't taken in by his act. I'd seen him in action when there was a particularly bad fight in the club. A couple of Scandinavian sailors spaced out on some unknown substance had taken it in mind one night to wreck the club and demolish anyone who stood in their way. Vince had leapfrogged spectacularly over the bar and thrust a metal-tipped umbrella through the stomach of one of them, rupturing his spleen, before dispatching the other with a swift left hook that put him in the Walton Neurosurgical Department for two nights' observation.

'And Joyce Grenfell. Now there's a rapper if ever I heard one.' He laughed lightly and I promised to play him something from *King's Rhapsody* on Monday's show.

I took my drink to a corner table as far as possible from the speakers and waited for Jim Burroughs. He arrived half an hour later, marching across the club looking the epitome of a policeman, tall and square with his steel-grey hair cropped to the skull and that arrogant air of authority they all have. I suppose it's all that training in police brutality. Unfortunately, I could remember him singing 'Be Bop a Lula' in the wrong key at the Orrell Park Ballroom in 1965, which ruined the effect somewhat.

I fetched him a pint of Newcastle Brown and myself another Scrumpy Jack.

'I never reckoned you as a private eye,' he said, supping the foam from the top of his glass.

'I never reckoned myself. But then, I never reckoned myself as a DJ till I found that operating a Dansette record player was a helluva lot easier than bashing the drums, and look what that led to.'

We got on to music then and talked about the sixties. 'Did I tell you our group are thinking of reforming?' he asked me.

Remembering the discordant performances of the Chocolate Lavatory, I wasn't enthused by the news, and the idea of them all middle-aged, with beer bellies and receding hair, cavorting round a stage singing about teenage romance was particularly off putting.

'Yes, we've been asked to do a concert for Merseycats. I've been in touch with the other guys and they're quite keen.' Merseycats is an organisation formed by some members of the old sixties groups who've got back together to do shows for charity. The thing has taken off in a big way and they've raised several thousand pounds over the last few years as well as giving a lot of menopausal men the chance to relive their youth.

'Let me know when it happens,' I said, 'and I'll put you on the show.' Another favour I figured he could owe me for. 'I can't see The Cruzads getting back together, especially with this trouble with Mally.' I was anxious to get down to the business in hand. He took the hint.

'Do you know something about this business that I don't?'

'I know nothing, Jim, other than what was in the *Daily Post* report.' Was it only this morning I'd first read about it?

'You must have some angle.'

'Only the Mally connection plus a certain curiosity. The ears, I suppose. Not your average mugging. Maybe I watch too many American B-movies on afternoon TV and I want to be Alan Ladd. When I saw the name Scrufford, it gave me a kind of personal reason to get involved.'

Jim Burroughs' expression hardened. 'I hope you're *not* going to get involved. Police work is a team job for trained professionals, not a fun afternoon for meddling fucking amateurs.'

'For God's sake, Jim, do I look like Miss Marple?'

'So what ideas have you come up with?'

I hesitated, trying to crystallise the thoughts that had been going round my head all day. 'What are the most common reasons people get murdered? Robbery, jealousy, crime of passion, revenge, rivalry? Nothing there likely to apply, is it?'

'No?'

'Well, no money was taken, there was no jealous husband or spurned lover. He was at university, for Chrissake. He's hardly likely to be killed because he was top of the class in meteorology.'

'Go on.'

I remembered what Maria had said. 'Is it possible he'd got in with a bad crowd and upset them in some way?'

Burroughs shook his head. 'Not as far as we know. We've spoken to his friends and some of the other students. He seemed a pretty decent, sensible lad. Wasn't on drugs, didn't skip too many lectures. No suggestion he was running with any scallys.'

'Perhaps he was in the wrong place at the wrong time. Saw something he shouldn't and was killed for it.'

'Or *heard* something. Remember the ears.'

'Could be. But then why send them to Mally?' I took a swig of the cider. 'What about a maniac? Another Fred West or Yorkshire Ripper.' Since the government introduced this Care in the Community scheme and shut most of the mental hospitals, I've noticed the streets are full of nutters. Indeed, looking around the club, rapidly filling up with the evening's flotsam, they seemed to be all around us.

'But that would have been a random killing and this one was obviously well planned. No, the kidnap has to be favourite.' He took out a packet of Regal and offered me one. I declined so he lit his and blew out a mouthful of smoke. 'I think Mal Scrufford got a phone call on the Thursday teatime. I think he told them to fuck off so they sent the ears to show they meant business.'

'Bit soon, wasn't it?'

'The sooner the better for them. Get the money, send back the kid and scarper.'

'So, what went wrong?'

'Old man Scrufford opens the package the next morning and straight away rings us. We send a couple of officers round. The kidnappers probably had someone watching the house, saw our lads and panicked. Killed the boy and got rid of the evidence.' Jim Burroughs picked up the empty glasses. 'My shout,' he said, and pushed his way through to the bar.

The DJ had moved from reggae and was now playing

seventies disco music. The dance floor had filled up and the air was thick with smoke. At least I couldn't smell the cats any more.

I checked my watch. Nearly midnight. The sound of Candi Staton's 'Young Hearts Run Free' filled the room and I was suddenly reminded of a night at the Beachcomber with Hilary in 1976 when they'd played that same record. It was a week after I'd proposed and a night when I was the nearest I can recall to being in love. A fortnight later, I had broken off the engagement, realising I wanted to stay single and not be answerable to anyone in my life, neither a boss nor a wife.

The surprising thing is that Hilary has stuck around. She's worked at her career and is now a sister at the new Royal Liverpool Hospital and we've carried on much as in the earlier days of our relationship. The best description I can come up with, and I often try to analyse it, is 'loving friends'. We're friends, we make love but there are no ties on either side. So far, neither of us has felt the urge to marry anyone else and the chances are we never will. It may not be a situation many people would choose, but it gives us space and we remain each other's closest confidant.

Hilary has an admirer called Barry who takes her out occasionally. He's an eye surgeon at her hospital, about my age and divorced. She says it's platonic but, given Hilary's enthusiasm for sex, I think this is unlikely. For some reason, this aspect of their relationship doesn't worry me but I sometimes wonder if I'd mind if she were to fall in love with him. I've got used to having her around.

Jim pushed his way through the crowds. 'There we are. One Scrumpy Jack and one Newky Brown.' He put them on the table and sat down. 'Well, what do you think of the theory?'

'It sounds like something made to fit the facts rather than something that actually happened.'

'That's how the best scientists make their discoveries. Look at Darwin. Went out for a bevy one night, took one look at his missus's face when he got back and realised it reminded him of a gorilla he once knew and there he had it – the theory of evolution.'

I laughed along but I had a nasty feeling that this was probably the way the police approached most of their cases.

'Hiya, I've found you at last.'

We looked up to see a small blonde girl with a big smile dance up to the table. She wore a tight top in citrus green, a matching lace miniskirt and high, side-buttoned boots.

Funny how you still say 'girl'. I've heard old ladies in nursing homes refer to their companions as 'girls' when they're well down the queue for the crematorium. Hilary is thirty-something although she's slim and still looks youthful.

'Hil! I wasn't expecting to see you tonight.'

'I only just finished work and didn't feel like going home to a lonely bed. At least, not mine. I thought I might find you in here.'

'You know Jim Burroughs, don't you, the next Chief Constable and virtuoso bass player? Hang on, I'll get you a drink.'

I fought my way back to the bar for Hilary's gin and tonic. When I returned, she and Jim Burroughs were chatting like old friends. Hilary is a gregarious girl.

We stayed awhile longer in the club. I didn't mention matt Scrufford again and when Jim left around one o'clock, Hilary and I had a few dances. The DJ had moved on to the slow stuff and the floor was packed with groping couples.

'Jim's been telling me about this ears case,' shouted Hilary above the music. 'I saw it in the *Echo* but I never associated it with you.'

I explained about The Cruzads. My days as a pop star

were before her time. 'Jim thinks it's a kidnap gone wrong.'

'I know, he told me. And you don't?'

'No. But I don't know what the hell else it can be.' She held me tighter and we ground our hips against one another in time to the slow rhythm in the manner of people who are acquainted with each other's bodies.

'Your place?' she whispered mischievously as the record ended.

We got a cab back to the apartment. I checked the answerphone whilst Hilary made us a nightcap. There were two messages. The first person had rung off but the second was a voice I didn't recognise. It sounded young, male and frightened.

'Er, I heard your programme tonight. I'm in the same study group as Matt Scrufford at John Moores and I think I know who might've killed him.' A pause. 'I'll ring again in the morning. Don't tell the police. I'll explain when I see you. Don't tell the police. He might kill me.'

Chapter Four

Hilary brought over two glasses of Southern Comfort and lemonade with ice and we sat in bed, half watching an old gangster movie on Sky TV, the sound turned down as we talked about the message.

'It'll be a hoax,' I said. 'We get a lot of crank calls. Wonder how he got my home number?' I'd checked the call display but there were no numbers stored.

'It didn't sound like a hoax to me. He sounded pretty frightened.'

'Then he'll ring back.' Suddenly, I'd had enough of Matt Scrufford for one day. Not the attitude of a dedicated private eye, I realised. Maybe the Scrumpy Jacks were taking effect or maybe I had more pressing things to think about.

Hilary had removed her top clothes and wore just her bottle-green Wonderbra and matching knickers, her knees hunched under her chin. I was down to the black-silk boxer shorts she'd bought me last Christmas.

I put my empty glass on the bedside table and clicked the remote to switch off the TV. 'It's ages since you've been round.'

She laughed. 'Oh yes, at least two weeks.'

'Precisely. Ages.'

'And how's the lovely Maria? I must say she's lasting well.'

I took her in my arms and lifted her boobs out of the bra. They were warm and soft. 'And we go on for ever,' I reminded her as we rolled across the mattress.

She licked my ear, then fished an ice cube from out of her glass and reached down beneath the covers. I cried out as the cold seared along my upper thigh. She laughed and held the melting ice firmly against me. I found another ice cube and pressed it between her legs until it was out of sight.

'For ever,' she laughed. 'I might hold you to that.'

We slept late. Kenny Johnson's country music show on Radio Merseyside was well underway on the bedside radio alarm. He was playing 'Today' for somebody's wedding. He plays it most weeks, possibly because he wrote it, but more probably because people like it. I don't know whether it was that which woke me or the warbling of the phone.

Neither woke Hilary.

'Johnny Ace.' My tongue felt thick and furry as I spoke into the mouthpiece.

'I rang last night.' It was him. I was suddenly wide awake.

'What's your name?'

He hesitated, then, 'Jordan. Jordan Crook. I'm at the uni with Matt Scrufford, or rather *was* with him.'

'And how do you know who killed him?'

'I don't. That is, I know who might. Look, can I meet you somewhere?'

'Where are you speaking from?' I checked the number on the call display screen but it read 'Unavailable' so it was probably a phone box.

'A phone box by the Town Hall.'

'Do you know Rumours in Stanley Street, opposite Radio City?'

'The coffee bar?'

'That's it. I'll meet you there in half an hour.'

I scrambled out of bed, took a quick shower and dragged on a clean pair of jeans, a denim shirt and my leather jacket. Hilary slept on. I left her a note on the pillow, 'Back in an hour for breakfast', and dashed out of the flat.

I got to Rumours first and ordered tea with a bacon sandwich. There were a couple of guys in from Radio City that I knew slightly. Crook came in shortly afterwards. He wasn't hard to identify by the nervous way he looked over his shoulder like a fugitive in a Clint Eastwood film. I half expected masked gangsters with sub-machine-guns to burst through the door behind him and flatten us all.

He came up to the counter and ordered a coffee. I went across.

'Jordan?' I said. He nodded. 'I'll get that.' I paid for his drink and led the way to the corner table.

'OK. Tell me the story.'

He took a sip of coffee and I feared for a second that he might change his mind. He couldn't have been older than nineteen, thin and gangly like a twisted walking stick and with an interesting selection of pimples suggesting a delayed puberty. He wore a grey anorak, sloppy sweater and faded jeans. His hair was cut fashionably short, 1950s GI style.

'Look, I don't know if there's anything in this but Matt was doing the same General Studies course at university as me and one of the tutors is a guy called Colin Bennison. Matt had found out something about him.'

'Like what?'

'I'm not sure but I think it was to do with exam papers. There was some sort of fiddle going on.'

'And Matt was blackmailing him?'

'God, no! Nothing like that. Matt was dead straight. No, Matt was going to confront him about it.'

'And did he?'

'He might have done. It was last Wednesday when he told me and I never saw him again.'

I ate the last piece of bacon and wiped the fat from my fingers on the napkin.

'So you think he could have had this confrontation

sometime on Thursday and Bennison could have silenced him?'

'I don't know but you wanted a motive.'

'But if he just wished to silence him, Jordan, why all the business with the ears?'

'To make it look like a kidnap perhaps. Make sure there's no connection with the uni.'

'Why didn't you go to the police?'

He hesitated. 'I got busted for drugs last term. Only cannabis, nothing serious, but, well, I'm not overfond of the law so I stayed out of college when I realised they'd be coming round.'

'And did Matt do cannabis too?'

'No. He wasn't into drugs at all. Or drink, come to that. Far too serious. Keen on his exams.'

'Sounds like a pious wimp, your friend Matt.'

'Not really. He was a good laugh and all the women fancied him.'

'I thought he was engaged.'

'He was but that was just a challenge to most of them.'

'And did Matt succumb to their advances?'

Jordan shrugged. 'Dunno. He was pretty shy with girls. Anyway, I didn't see him much outside of college.' I thought of Mally's predilection for women. Had it carried on to the next generation? Did that make Sarah a suspect if she found Matt had been unfaithful?

'Getting back to Bennison, do you think Matt mentioned his suspicions to anyone else at college?'

'Not as far as I know. Nobody's said anything to me.'

'Has Bennison been attending classes since Matt's disappearance?'

'No. They say he's on leave, whatever that might mean.'

'Do you know where he lives?'

'Somewhere in Formby, I think.' Near Maria's sister, I thought. 'But I can tell you where he'll be tonight. He's in some amateur drama group, the North End Players I think they're called, and they're doing *Annie Get Your Gun*.'

A night at the theatre was looking good. 'Where can I get hold of you if I need to speak to you again?'

He gave me an address in Kensington, where he shared a house with three other students, and promised to get in touch with me if there were any new developments.

Hilary was up and dressed when I returned and halfway through a bowl of Force flakes. I recounted the meeting to her but she was not impressed. 'I can't see a university lecturer resorting to murder, can you?'

'I certainly can.' I could remember a lot of masters at my old school who would have matched Genghis Khan for mass sadism so I was quite prepared to accept Colin Bennison as a common or garden murderer.

'So it's a night at the musical, is it?'

'I thought I might go along after the match, yes.'

'Ah! You'll be able to take the lovely Maria.' Hilary smiled sweetly and I threw a cushion at her. 'I'm on a late tonight.'

It was a trip I wanted to make alone. It didn't promise to be pleasant. We talked awhile then she left to do her weekend shop. I promised to call her.

I took my seat at Goodison at three o'clock. The visitors, Sheffield Wednesday, had been top of the Premiership a month ago but, like Everton, had suffered a slump in form.

Nonetheless, there were 30,000 or so spectators present, all doubtless hoping for better things. It wasn't an outstanding game, the strong wind saw to that. Wednesday were rubbish and Everton not much better. I'd seen more class on a Subuteo table. Goals from Kanchelskis, our star player, and Stuart gave us the three points.

It was dark when I left the ground and called in The Winslow opposite for a half of cider. The place was packed with vociferous Everton fans holding their post mortem on the match. The 'Royle out' faction seemed to have been temporarily silenced by the result, apart from the odd carping voice.

'He's fucking useless,' opined a man with a bulbous nose and matted grey ponytail poking from beneath a blue-and-white bobble hat. He was in his late sixties. 'John Major could do fuckin' better.'

I couldn't quite see it myself but didn't say so.

An hour later I walked across to Moorfields Station and caught the electric train to Formby on the Southport line: not an edifying journey. Groups of youths clambered into the carriage at Sandhills, shouting obscenities as we rattled through areas of derelict dockland. Nobody dared to challenge them.

After Blundellsands and Crosby, the scenery changed to fields and by Formby we were in the Northern equivalent of Betjeman country, leafy suburbs in a 1920s time-warp.

The North End Players performed in a wooden hut a few hundred yards from the station and I was just in time for the evening performance. 'You're fortunate to get a ticket,' explained the elderly gentleman at the paybox, who looked like Margaret Rutherford in drag, 'only we had an unexpected cancellation.'

I bought a programme, a flimsy pink sheet of paper with typewritten names of the cast, and passed through a curtain into the theatre. There were twenty rows of red plush seats which ran down almost to the stage. I was on the aisle midway down.

As amateur musicals go, I've seen worse. The singing and acting were surprisingly good, the costumes colourful and the five-piece band enthusiastic. What spoilt it, like every amateur production, was the age of the chorus 'girls', which seemed to average out at around fifty. Twelve of them thundered on stage at regular intervals, gingham dresses flapping incongruously over elephantine blue-veined thighs, with bulbous bosoms straining for the floor like giant medicine balls.

Colin Bennison was playing Buffalo Bill. He was a tall, slightly stooping man heading for his fifties. He didn't look like a killer, but then he didn't look like Buffalo Bill either, even with the wig, the white beard and the stetson.

When the final curtain fell, I headed for the bar, hoping the cast would make their way there. I struck lucky. It was last night and there was a show supper for all members.

The bar area was half the size of the theatre and the wooden walls were lined with photographs of past productions, the usual mix of Ayckbourn, Christie, Rattigan and Durbridge. Behind a serving hatch, an elderly lady with a tight, iron-grey perm dispensed coffee from a steaming silver urn. Eventually, sandwiches and cold quiche slices were brought round. I took a tuna on brown and joined the fringe of a group which included Bennison.

'You must be Gilbert's friend,' said an angular woman in a green frock. She had high cheekbones and teeth like Mister Ed. 'I hope someone's looking after you.' I assured her I was and they were and we fell into a conversation about the merits of Suzi Quatro in the 1986 London production.

I commented that I'd always liked Suzi Quatro from her glam-rock days.

'Not a patch on Betty Hutton,' said Colin Bennison, breaking into the conversation. I quickly agreed with him and for a while we all discussed the respective merits of forgotten musical divas.

A military-looking man with a grey pencil moustache and matching hair barged his way through, gin and tonic in his hand.

'Gilbert, at last,' gushed the green frock lady and took his arm. 'I wondered where you'd got to.'

I moved quietly away. 'Enjoyed the performance,' I said, sidling up to Bennison at the back of the group. 'Can

I get you one?' His cowboy costume had been replaced by cavalry twill slacks and a tweed jacket with the teacher's regulation leather patches on the elbows. His temples hinted at Grecian 2000 and his sparse hair was brushed forward at the front to conceal his receding hairline.

'Very civil of you. I'll have half of lager.'

There was a limited bar which did not include cider so I ordered two halves of lager. Next to me, a couple of ladies in cloche hats were bitching loudly about the performance of one of the actresses.

'Absolutely ridiculous giving her that part. She's far too old.'

'Just what I said, dear. You were perfect for it. If that isn't favouritism, I don't know what is.' She lowered her voice to a bellow. 'Of course, everyone knows she's been sleeping with Hughie for years. His wife's dyslexic, you know.'

I took the drinks back to Bennison. 'They tell me you're a lecturer in real life.'

He laughed. 'Real life! I wonder which is which sometimes.'

'At John Moores, isn't it?' He nodded. 'A friend of mine's son goes there. Or should I say, did. Matt Scrufford. I used to play in a band with his father. Did you know him by any chance?'

I might just as well have asked him if he'd had carnal knowledge of the Pope. The colour drained from his cheeks and a nervous tic appeared in his left eye. He took a long gulp from his drink and I noticed his hand trembled.

'Er, I believe he was in one of my General Studies groups but I never had any personal contact, on a one-to-one basis, that is.'

'That's odd. I could have sworn Mally said he'd mentioned your name. Obviously I've got it wrong.'

'They all look alike after a while.'

'Like Red Indians,' I said. He looked puzzled. 'Buffalo Bill.'

'Oh yes.' His laugh was one of relief that the subject was closed. It wasn't.

'I'm told there's been a bit of a scandal at your place, something to do with exam papers.'

'Look, who are you?'

'Like I said, I'm a friend of Mally Scrufford and I'm curious to know how far his son was involved in all this.'

'All what? There's no scandal, you're talking rubbish.'

'In that case, it won't bother you that the university authorities are about to receive a letter giving full details of these alleged irregularities.' If you're going to bluff, go for broke, that's my motto.

'What irregularities?'

'And I want to know how many of them might implicate my friend's son.'

'Look, Matt Scrufford's dead and—'

'And someone had a reason for killing him.'

Bennison slurped down his lager and slammed the glass viciously on the table. 'I don't know what you're after, my friend, but I'm not staying here listening to this drivel.' He pushed through a crowd of people to get to the door.

'Really!' exclaimed the green-frock lady, reaching up to readjust her perm.

Gilbert, beside her, raised an eyebrow. 'What's the matter with Colin? Having one of his tantrums?'

'Does he get them often?' I asked.

'Well, you know what they're like. They might make good actors but they're all prima donnas, aren't they?'

I supposed they were. I left the rest of my lager and followed Bennison out of the door. He was nowhere to be seen but an old Escort with a leaking exhaust was turning the corner.

Well, something had touched a nerve but had I frightened him off? And I still didn't know if he was fiddling the exams, though certainly something was bothering him.

The rain that had threatened all day started to bucket down as I walked towards the station and I was glad I'd brought my parka. Even so, I was soaked before the train arrived to take me back to the city.

The night was just beginning.

Chapter Five

Tommy McKale was at the door of the Masquerade watching a party of Irish navvies vomiting in the gutter. 'Must have been the caviar,' he said. 'I told them to stick to beefburgers. You know where you are with mad cow disease.'

I followed him inside and handed my sodden parka to the cloakroom girl. Tommy eyed my suit wonderingly. 'Christ, Johnny, you look smart! Where have you been? There's a guy inside looking for you.'

'For me? What's he look like?'

'His hair's like one of those brushes they used to shove up chimneys.'

'Sounds like Badger.' I wandered into the club and there he was, chatting to a Kate Moss lookalike. He was wearing a bright yellow jacket, royal-blue shirt and navy trousers. I stopped worrying about being overdressed.

He saw me and came over. 'Hi, man. I've been looking for you.'

'Don't tell me, next month's rent?'

'Better than that. I've got something on your chummy.' It was more than I'd expected, and sooner. 'Have you heard of the Stripes Club?'

I know most of the clubs in the city, legit or not, but I didn't know this one.

'It ain't no proper club, like they don't have premises. They just hire places when they have meetings.'

'And do they have many meetings?'

'What are we doing standing here? Let's find a seat and I'll have a large brandy.'

Obediently, I got the drinks in and followed him to the back of the club, away from the usual million decibels. Saturday night was rave night.

'Do you remember in the eighteenth century, the Hellfire Club?' This was Badger the academic. I nodded. 'And in the sixties, the Whiplash Club?' I was old enough to have lived through the Christine Keeler episodes and subsequent government scandals, which somehow seemed to be more prevalent than ever in the nineties.

'Well, the Stripes Club is like those, man. A place where people of similar sexual proclivities can meet and indulge themselves in those perversions that take their fancy.'

'In this case . . .?'

'In this case, some serious flagellation, hence the name.'

'Why the secrecy and changes of venue?'

'Apparantly, not all the participants are willing. Makes it more exciting for the members if a few strangers get mutilated in the name of entertainment.'

I took a mouthful of cider. 'So what has this got to do with Matt Scrufford?'

'He was there the week before he was killed. They had a meeting at a house in Princes Drive, one of the refurbished Victorian mansions. There's a huge cellar down there that makes the Adelphi Hotel look like Joe's Café, panelled walls, chandeliers, the lot.'

'You've been?'

'Last night. Personal invitation; they seem to think I'm loaded.'

'They're not your landlord.'

He smiled. 'This is how they operate. The members bring along women looking for a good night out, right?'

'Right.'

'Women who are goers.'

'I get the picture, Badger.'

'So they fuel the women up with a few doubles, then they get one of them up on stage and along come these guys with the big bankrolls and they start bidding like they're playing strip poker only without the deck.'

'Go on.'

'Well, a few pounds change hands and eventually the girl gets stripped off and they handcuff her to a wall and tell her its OK, she won't really get hurt but how about letting this guy whip her. Just one stroke, you understand, nothing heavy.

'So there's this guy standing there on stage with a whip in his hand and up gets this Arab waving a ten-pound note and the girl says OK, one stroke, and a minute later there's a big red weal on her ass but a tenner is a tenner. Then another guy gets up and offers twenty for another stroke but on her tits. And she's not too happy but, well, it's twenty pounds, man. You get the picture?'

'I think so.'

'I mean, she's handcuffed, man, the chains are on.'

'And no knights in shining armour are in the audience to rescue her?'

'You're kidding. That's what they're there for; they're loving it. It's like the Roman games. Bring on the Christians.'

'What about the boyfriend?'

'Come on, get real, man. He's the one collecting the bread and, besides, he's probably getting off on it himself. So what if she's yelling a bit? A couple more lashes won't hurt.'

'Until . . .?'

'Until the serious pain starts and he gets a bit nervous but this is where the other punters come in and wave the big money and so the show goes on.'

'So what's a nice boy like Matt Scrufford doing in a place like that?'

'And with such a nice girl too.'

'What!' This was a turn-up. I hadn't met Sarah but from what I'd gathered, she didn't strike me as being the bondage type. 'What did she look like?'

'From what I've heard, Whitney Houston.'

'You mean she was black?'

'As my ass,' grinned Badger. I tried to come to terms with this new information. Matt was with another woman. This was a new ball game. What would Sarah think of her fiancé's secret life?

'How do you know it was Matt Scrufford?'

'I've seen the visitors' book.'

'Anybody could have signed his name.'

'It was him.' He pressed his finger to his nose. 'I have my sources.'

'When's the next meeting?'

'Wednesday night. Do you want an invite?'

'Can you get me one?'

'It'll cost you and you'll have to bring a woman.'

I couldn't see Maria at the Stripes Club. I wondered if it was Hilary's night off. 'So long as she's not part of the floorshow.'

Badger swirled his brandy around the bottom of the glass. 'Do you think we're on to something here?'

'I don't know, but there's another angle as well.' I told him about Colin Bennison.

'I knew all them exam boards was crooked and I still managed to get my MA! So was No-Ears after a dropsy?'

'Apparently not. He's dead straight; he wanted to warn the guy off.'

Badger nodded sagely. 'Oh yeah, he's dead straight, that's why he's partying at the Stripes. Seems to me there's more to chummy than meets the ear.'

'Very droll.' But he was right. Suddenly, all sorts of unexpected avenues were opening up.

'Listen, man, I can't sit here with you all night, I've

got some serious fucking to take care of.' I observed the skeletal creature still hovering by the bar, surrounded by a coterie of middle-aged lechers. On closer inspection, she was a little old to be a model. She looked at least fifteen. 'Call round Wednesday teatime; I'll know the venue and I'll get your pass.'

He danced through the crowd, glass in hand. I sauntered across to the door.

'Ever heard of the Stripes Club?' I asked Tommy McKale.

He looked startled. 'You're not in trouble with them fellas, are you?'

'No, I don't know them.'

'Very heavy crowd. Shooters, drugs, you name it. They're an inter-city mob, fellas in from the Smoke, Newcastle, Manchester . . .'

'They give you any trouble?'

'Let's say we treat each other with respect and stay out of each other's way. How come you're interested?'

'Someone I know mentioned this Stripes Club.'

'You keep clear, Johnny. You don't need it.'

'I'll try.'

He lowered his voice. 'If you ever need any help . . .' he said. I remember when a chef attacked his brother, Denis, ripping out his intestines with a French knife. The sort that curves. Even in intensive care, with the priest waiting to read the last rites, Denis refused to name his assailant to the police. Much later, when Denis had recovered, the chef was found in the early hours of the morning, crushed to death on the verge of the East Lancs Road.

Witnesses spoke of a big dark Jaguar. Tommy O'Kale drove a dark-blue XJ6. Nobody was ever arrested in connection with the 'accident'.

I knew he meant it. 'Thanks, Tommy.' I looked at my watch. 'One o'clock. Time I had an early night.'

* * *

I suppose there are places where you can wake up on a Sunday to the sound of church bells and skylarks. Liverpool isn't one of them. I get just the odd burst of a ship's hooter and the roar of traffic making its way to the Sunday market in the old Stanley Dock. That's what comes of sleeping with the window open.

I got up about ten, had a shower and made breakfast. I have this receipe where you put All Bran, Bemax wheatgerm and Force wheat flakes in a bowl and add a beaten raw egg, honey and boiling milk with a sprinkling of nutmeg on top. Does wonders for the system.

I ploughed through a few sections of the *Sunday Times*, half listening to *The Archers*. Frankie Dettori had gone through the card at Ascot and given the bookies their biggest roasting for years. Before *Desert Island Discs* came on, I wandered along to the market myself.

It amazes me that the big stores in town take any money when you see the prices down there. Of course, a lot of it is bootleg gear and there's a fair amount of crap but you can pick up some decent bargains. I bought a pair of trainers, ostensibly Adidas, for a tenner, and splashed out another £15 for a sweater remarkably like Mally Scrufford's.

I walked back along the dock road to the Pier Head and caught a ferry. At one time, the Sunday ferries would be packed with day trippers off to the sands and fairground of New Brighton but that was before the tower burnt down and the sea washed away the landing stage and New Brighton became a posh suburb instead of a seaside resort.

Nowadays, the boat commutes between Liverpool, Birkenhead and Seacombe but all the serious passengers take the Underground, leaving the boats deserted for most of the time. At weekends, they lure a few tourists on board.

There weren't too many tourists this September Sunday. I sat alone on the open top deck of the *Mountwood* as the boat pulled away, glad of my waterproof parka to counteract the spray blown by the cold east wind.

It was a good place to think and I had plenty to think about.

I couldn't see Bennison as the killer, even if he did have a motive. He might want to kill Matt to shut him up, but why bother with the ears?

On the other hand, all sorts of perverted things could be going on at the Stripes Club. Removal of the odd pair of ears might hardly be considered untoward. In fact, a live amputation performance would probably merit a gala night and an increased entrance fee. The thought came into my head whimsically but I shuddered when I realised there could be some truth there.

Who could the black girl have been?

In reality, all my investigations had just clouded the picture. It wasn't a simple botched kidnap any more. So what the hell was it?

The Liver Buildings were receding into the mist as the boat neared the Woodside pier at Birkenhead. A couple of people got off and an old lady boarded.

A tug chugged past, like the one Billy Fury once worked on. It's funny how, in abstract, I always visualise the city as it was in the sixties. I still expect to see the Royal Iris crossing the Mersey and there are days I walk down Mathew Street convinced The Cavern will still be there with Paddy on the door and Bob Wooller spinning the discs.

The old lady climbed up to the top deck and took a seat beside the rails. From a battered shopping bag, she produced a loaf and broke bits off to throw to passing seagulls. The birds obviously knew her because they clustered round and one or two braver ones landed on her arm.

I thought of Matt Scrufford lying at the bottom of this water, only a mile or two down river. Who had put him there and why?

The one person I really wanted to talk to was Sarah, Matt's girlfriend, and she was in Chiswick till Friday. I couldn't wait that long. I decided I'd drive down in the morning and see her.

By the time we'd got back to Liverpool it felt like early evening though it was only four o'clock. Low clouds and drizzle had brought the night on early. I walked back to the flat and phoned Mally Scrufford for Sarah's address.

He didn't seem overjoyed at my call.

'The police have already spoken to her, Johnny. She knows nothing.'

'I know. But I found out something interesting that nobody's mentioned. Did you know that Matt's lecturer at university was on the fiddle and Matt had threatened to shop him?'

The silence told me he didn't.

'Pretty straight, your lad, you ought to be proud of him.' I didn't mention the Stripes Club. 'So I thought Sarah might be able to tell me something about this fellow.'

More silence then, 'Oh, please yourself. Whatever you do it's too late for Matt.' I waited whilst he gave me the address. 'I'm sorry, Johnny. All this is getting to me. I appreciate you trying to help.' His voice hardened. 'And if you think this chap had something to do with my son's murder, I want to know before the police do.'

I murmured something appropriate and cut the call. It was time to fix arrangements for the evening and I'd still not rung Maria as promised. I caught her at her flat and agreed to pick her up at seven.

We went to L'Alouette in Lark Lane and, as we ordered, I brought her up to date with events.

'So Matt Scrufford may not be all he seems,' I said, thinking of the Stripes Club.

'What do you expect?' replied Maria. 'I mean, with his upbringing.'

'In what way?'

'Parents splitting up, him shipped off to the Isle of Man without his dad.'

'But they weren't not speaking. He'd been living with Mally since he came to uni.'

Maria put on her serious social worker look. 'There's this theory now that divorce isn't good for kids after all, and it's better to have both parents together, no matter how much they might row.'

I wasn't sure I agreed with that. When I was a kid, I couldn't wait for my father to leave the house as he spent most of his time in it battering my mother.

'You see, a person's self-esteem comes from the knowledge that he's been created as an expression of his parents' love for one another. It gives him a reason for his existence.'

'So you're saying that if a girl goes out one night, gets drunk and ends up pregnant by a stranger that she never sees again, then that child will have no self-esteem, no matter how well she brings it up and loves it?'

'Yes, I'm saying exactly that. It will still feel deprived of its father. This has been proven in black communities in America where family life has broken down almost completely.'

I drained the last of my soup and sat back. I could have asked what effect her own divorce had on her son but I didn't feel like getting into a big socio-anthropological argument.

We moved on to safer subjects but then she brought up the visit to her sister's again. 'If you've nothing on next Sunday night, Kaye and Alex have invited us round for a meal.' I told her I wasn't sure I wanted to meet her relations just yet.

'We're only going for a meal, Johnny, I'm not proposing.'

'I know. It's just that I feel they may read more into our relationship than there is.'

'I don't think they will but would that be a bad thing anyway? I mean, all relationships have to progress, don't they?'

I didn't think they did. 'Why can't they reach a plateau where both parties accept things the way they are?'

'Because most people expect them to lead somewhere. They get married or live together or they call it a day and find someone else.'

'You've had one marriage that didn't work out. Why go into it again?

'I don't want to be on my own for ever, I guess.'

This was the very thing I valued, to have my own place, to be free to come and go as I pleased.

'Robin's left home now; it could be time for me to make a new start.'

'But who says you can't just carry on the way you are?'

The waiter came to remove the soup dishes. Maria leant across the table. 'Because things change, Johnny. People change. But they don't for you, do they? I've noticed it for awhile. Half the time your head's in the past.'

'Strange you should say that. I was on the ferry this afternoon and I half expected to see the *Royal Iris* pull alongside. We used to play on it every Saturday night; there were terrible fights.'

She laughed. 'You see, you're doing it again.'

'But the past is always with us.'

'No it isn't. All those people on that boat when you played there are living different lives in different places. All you have is a memory, not reality.'

'Marc Bolan said thought was the only reality. My trip this afternoon is no more real than my memories. They're both only thoughts in the end.'

'But what happened to the girls you took out in those days? They'll all be married with families now; they'll have long forgotten you. And what do you do? Just carry on the same as always. A new generation of girls to take out, all interchangeable, no commitment and they too will move on in time. You haven't moved on at all. How long can it go on?'

'For ever, I hope. I'm happy with my life as it is. Look, Maria, I enjoy your company. I find our conversations stimulating. I enjoy sex with you. But there is a girl called Hilary I have known for twenty years that I see from time to time and will continue to do so. And if I met someone tomorrow that I fancied taking out, I like to feel I'd be able to do so without any guilt.'

She opened her mouth to say something but I carried on. 'But that doesn't mean I don't want to see you. I do. But, I accept that this means I have no right to object if you want to see someone else. I just hope that you'd want to carry on still seeing me.'

'And if I didn't?'

I shrugged. 'I suppose I'd meet someone else, like I always have done.'

'That's so arrogant.'

'It's honest. No one woman, or man for that matter, can satisfy every facet of their partner's personality. Most people accept this and settle for less. Then they find themselves unfulfilled, seek diversions and end up in the divorce courts.'

'Well, I can't say I haven't been warned, can I?' She gave a brittle laugh. 'Anyway, does all this mean you won't come on Sunday at any price?'

'After all I've said, I think it would be very churlish of me not to accept,' I said solemnly. 'So long as you don't order a wedding dress on the strength of it.'

We both laughed, glad to relieve the tension. The main course arrived and the rest of the evening passed pleasantly. I dropped her off at Crosby just before midnight, declined the offer to stay the night and drove straight back home. I wanted an early start.

I parked in my usual spot. There was a metallic-blue

Shogun I hadn't seen before and I assumed one of the neighbours had visitors.

I was putting the key in the lock when the two men jumped me.

Chapter Six

I figure they'd been hiding round the corner of the corridor and checked me when they heard the lift. The first blow struck me in the kidneys, knocking me against my front door. Before I reached the ground, the other bloke pulled me round by my hair and kicked me in the mouth with the toe of his Doc Martens, splitting open my lip.

I grabbed for his leg and held on to give myself breathing space. He was dark-skinned, not black but certainly of mixed race. I figured as long as I was close to him, he couldn't get any distance in his punches but I still had the first guy to deal with and a stream of blood was running down my chin. This guy was white but wore a navy woollen balaclava that hid most of his face and also made him look more menacing.

I looked up to see him coming towards me with a knife. It was his big mistake. He lunged towards me, his arm curved in a vicious arc as he slashed down at my face. Quickly, I twisted away. He couldn't stop the trajectory. The blade ripped through the jeans of the Doc Marten man, who fell to the ground screaming in agony as it sliced into his groin.

He didn't get up.

Whilst the first man stopped in momentary horror, I hit him as hard as I could on the temple with my fist and he joined his companion on the floor.

It was suddenly silent. Nobody came out on to the landing. If they had heard anything beyond their solid front doors, they probably thought it was somebody's television.

I looked down at my two assailants. I didn't recognise either of them but I didn't expect too. Both wore dark sweaters and blue jeans. I pulled away the balaclava from the white guy's face. He was about twenty-five, with designer stubble, a gold ear stud and thin, bloodless lips.

I let myself in the flat and dialled the police. It wasn't an instant decision. I didn't really want to draw attention to myself and I knew it would antagonise whoever had sent the two roughnecks.

Also, of course, in the current climate of liberalism that is strangling British law and order, it occurred to me I could be charged with assault myself. In fact, if they sued me, I'd probably end up paying them damages.

In the end, however, the thought of having to dispose of two heavy bodies, albeit living ones, was the deciding factor. I was getting too old for humping and carrying.

As an afterthought I ordered an ambulance. The guy with the damaged wedding tackle wasn't looking like he'd last too long. I went into the bathroom to wash the blood off my face. Luckily, the cut wasn't deep. I returned to the lounge and sat down to wait for the inevitable cross-examination.

The police beat the paramedics by thirty seconds, by which time the first of my assailants was staggering to his feet.

'You take him, we'll have this one,' suggested the ambulance driver cheerfully. Neither policeman appreciated the humour. They rarely do. I noticed a pool of darkening blood on the landing carpet as the second thug was dragged away and wondered if the service charge would cover the cleaning.

'Would you like to explain what happened?' the first policeman asked after he had established it was I who had summoned them.

'Muggers,' I replied. 'Waiting for me at the top of the stairs when I came in. So much for the security car park.'

'Why were they waiting for you? Are you carrying anything valuable?'

I had to be careful here. I wanted to be the accidental victim of street crime not a gangland target. 'I think they were about to break into my flat when I came back and disturbed them.'

His companion broke in. 'Did you find it absolutely necessary to rip his bollocks open . . .' he forced the word out, 'sir?' He looked more like a villain than my attackers but they do say police and criminals swim in the same cesspool. It's just that when the fishermen arrive, one lot come out the other side of the net.

'The other man did it, by accident. He was aiming for me but I managed to swerve out of the way.'

'I suppose he knocked his pal out as he fell?' I wasn't impressed. I've always regarded sarcasm as the refuge of the woefully dense. It's a policeman's favourite weapon.

'I did that,' I said, 'in an act of self-defence.'

'Oh, really?' He didn't look convinced.

'Look, it's nearly one o'clock. I have to be up at six. I can't tell you any more than I have. If you want to get in touch with me again, here's my card.' I handed him one of my expensive plastic business cards and he studied it carefully.

'Johnny Ace. I thought I recognised the voice. This'll be a story for the tabloids.'

'Not from me it won't. I'm not interested in publicity, especially that sort.'

It must have been something in my tone. The first policeman quickly stepped forward. 'Don't worry, Mr Ace. We'll sort things this end and we can get in touch with you at this address, I take it? We'll need a statement from you at some time.'

'No problem.'

They left and I shut the door in relief. Someone had tried to kill me. But who? One thing was for sure. Matt Scrufford's death was looking less like a kidnap than ever.

I had a shower, put some Savlon on my mouth and got into bed. I felt like I'd been ten rounds with Dolly Parton. I soon fell asleep.

I was on the M6 by six thirty. My mouth was swollen and slightly sore but I figured I was lucky to get off so lightly. By eight o'clock I was stuck by the Walsall turn-off along with what seemed like the rest of the British population. There was no point in fretting. Short of racing along the hard shoulder there was nothing I could do about it. I sat back in my seat. I had Confederate Railroad's 'Trashy Women' blasting out in the cabin, a cardboard container of hot tea from the Hilton Park services in the cup rest and a copy of the *Sun* opened out on the steering wheel. Every few minutes I edged several yards forward then went back to the football reports.

A bit like travelling on the train really.

The Birmingham rush-hour traffic added a good half-hour on the journey but I made up time on the M40 and pulled into Chiswick before ten.

Sarah and her parents lived in a tall semi-detached alongside Turnham Green, just off Chiswick High Road. A large church stood in the middle of the green giving a village feel to the area. The houses were probably built in the twenties, in Accrington brick, but with no garages. Consequently, the first parking space I found was a few hundred yards along the road.

I rang the bell a couple of times before someone stirred. Sarah had obviously still been in bed as she was rubbing her eyes when she opened the door. She wore an ankle-length towelling robe and her long, straight blonde hair was pulled back and held in a ponytail by an elastic band. There were no signs of night-before make-up and she looked every bit the archetypal student.

I introduced myself as a friend of her boyfriend's father and she invited me into the kitchen, a tall, narrow room at the back of the house. Brass pans stood on a large Aga, the units were antique pine and pots of growing herbs were dotted round the room on every available surface. An old-fashioned clothes rack was suspended against the ceiling, mostly full of underwear, socks and tights. I suspected it was an original feature of the room like the bells in a case over the door, relics of the days when the kitchen housed the servants' quarters.

'You must have left Liverpool very early,' she said. 'What time is it?'

'About ten o'clock.'

'Have you had any breakfast? Would you like some toast?'

'Love some.'

'Tea or coffee?'

'Tea, please.'

She set about making it and I took a seat at the solid kitchen table, more antique pine.

The toast was wholemeal, smothered in butter and marmalade. She brought over two mugs of tea and sat beside me. Now that I'd got here, I wasn't sure how to start. I didn't want to mention that the dead boyfriend, whom she had presumed faithful, had been escorting an unknown black woman to deviant sex orgies. At least, not to begin with.

What did the Greeks say about shooting the messenger?

'My parents are at work,' she said. 'I thought I'd have a lie-in. I don't get much chance when I'm in Liverpool.'

'I don't blame you. Look, I came to talk to you about Matt,' I began. 'I know it might be upsetting for you but I'm not sure his death is quite what it seems.'

'Oh no? So what does it seem like?'

I was unprepared for her tone of self-assurance. As she picked up her cup, her dressing gown fell open to the waist exposing large unfettered breasts swinging beneath a loose *Les Miserables* T-shirt and I was lost for a reply.

'You mean you don't believe it was a kidnap attempt?' I took a sip of tea to compose myself. She was very fanciable and I had to remind myself she was just two years out of school and of a generation that sues for sexual harassment if a man offers his seat on a bus.

She pulled the dressing gown into place without embarrassment.

'I'm sure it wasn't. That's why I came to see you. To see if you had any suggestions.'

'Like what?' I felt she should have been studying Law, not Geography. She'd have made a great barrister.

'Well, for a start, had he upset anyone? Was he running with the wrong crowd? What do you know about a lecturer called Bennison?'

'Whoa. That'll do for starters.' She looked into my eyes. 'The answer is no to the first two. As for the third, Bennison tried to grope me in the lecture theatre one night when everyone had gone home.'

'I take it he didn't get very far?'

'What do you think?' Her scornful tone suggested he hadn't.

I started on the toast and marmalade. 'Did you tell Matt?'

'Of course. He wanted to batter Bennison but I told him not to bother. The worm wasn't worth it.'

'Was Matt very affected by it?'

'He was angry at the time, obviously, but I don't think he was brooding about it. Anyway, if there'd been any revenge, it would have been Bennison floating in the river, wouldn't it?'

'Not necessarily. You see, Matt had another disagreement with Bennison. He found out he was fiddling exam papers.' I studied her expression to see if it registered any recognition of this news. It didn't. She looked amazed.

'No! What a turn-up! Was Matt sure? He never said anything to me.'

'Apparently, he was going to confront Bennison with the evidence.'

'And what happened?'

'I don't know, I wasn't party to the conversation. One of Matt's chums at college told me about it.'

'So did Matt challenge him or not?'

'We'll never know. Unless Bennison tells us. This only happened on the Wednesday, the day before Matt went missing.' There was a silence. I took advantage of it to broach the more difficult subject.

'Did Matt ever mention a club called the Stripes?'

She pursed her lips. 'No. And I don't think I've heard of it. Is it in Liverpool?'

'Princes Drive.'

She shook her head. 'What's the significance?'

'Matt went there.'

'So?'

'You didn't know?'

'I wasn't his keeper. He did go out without me, you know.'

'With other girls?'

Sarah jumped up, tossing her ponytail and stood in front of me. 'Look, I don't know what you're playing at, coming here bothering me with all this crap.'

'I'm sorry. I didn't know exactly how serious your relationship was.'

'We were engaged to be married.' She spat the words out. 'He wasn't unfaithful and I wasn't unfaithful. Right?'

I picked up the last piece of toast. 'Right,' I echoed. I wasn't going to argue but, whether it was the way she avoided my eyes or whether it was the too aggressive tone of her voice, I didn't believe her.

She remained on the offensive. 'So what makes you think he might have had other girls?'

'I don't. I was just asking.'

'You must have had a reason.'

'He was in a nightclub. Fellas usually go to clubs to pick up women.'

'God, how bloody sexist. He probably went there for a drink with some guys from the uni.'

'You're right, I'm sure.' I didn't want to antagonise her further. 'So, apart from Bennison, we don't know of anybody with reason to harm Matt?'

'I've told the police and I'm telling you, no, no, no. And now I think perhaps you'd better leave.'

I didn't feel I had a choice and there was no way I could bring myself to mention the Whitney Houston lookalike. I drank the rest of my tea quickly and stood up.

'I'm sorry if I upset you. I'm just trying to find out anything that might account for his death and this club might have been a lead.'

'Well, it means nothing to me. I've never heard of it.'

I made my way to the door. 'You're coming back for the funeral, I believe?'

'Of course. I live in Liverpool now. I've got my course to finish. I just wanted a few days at home away from everything.'

'I understand that. I may see you at the service then.' Matt was being buried at St Peter's. She nodded and opened the front door. I felt there was more I should say but nothing came to mind, so in the end I walked down the street to the car.

It was not yet 10.30 a.m. Seven hours' round trip for a thirty-minute interview that had produced . . . nothing. That was bad time management. I felt I wasn't doing very well as a detective.

Chapter Seven

On the way home, I stopped at the services outside Bicester and bought *The Times* to read over a cup of tea. It's only ten pence on a Monday so I feel inclined to support Mr Murdoch's benevolence. I read the football reports over a pot of tea. Joe Royle said Saturday's result had put Everton back on track but I couldn't see it myself.

Driving back up the M40, I considered what had happened to me since I first got involved in the Scrufford case. The fingernails disturbed me. They must have been sent on the Thursday before I even knew about Matt's death, yet I felt sure there was some connection.

And what about the heavies? Bennison was the only person who knew I was involved in any way with the Scrufford case so logically it must have been he who had sent them. He didn't look the type to hire muscle but was there a 'type'? Maybe Jim Burroughs could find out something for me.

I dialled his number as I roared along at eighty towards Birmingham. He didn't seem pleased to hear from me.

'What the fuck's going on with you? I thought I warned you about getting involved in police work.'

'What are you talking about?'

'You'll be glad to know Sonny Loumarr's going to survive though there's some doubt as to whether he'll ever expect a card on Father's Day.'

'Sonny who?'

'The joker you had an altercation with last night.'

'He's OK then?'

'Oh yeah, he's fine, just fine. There's a whole new career opportunity just opened up for him doing Aled Jones on *Stars in Their Eyes.*'

'Who the hell were those guys, Jim?'

'Muggers, so you told Sergeant Britton. Common or garden muggers. Picked you out at random, you said.'

'Isn't that likely?'

'Hired muscle, that's what they are, so don't try and tell me this was a coincidence. I'm not fuckin' stupid. The other fellow's Teddy Twigg, night club bouncer with a long list of form, GBH, ABH, you name it. I want to know why they were after you.'

I slowed down to negotiate the turn-off for the M42. The traffic was getting heavier. 'How do I know? I've never heard of Sonny Loumarr. What's his line?'

'Anything that makes money, which usually means drugs, sex and insurance.'

'Insurance?'

'They used to call it protection. Even the underworld is politically correct these days. So what's it all about, Johnny?'

'I'm not sure, Jim. Look, if he's a hit man, who hired him to hit me?'

'That's what I just asked you.' His voice sounded exasperated though it might have been the static on the mobile.

'I was hoping you'd have found out. You're the detective.'

'It's about time you remembered that. I want you at the station in half an hour.'

'Sorry, Jim. I'm in London at the moment, on the North Circular,' I lied. 'But I'll ring you when I get back.' I switched the phone off quickly. The M42 turn-off was a mile away. Barring traffic jams, I'd reach Liverpool in just over a couple of hours.

The M6 was clear for once and I was back at the flat

for two thirty. The security guard saluted as I drove in. Where had he been last night?

I ran a hot bath scented with some aromatherapy oils Hilary had bought. After the struggle with Sonny Loumarr and his pal, plus the seven hours' driving, I needed something to sooth my muscles. I lay in the water for an hour, taking occasional sips of chilled Southern Comfort and lemonade and dozing off in between. Finally, I had a quick cold shower to wake me up.

I didn't fancy starting cooking so I put on some clean clothes and walked across town to Tess Riley's in Great Charlotte Street. Clayton Square was packed with early Christmas shoppers. September was not yet over and already the shops were full of next year's diaries and Christmas cards and fancy wrapping paper. Beside the open café in the upstairs mall, Glenys Carroll, dressed in a black afternoon frock, was playing 'As Time Goes By' on a grand piano, drowning out the distant sound of records playing inside the Virgin Megastore. It could have been 1930 except for the pile of her cassettes for sale on top of the instrument. In fact, thirty-five years ago, Nems record shop was on this spot where Brian Epstein stocked every record ever released. Two years later he was managing The Beatles and I was playing in The Cruzads.

Inside Tess's there were fewer people. Being only four thirty, it was too early for the after-work, early dinner crowd although a few hardened daytime drinkers were still clustered around the bar.

The blackboard anounced the lunchtime special was chicken curry with mushrooms, peppers, sultanas, tarragon and anything else the chef could find to throw in. I ordered it with rice and took a glass of cider to a quiet corner. The meal was good. I had a cappuccino afterwards and felt well refreshed.

Happily, there were no more Jiffy bags waiting for me in the mail at the station when I arrived to do the show; just the usual request letters for birthdays and anniversaries and a couple of promotion CDs.

I dug out Dawn's 'What are you doing Sunday?' and played it for Maria, following it, in a moment of whimsy, with 'All Alone am I'.

At seven, I handed over to Godfrey Withers, who has a two-hour slot on a Monday evening, playing big band music and stuff from the thirties and forties. Godfrey is an excrutiating presenter. He's about seventy-six and speaks very slowly and correctly. I swear his programme is aimed at pensioners with cataracts who can no longer see *Coronation Street* on their television screens so are resigned to Godfrey on the wireless.

Jim Burroughs was waiting in Reception. 'Good job you're easy to find.' He smiled grimly and I cursed that I hadn't gone out the back way through the car park. The last thing I wanted was an interrogation. 'Come on, I've got my car round the back.'

He was in a plain clothes Mondeo. I sat alongside him and we drove through town, past the Pier Head and into the Albert Dock car park. He stopped at the far end, overlooking the river, where there were no other cars around.

'So, Johnny, what's it all about?'

'Cross my heart, Jim, I don't know. These two fellows jumped me when I got home last night. There was a Shogun parked outside that I didn't recognise. It could have been theirs.'

'Are you still nosing around this Scrufford case?'

'I don't know what you mean, Jim. I've hardly stopped since I last saw you. I was at the match on Saturday, went to the theatre at night. I was out with a girlfriend yesterday and I've been in London all day today buying CDs for the show.'

He didn't look convinced. 'I find it very strange that two days after our conversation, in which you seemed unhealthily interested in one of my murder cases, two lowlifes find it necessary to pay you a visit.'

'But it was just a casual interest, Jim, with me knowing the lad's father.'

'I hope that's what it was, Johnny. If I find out—'

'There's nothing to it, I tell you. Anyway, what's happening to the muggers?'

'You're supposed to be making a statement for Cecil Britton. I doubt if the Director of Public Prosecutions will go for it, though. You're not hurt, nothing's stolen.'

'I'll go in and see Britton tomorrow.' Jim seemed satisfied. I considered telling him about Bennison and about the Stripes Club but decided against it. After all, he'd told me not to interfere.

He dropped me off at my flat. I didn't go inside but got the RAV4 out and set off for Kensington. I decided I needed another chat with Colin Bennison, and Jordan Crook was the only person who could lead me to him.

The house Crook shared was a two-up, two-down terrace on a street behind Kensington Library. Most of the houses had graffiti on the walls and the gutters held a week's litter. A group of young kids ran up as I pulled into the kerb. 'Mind yer car, mister.'

There were five of them, the eldest no more than seven or eight and the youngest hardly out of nursery but already they looked like extras from *Lord of the Flies*. Their parents were probably at bingo or the pub. Or out mugging.

I gave the leader ten pence. He had a shaven head and an earring at the top of his right ear. 'You'll get another if it's untouched when I come back.' You get to learn the rules. No money and the car gets broken into or vandalised. Pay them and they disappear and you take your chance on someone else coming along wrecking it instead.

'Give us that,' screamed one of the smaller children, a girl, trying to prise the coin from the boy's fingers.

He pushed her away. 'Fuck off.'

'Fuck off yourself.' A fight broke out. No wonder school teachers are retiring early with stress. I turned away and walked to the door of Jordan Crook's house. A piece of wire hung loose from the wall where the bell had once been. I knocked hard on the door.

Jordan himself opened it. He wore the same clothes he had worn at Rumours on Saturday. His expression was not welcoming when he recognised me but I strode past him into the front room, saving him the embarrassment of talking on the doorstep.

There were two other guys sitting on an old leather settee, both smoking, and the air was heavy with the scent of cannabis. They nodded disinterestedly at me and continued sucking in the smoke and staring into space.

Jorden belatedly followed me into the room. 'Er, this is Timothy and Simon. Er, Johnny Ace.'

They nodded again and said nothing. Jordan ushered me into the back room which served as a kitchen. Unwashed crockery filled the sink and pans half full of baked beans and congealing soup stood on the stove. So much for New Man.

He faced me nervously. 'What is it now? Didn't you find him?'

'I'm curious, Jordan. Yes, I found Mr Bennison just like you said, at the theatre, but I didn't find him very frightening, even dressed as Buffalo Bill. Now this I find puzzling as you obviously seemed scared of him.'

He shuffled uncomfortably. 'Christ, Matt had been killed, for God's sake. Wouldn't you be frightened?'

'Can you really see your Colin Bennison as a savage killer?'

'No, but the people he mixes with might be.'

'Ah! The people he mixes with. You never mentioned them. Who are they?'

'I don't know who they are but the rumour was that he went in for the rough trade.'

Suddenly, something came back to me, a comment in the theatre bar from Gilbert. *You know what they're like. They're all prima donnas, aren't they?*

'You're telling me Bennison's gay?' And yet Sarah had said he'd tried to grope her.

'Of course. Everyone knew it.'

'You never mentioned it before.'

'Sorry, I never thought.'

'So what's this about rough trade?'

'You know. He'd go with seamen down the docks, get himself roughed up a few times in public lavatories, that sort of thing. Well, if he's hanging around with those sort of people, you wouldn't want to cross him, would you? Next thing you know, you'd be getting a visit.'

I knew all about visits.

'So your theory is, Matt confronted him with the examination scam and Bennison put some of his rough friends on to him. Only they went a bit too far.'

'Something like that, yes.'

I thought about it. If that were the case, Bennison should have been shitting himself because he'd know that if the police found the killers, the trail would lead back to him. So the obvious thing to do would be to disappear in case they shopped him or, worse, tried to blackmail him.

Yet he'd looked sanguine enough at the theatre on Saturday, that is until I started to question him. So, he'd set the killers on to me. What hold did he have over them to command the loyalty of men like Sonny Loumarr?

'You've not met any of these "friends" of Bennison's, have you?'

'No way. I tell you, it's just talk, but after Matt's death and with him telling me about the exams, I mean, who else would want to kill Matt Scrufford?'

That was the big question. Who else would? The police had nobody in the frame. Bennison was the only contender. He had the motive and, it seemed, the means. How could I prove it? If he had to hire his muscle, that suggested he wasn't too handy with the physical stuff himself. Maybe he would confess if enough pressure was put on him.

'Have you no idea where Bennison lives?'

Jordan shook his head. 'You could find out from the college office. Or maybe from his theatre club.'

'Is he still on leave?'

'He's not been in today so I suppose so.'

'Right.' There was nothing more here for me. I was tired. I'd had less than five hours' sleep since I was attacked, I'd driven to London and back, done the show and I'd had enough. I just wanted to get my head down. I made it into bed for ten and I slept the clock round.

Tuesday morning was fine and mild. I went down to The Diner for a late breakfast. The suits were having their morning tea breaks but I found an empty seat near the fountain and took my tray over.

The *Post* had a mere paragraph about the Scrufford case saying the police were pursuing certain lines of enquiry. God knows what they would be. All the headlines were about the long-running Liverpool docks dispute.

I had no plans for the day. I didn't know if anyone's thugs would still be looking for me but I'd no intention of going into hiding.

I finished my breakfast and went back to the flat. I was restless. I switched on a morning chat show on TV in which a group of people were seriously debating the wisdom of giving Action Man a penis in view of the fact that a Barbie doll had breasts.

A lady head teacher said it would encourage an unhealthy obsession in gender in the unformed minds of infant males. A woman sociologist with bushy nostrils agreed and, furthermore, wasn't too keen on Barbie either, believing the toy was only one step away from those inflatable women advertised in the salacious sections of the tabloid press.

The only bit of sense came from the financial manager of a plastics company who pointed out that an extra eighth of an inch on every model would cost the company half a million pounds a year in increased production costs and as far as he was concerned, if the kids wanted their Action Man to have a dick, they could get some Plasticine and stick one on him themselves.

I switched the set off, went over to the piano and doodled a few tunes. It's interesting how one tune leads to another by association of ideas. I started playing 'As Time Goes By' from *Casablanca*, which starred Humphrey Bogart, who also appeared in *Key Largo* . . . 'Key Largo', the Bertie Higgins country hit . . . 'We had it all, just like Bogie and Bacall' . . .

The phone shrilled out and interrupted my reverie. It was Badger. 'OK, man. I've got your tickets for tomorrow night. It'll cost you fifty.'

'Fifty pounds!'

'Don't worry. Just throw away the cheque I gave you and we're straight.'

'Good job I never banked it. Where's the venue?'

He gave me an address in South Albert Road, obviously another large Victorian mansion. I know because I own a house down there myself.

'Can you pick the tickets up now? I'm going away for a couple of days and I gotta leave pretty soon.'

'Yeah, OK.' I had nothing else on. I set off for Livingstone Drive. On the way, I made a detour down South Albert Road. The house looked like any others in the street except there were shutters across the downstairs windows. I passed my own property but didn't go in. If the tenants see you, they feel the need to complain. Best to stay away.

Badger was waiting for me at the front door. 'You

only just caught me. My plane leaves at two.' He was wearing a camel coat which reached mid-calf above cream trousers. He handed me two handwritten tickets. 'Remember what I told you, man. Don't you be getting up on that stage by mistake unless you fancy yourself as Fletcher Christian.'

I put the tickets carefully in my pocket. 'I won't. Where are you off to?'

'Only Bermuda. A bit of business I have to attend to.' He said it as if it was a short bus ride along Upper Parliament Street. 'I'll be back by the weekend. Let me know how you get on.'

I promised I would, then headed for the Everyman Bistro for lunch, which, in the sixties, was known as Hope Hall, home of The Mersey Poets and bluesy bands like The Road Runners.

The campus of John Moores University (ex-Liverpool Polytechnic) intermingles with that of Liverpool University. I had to walk a mile before I found the administrative offices.

The lady in charge was puzzled that I should want Colin Bennison's address and very disinclined at first to give it to me. She was touching fifty but was fighting it with blonde highlights, contact lenses and a loose-fitting Laura Ashley creation to hide her spreading figure.

'I have some documents I want to send him,' I explained.

'You can address them to the college.'

'He's on leave at the moment and it is important he receives them tomorrow.'

It was touch and go for a minute. I smiled my most enigmatic smile and waited. My next step would have been a ten-pound note but I figured the smile was my best shot and I was right.

'I don't suppose it will do any harm.' She brought the directory up on her screen and wrote an address on a sheet of paper which she folded conspiratorially in half and handed to me. I smiled again and thanked her. When I got outside I checked the address. It was near the pinewoods in Freshfield, a couple of miles from the Formby theatre.

I decided not to go until after the show as I figured my little chat with Mr Bennison might take some time. Besides, it was Tuesday afternoon when I usually go down to my office to check things with Geoffrey.

Geoffrey looks after the flats. I suppose he'd describe himself as a Property Manager on his c.v. He served his time as a plumber, obtaining his Corgi registration, picked up some electrical knowledge and a bit of joinery along the way and started out doing odd jobs for me on the properties.

As I acquired more flats, so he became more involved until now I give all the tenants his number and he sorts out all the repairs and problems.

As the rents are all paid by banker's order, all that's left to me to do is show the flats when they become empty, a job I hate but which I'd trust to nobody else.

My office is above a parade of shops in Aigburth Road. Punters rarely call there but it keeps the office machines and paperwork out of my flat and gives Geoffrey a base to work from.

He was on the phone when I walked in, sitting behind his big oak desk, disputing a bill with Manweb. 'Come and read the meter yourself if you can't take my word for it, pal.' Geoffrey speaks in broad Scouse and is built like the hull of one of the old liners. He's six four, wears his hair short, sports an earring in his left ear and weighs in at two twenty. He's very useful in certain cases of eviction and debt collecting where he is more effective than the threat of a bailiff.

Unfortunately, Geoffrey has appalling taste in music. He's into The Police and Elvis Costello, as befits someone who was a teenager in the post-punk eighties, but

I've tried not to hold it against him. He, in turn, thinks anyone who can listen to more than five seconds of New Country without throwing up should be reserving their bed in Ashworth Hospital. So we agree to disagree.

'All right, boss,' he said eventually. He indicated the phone. 'I'm not letting them twats put one over us.'

'Quite right,' I said.

'There's been some comedian on for you. Something about nails.'

The hair on my neck stood up. 'Nails? What about nails?'

'Nothing. Just did you get them. Didn't give his name. Sounded local.'

Nothing added up at all. Where did the nails fit in?

'Probably a joker,' I said.

'Must have been. You couldn't knock a nail in a sheep's ass from six inches. The day you take up carpentry, I'm resigning.'

We spent a couple of hours going over things then I left for the station, just in time to stop Ken, my producer, having apoplexy in case he had to present the show himself.

I started the programme with an old Police track for Geoffrey then I played the brilliant 'Lonely Too Long' from the new Patty Loveless CD, for which she'd just won this year's CMA award.

I went on to a couple of dance tracks from the 'Toe The Line' line dance album. All the menopausal women who used to go to aerobics are now into country music and line dancing, although most of them wouldn't know George Jones from Tom Jones. The church halls are full of them. It's amazing. Probably, I thought, the women in the North End Players chorus line would be line dancers. They certainly looked the part.

I finished the show with a track from one of the new promo CD's from Ace Records, by a 'new R & B sensation' called James Hunter. Van Morrison was singing with him which showed how respected Hunter was. Either that or Morrison's star was waning and he was anxious to be associated with up and coming talent.

It was eight o'clock when I drove over the level crossing gates at Freshfield Station. The line of trees shading the streetlights made it even darker as I drove up to the pinewoods. In the daytime, hordes of sightseers come to see the red squirrels and the woods are owned by the National Trust. Behind the woods are the sandhills, home to a protected species of toad, and the beach, washed by the polluted waters of the Irish Sea.

I turned off just before the entrance hut into a road of palatial houses which backed on to the woods. Bennison's was seventh or eighth along, a substantial Tudor-style detached. According to Crook, he lived alone so perhaps it had been his parents' home and he'd stayed on after they died. It was certainly not a property he'd buy on a lecturer's salary.

The house was in darkness. I let the car glide quietly up to the gate and walked purposefully to the front door. I hoped his hired thugs wouldn't be around. I rang the bell and knocked a couple of times but nobody stirred.

I went round towards the back door but the side gate was locked. I peered in the window of the detached garage and recognised the old Escort there that I had seen drive away from the theatre. I felt suddenly apprehensive. Somehow I knew I was going to find something awful here.

[illegible] with him [illegible] how [illegible] and he was [illegible]

It was eight o'clock when I drove over the level crossing [illegible] Station. The [illegible] shining [illegible] and [illegible] the [illegible] and the [illegible] by the [illegible] home [illegible] by the [illegible] of the [illegible]

I [illegible] the [illegible] had a great deal of [illegible] was [illegible] perhaps it had been [illegible] then [illegible] in [illegible] on a [illegible]

The [illegible] little to me from [illegible] of [illegible] and [illegible] front door [illegible] was [illegible] by the window [illegible] the [illegible] I had [illegible] away [illegible] suddenly [illegible] now I [illegible] going to [illegible] up [illegible]

Chapter Eight

What I found was the body of Colin Bennison.

It was in the front bedroom. Having clambered over the side gate, I noticed that the kitchen window had been left slightly ajar. Pulling it open was easy: So was climbing through. Not something I'd normally do, but I'd come this far . . . Luckily, the house was not overlooked and the burglar alarm was not switched on. Bennison probably just bought the box as a deterrent, I thought, the cheapskate. Not a good idea.

I put the lights on as I walked through the rooms. Nothing is more suspicious to a passer-by than a torch flashing around a darkened house.

There wasn't anything out of the ordinary. In the kitchen, an empty mug and a plate lay on the kitchen table next to half a packet of cream crackers and some crumbs of Lancashire cheese on a piece of clingfilm. I felt the kettle on the hob. It was stone cold. It was some time since he'd had that snack.

The lounge and dining room were empty. I went upstairs and into the front bedroom. The curtains were pulled across and they were thick because there was no glow from the street lighting. I felt for the light switch and straight away I saw him.

He wouldn't be playing Buffalo Bill again.

He was sprawled across the double bed, dressed in a pair of gold and red striped pyjamas and a brocade Noël Coward dressing gown. Theatrical to the end. One velvet slipper had fallen on the floor, the other hung from his toes.

There was a gash on the side of his head outlined by the coagulated scarlet blood that had matted in his thinning hair and some blobs had dropped from his skull on to the yellow and pink duvet cover. His pallid skin was waxen and from the offensively sweet odour of decaying flowers that permeated the room, I guessed he'd been dead for some time.

On a white bedside cabinet lay a bottle of pills. I checked. It was three-quarters empty.

I had another look at the body then stepped quickly outside and made my way back to the kitchen. What now? Why had Bennison been killed? Had Loumarr and Twigg decided to cut the connection between Bennison and themselves and thus any trail back to Matt Scrufford?

And should I phone the police and have a repeat of Sunday night's unpleasant interlude with the law or would I be better creeping quietly away? But I couldn't do that because there'd be fingerprints and my car was parked openly outside for anyone to see, and the RAV4 was not the most anonymous of vehicles.

Christ, I thought. What was I doing getting mixed up in all this? If I was that bored, why hadn't I taken up basket weaving or scuba diving? Talk about being up Shit Creek without a paddle.

In the end, I took the only option I really had. I rang Jim Burroughs.

He wasn't so thrilled to hear from me. 'You're not in more trouble, are you? Don't say your so-called muggers have been back?'

'Jim, listen. I'm at a house in Freshfield. Actually, it's Matt Scrufford's tutor's house.'

There was a sound like a small explosion at the other end of the line. 'You told me you weren't messing around with that case. What the hell are you doing there?'

'I'll explain that later.'

'Too fuckin' right you will.'

'He's dead, Jim.'

'What!'

'Murdered. He's lying on the bed, blood everywhere.'

'Oh shit! Give me the address and don't go away. I want to hear the full story.' A thought seemed to strike him. 'Hey, you didn't chill him, did you?'

'Don't be stupid. He's been dead for days by the look of him.'

'Don't even leave the room. We'll be there in half an hour.'

He made it in twenty minutes. The Mondeo screeched to a halt and he came running up the front path with a long-haired man that I took to be his sergeant.

'Right, where is he?'

I led them up to the bedroom and went back to the kitchen to find a drink. I felt I needed one and Bennison would certainly not be using his fridge again. All he had was a four pack of Castlemaine XXXX but it was better than nothing and I helped myself to a can.

By the time I'd drained it, Jim Burroughs was back down, his mobile phone in his hand. 'The doctor and the forensic team are on their way down but for someone who fancies himself as a detective I'd say you were pretty crap.'

'What do you mean?'

'That isn't murder up there, sunshine. The old queen's topped himself, hasn't he?'

'But his head's cut open.'

'My guess is he took the tablets, lost his balance, fell against that cabinet and cut his head open. Maybe he passed out, maybe he just lay there waiting for the drugs to take effect, I don't know. But I'd lay a month's salary the dope did for him.' He came across the room and stood over me. 'The question is, Johnny, why does Matt Scrufford's tutor do this and where do you fit in?'

'How do you know he's an old queen?'

'Oh come on, Johnny. Wise up. His local lavatory's

one of the top meeting places in the Gay Tourist Guide to Merseyside. He's passed through our hands numerous times, figuratively speaking, of course.' He eyed my empty can. 'Are there any more of those?'

'In the fridge.'

He went across, pulled the other three cans out and handed one each to me and the sergeant. 'Might as well drink them, no use leaving them for the burglars. You don't know Kevin here, do you? Kevin Payton, used to play lead guitar for a thrash band at university. One of our educated coppers. This is Johnny Ace, ex-drummer and radio personality who now thinks he's a fucking detective as well.'

Kevin nodded to me wordlessly and proceeded to open the Castlemaine with his teeth. There was a Neanderthal quality about him undiluted by his educational prowess.

'Right then. Let's hear it from the beginning and it's no use pretending it's a coincidence that you're here.'

I filled him in with the Jordan Crook part of the story. I didn't mention the Stripes Club. I didn't think he was ready for it.

The two men guzzled their lager noisily as I told my story but didn't interrupt. When I'd finished, Jim Burrows tossed his empty can across to the sink and turned to me.

'Let's get this right, then. After speaking to this kid Crook, you've got Bennison in the frame for fixing exam results, ordering the kidnapping, mutilating and drowning of Scrufford Minor, if not actually taking part in it himself, when he thinks young Scrufford's on to him, and then sending Loumarr and Twigg to see you off when you start asking your awkward questions?'

'I suppose so.' It didn't sound so plausible the way he expressed it.

'Well, that's what you've told me. But if I'm right about the cause of death, bearing in mind I'm only the policeman here, of course, then can you tell me why he should do himself in at this stage?'

'Not offhand,' I said. 'But give me time.'

The front doorbell rang and Jim Burroughs turned to his sergeant. 'Take a statement from him, will you, Kev, while I take the medics up?'

I repeated my story to Payton. It sounded even less likely the second time round.

By the time we'd finished, Jim Burroughs reappeared with a white-haired man he introduced as the police doctor.

'I was right, Johnny. Suicide it was. A hefty overdose, enough to kill six elephants so Dr Womersley here says, or was it six gerbils? Anyway, the interesting thing from your point of view, is the time of death.'

'I don't see—'

'Colin Bennison died around midnight on Saturday, give or take an hour or two. Now you say you saw him driving off from the theatre at eleven thirty? So it looks very unlikely that he'd had time to organise his heavy friends to go round and duff you up.'

'I don't understand.'

'Maybe you're not telling me everything or it's just someone who doesn't like your radio programme. Either way, you've obviously got more enemies than you thought.'

I thought of the nail clippings. That was another thing I hadn't mentioned. They'd been posted before I spoke to Bennison. I was beginning to feel nervous.

The forensic people arrived with cameras and equipment. Eventually, I said I was leaving and Jim Burroughs made no move to stop me.

'Watch out when you walk round corners,' was his parting shot.

I took his advice when I got to my building but I reached the flat unscathed. Now I was seriously worried. If Bennison hadn't set the monkeys on me, that only left the Stripes Club mob, though I wasn't aware they knew about me and my investigations. Still, if Tommy McKale was to be believed, they weren't people to cross.

I remembered the tickets in my pocket and rang Hilary. 'Can you make tomorrow night?' I asked. 'I've a couple of tickets for a club.' I was lucky; it was her night off. 'It's not a normal club,' I ventured and the tone of my voice alerted her.

'What do you mean, not normal?'

'It's a sort of strip club but very upmarket. Matt Scrufford went the week he died. Look, I'll explain when I see you.' We agreed she should meet me at the station after the show.

Then I rang Maria and told her what had happened since I last saw her. It was only two days but it seemed like a month. I don't know why I rang her but I needed someone to talk through the possibilities with and Maria has an analytical mind.

'You sound like you've had a bad time,' she said. 'Do you want me to come over?'

'It's gone eleven.'

'That's all right. I'm doing nothing. Shall I bring a nightdress?'

I didn't think she'd need it. 'I'm hungry,' I said. 'I was going to send out for a pizza. Do you fancy one?'

'Vegetarian with pineapple. I'll be half an hour.'

I opened a bottle of red wine to let it breath and got out the plates and glasses. Maria and the delivery girl arrived simultaneously and we ate the pizzas whilst they were hot.

'Right then,' she said eventually. 'So tell me exactly what happened.'

I poured us each a glass of wine, led her to the settee and went over the events of the past two days. When I'd finished, she was silent for a few moments then, 'Bennison could well have killed himself because he thought his scam with the exam papers might be exposed.

In fact, his going home and doing it soon after you spoke to him suggests that's what happened.'

'But Matt Scrufford had already challenged him so he knew his cover was blown.'

'Well, first of all, we don't know Matt did confront him, we only know he was going to. And if he did, then perhaps Bennison did have him killed. Then, when you saw him at the theatre, he realised he couldn't keep the lid on it any more.'

'Which leaves the question, who had me attacked and why? Oh, and then there's the fingernails.'

'The what?' I fetched the Jiffy bag and showed her the contents.

'Oh, at least they're only clippings. At first I thought you meant they were whole fingernails pulled out with pliers or something.' She shuddered. 'When did they come?'

'Friday. The day before I met Bennison so they're nothing to do with him. But then, I knew nothing about Matt Scrufford before Friday so I can't see how they're connected with him either because they must have been posted on Thursday or earlier.'

'It's probably somebody's idea of a practical joke. You are an open target for nutters, aren't you, with your show?'

'I suppose so and I wouldn't have thought twice about it until . . . until the ears. And then there was a phone call about them at my office, something about did I get the nails. I mean, what'll come next – Parcel Force at the door with the fingers and thumbs?'

'If they rang once, they'll ring again and then you'll find out.'

'I suppose so. If the hitmen don't get me first.'

I filled up the glasses and we chatted about other things. It was time for bed but I was aware of our conversation of two nights ago and realised I had to lighten the mood.

'The wine's finished,' I said, picking up the empty bottle. 'Do you realise, we've been out twice in three days, it must be time for the honeymoon.' I took her hand. She laughed and allowed me to lead her to the bedroom.

The lovemaking was good. We got to sleep around two and I felt all the tension gone from me. I didn't wake until ten o'clock, feeling fully refreshed. Maria had left for work but there was an enigmatic note on her pillow. It had a drawing of an engagement ring followed by an exclamation mark and 'Enjoyed the honeymoon, see you Sunday' with another exclamation mark and a kiss.

I smiled. She was a bright girl. She'd committed me to the Sunday dinner but she was also letting me know she was accepting my terms for the relationship, for the time being at any rate. It had been a good night but I wasn't looking forward to the next one, at the Stripes Club.

I spent the day cleaning the flat until it was time to go to the station to do the programme. I played 'Anything You Can Do' from *Annie Get Your Gun*, the Suzi Quatro version, and P. J. Proby's brilliant send-up of 'Somewhere' from *West Side Story*. I had been going to play 'Maria' but I thought if Hilary was listening, she might read something into it and I didn't want any aggro tonight. The Stripes Club could be aggro enough.

Chapter Nine

I picked Hilary up at the hospital at nine. I was very apprehensive about the whole trip but it was the only lead I had left.

'Is this for real?' asked Hilary, as we drove towards Toxteth. 'I mean, a strip club?'

'It's not really a strip club. It's more like the old Hellfire Club, do you remember, in the eighteenth century?' Hilary looked blank. 'It was run by Sir Francis Dashwood in a ruined Cistercian abbey beside the Thames near Marlow. They used to hold orgies there for members of the aristocracy.'

'How come you know all this?'

'I read it up in the encyclopaedia.'

She laughed. 'We never did anything like that in history lessons. Sounds like fun.'

I wasn't so sure. Flagellation had never really appealed to me and there was the small matter of Sonny Loumarr and his pal who could well be in attendance at the club.

'Am I dressed all right for this?' I looked across. Beneath her coat she wore a miniskirt which, being thin, she could get away with, and a low-cut blouse allowing generous glimpses of her ample cleavage.

'You probably qualify for the floorshow,' I said, taking advantage of the RAV4's automatic transmission to rest my left hand on her knee.

The driveway of the house in South Albert Road was already full and, judging by the BMWs, Jags and

Mercedes parked there, it wasn't going to be a cheap night out.

We settled for a space three doors along and walked to the house, which was set back from the road, half hidden by trees. There was a light in the hall but the shutters kept the ground-floor windows dark.

I rang the bell and an elderly man dressed as a butler opened the door to reveal a large hall. A giant chandelier hung from the ceiling like a shimmering jewel, illuminating a wide polished mahogany staircase with life-size gilt-framed portraits adorning the walls.

Before I could be taken in by this show of stately home gentility, I observed two men in monkey suits hovering by the corridor who would have looked more at home in a Kirkby gym and knew we were in the right place.

The butler wished me 'good evening' in a BBC accent and held out a silver platter for my tickets. He returned the counterfoils and directed me to a cloakroom down the corridor where we left our coats. I was wearing a dark suit and regimental tie which seemed to fit in with the surroundings. I wasn't sure what regiment it was and the man at Stanley Market who sold it me hadn't known either, but it was silk and looked authentic.

We made our way into the main part of the club, which occupied the right side of the house from the front lounge through to a conservatory at the back. I was surprised to find it was set out as a casino with tables for roulette, poker and chemin de fer. The croupiers were all girls wearing uniform fishnet tights, black stilettos and, above the waist, just black bow ties around their necks.

'Bit old hat, isn't it?' said Hilary.

'The girls, you mean?

'Yes, it's the nineties now. Haven't they heard of the Chippendales? They should be having toy boys in posing pouches.'

'That's just wishful thinking on your part. Nowadays, it's all lap dancing. Peter Stringfellow's making a fortune out of it. Anyway, these punters look pretty traditional to me.'

'Mmm, I see what you mean.' The room was packed with middle-aged to elderly men, all accompanied by women unlikely to have been born in time to have known the joy of having Edward Heath as their Prime Minister.

'Let's go and see what's downstairs.' There was a gold-painted spiral staircase descending from the middle of the room. 'That must lead to the dungeons.'

'Dungeons? We're not in a castle.'

'Cellars,' I corrected, but I remembered Badger's account of the Princes Drive establishment and so it came as no surprise to me to be confronted by an array of stocks, whipping posts and chains, set out in individual stalls, like the Borgias had taken a concession in a Debenhams store.

Hilary's face was a picture of wonderment. 'It's like the Inquisition. Did you see that iron bra with the spikes?'

'I don't think it'll affect Marks and Spencer's sales.'

We walked through into the room beyond. A man dressed in the gold braided blue uniform of a commissionaire stood at the entrance. 'Next show in ten minutes, sir and madam.'

We were in a small theatre with tables and chairs taking the place of rows of seats. On each table was an ice bucket holding a magnum of Bollinger. Most of the seats were already taken but we found an empty table for two on the edge of the stage.

'What's going to happen?' asked Hilary.

'I don't know but we'll soon find out.' A waiter came over and, without asking, opened our champagne and poured us each a glass. He must have been seventy, had a slight limp, wispy white hair and he wore a lorgnette round his neck. Beside him, Sir John Gielgud would have looked like one of the Gladiators. It all added to the bizarre atmosphere of the place. We could have been in Phantom Manor at Eurodisney.

'Cheers,' I said, raising my glass. I glanced round the room, which was rapidly filling up.

'Who are you looking for?'

'Somebody who looks like Whitney Houston.'

'I won't ask why. There aren't any black girls here except for those two Chinese ones over there or don't those count?'

'They're yellow not black and they're not Chinese they're Japanese so no, they don't count.'

'Hang on, there's one now, just coming in over there, can you see, with that fellow that looks like a small Prince Philip.' I turned round and saw them. She was a good five inches taller than him, around five foot ten with a lot of it in her shapely legs. She was about twenty-six with a mass of black frizzy hair and did indeed bear some resemblence to Whitney Houston. I was sure it was the girl who'd spent that evening with Matt Scrufford.

'Look, Hil, I need to go and have a word with her. I won't be long. I'll tell you all about it when I come back.' Before she could argue, I jumped up and threaded my way through the tables to where the couple were about to sit.

'Excuse me,' I addressed the man. 'Would you mind if I had a word with your young lady? It's a private matter. I won't keep her a minute.'

He looked startled. He was in his late sixties and, closer up, in his charcoal suit he looked more like my old bank manager than the Queen's husband. The girl wore a peacock-blue floral sheath dress, slit to the top of her thigh.

'Er, well . . .'

I took the girl's arm while he vacillated and led her back into the dungeon room and to a quiet corner.

'I'm sorry about this but I won't keep you. A couple of weeks ago, you were at a club in Princes Drive with a nineteen-year-old university student called Matt Scrufford.' I sounded like a policeman. Perhaps I could do some foreigners for Jim Burroughs.

'Was I? Who said I was?' Her voice was wary.

'Were you?'

'I might have been. I don't remember.'

'Do you go to many of these, these . . . functions?'

'I go to all of them. I work here.'

'Oh.' This was something that hadn't occurred to me.

'I'm a hostess. I entertain clients.'

'Matt Scrufford was a client? He was only a lad. How could he afford any of this?'

'Matt Scrufford, you say?' Her accent was posh Liverpool. 'He was the guy that was murdered, wasn't he? The one that was kidnapped?'

'Yes.'

'And you think I had something to do with it? Are you the busies or something?'

'No. I'm a friend of his father and I can't understand how a lad who's happily engaged to be married and spends all his time studying for a degree, suddenly turns up in a sex club with another girl.'

'Engaged? Matthew?' She laughed. 'You must be joking. Matthew wouldn't be engaged. He was gay.'

'What?'

'Look, I don't know you and I can't stand here talking, I'll get into trouble.' I followed her glance towards the door and saw we were being watched by the commissionaire.

'What's your address? I'll call and see you tomorrow.'

'Give me some paper. I'll write it down for you.'

I gave her a business card and a pen and she scribbled on the back. 'I don't know your name,' I said.

'It's Davinia.' She flipped my card over. 'So you're the DJ? I thought your voice was familiar. I listen to your show sometimes.' She handed back the card. 'Make it afternoon. I don't get up till lunchtime.'

I watched her walk back to her companion.

'Sorry about that,' I said to Hilary when I returned to our table. 'But that girl dated Matt Scrufford the week before he died. She was with him in a sex club like this.'

'Are you still involved with that kidnapping thing? What happened about that student you went to see, the one that left the message on your answerphone?'

I was starting to bring her up to date with events when suddenly the lights dimmed and a tall man in a purple-velvet suit and a fixed smile strode on to the stage to a fanfare of taped music.

'Welcome to Stripes, ladies and gentleman, and another night of glorious entertainment for you. And to start the interactive part of the evening, we have a little cabaret. Please welcome Desiree.'

A young blonde girl was brought from the wings to loud applause from the audience. She was naked and had a curvaceous, almost Rubensesque, figure. I noticed she had rings through her nipples and her navel.

'What does he mean, "interactive",' whispered Hilary.

'I'm not sure. It'll probably be like sex on the Internet but with real dicks.'

'I think I prefer real dicks.'

The compere led Desiree to a post at the side of the stage and handcuffed her arms and legs to metal rings set at appropriate levels.

'Tonight's competition, ladies and gentlemen. We are going to call out numbers which will correspond with numbers on your entrance tickets. If you're number is called, you may come onstage and apply the whip to Desiree here. The first person to draw blood will win tonight's prize which is a weekend for two in Paris including a visit to the *Folies Bergère*.'

Applause greeted his offer and the first ticket was drawn out of the hat.

'Exciting, isn't it?' said Hilary, her face shining.

I was a little concerned. Hilary obviously didn't believe the girl would really get hurt but I wasn't sure, and I was finding the whole thing slightly disturbing. Badger was right. The atmosphere was redolent of the Roman games. 'She could be seriously injured,' I said.

'Well, she knows what she's doing and that's what the people have paid their money to see. It's only like boxers smashing each other's brains out.'

I'd seen worse things in the name of entertainment in Hamburg when The Cruzads had played in the Reeperbahn, but I still felt uneasy because I didn't entirely believe Desiree did know what she was doing. Most women involved in situations like this were smackheads waiting for their next score.

'At least boxers can defend themselves,' I said.

The promoters were certainly doing well out of it though. At £25 a head, that was two and a half grand in the coffers before the serious money started rolling in, and all they were giving away was a lousy weekend in Paris.

The compere called the first number. 'Seventeen.'

A woman of about thirty-five stood up waving her ticket and hobbled to the stage to claim her prize. She wore a white sequined cocktail dress that ended centimetres below her knickers and this coupled with the five-inch stilettos on her matching white shoes restricted her perambulation. Her ash-blonde hair was piled up high, thirty years too late for her to audition for the Ronettes.

'Congratulations, my dear. And what is your name?'

'Gaynor.'

'Right, Gaynor.' He handed her the whip. It was a long, flat leather affair. Not thin enough to cut easily. Obviously they wanted to prolong the event.

Gaynor stood back and lashed out at Desiree's buttocks. Desiree yelped as the whip cracked across them leaving a red weal but the skin wasn't broken.

Disappointed, Gaynor returned to her seat. The next number brought forward a man of Middle Eastern origin. He took a close stance and hit firmly but with not much vigour. Again, Desiree cried out but the mark made by the whip was slight. The atmosphere was building up. Nero would have loved it.

I watched in trepidation but, happily, our numbers were not called. I wasn't sure I'd have got up. It was the ninth 'contestant' who won, a woman of late middle age with wrinkled jowls, who dealt a savage crack with the whip that immediatly slit open a wound on Desiree's reddened and swollen cheeks and caused a trickle of blood to run down her thighs.

The woman received her prize with great exuberance, not even looking at the now crying girl. I'd always thought of women as being more bloodthirsty than men – the way grannies bay for blood at wrestling matches – and this seemed to confirm it.

'I think I need a drink,' said Hilary. She looked shaken.

I stood up. 'Come on, let's go. I've had enough.'

'Don't you have to see anyone else?'

'No,' I said. 'I've done what I came to do.'

Hilary took the champagne from the bucket. 'Shame to leave it.'

The commissionaire gave us a searching look as we passed him on the way upstairs to collect our coats, but he said nothing. We walked back through the hall to the front door. 'Not staying for the special events?' enquired the old butler.

I smiled at him. 'I'm afraid we have a holocaust to go to.'

The cold, night air was a relief. I took the champagne bottle from beneath my coat and offered it to Hilary, who took a mouthful and handed it back. I needed several swigs.

'I daren't think what'll be happening at the special events,' she said as we got into the car.

'From what I gather, they beat the living shit out of one another then go home poor, sore and happy.' Badger had told me enough for me not to regret missing it.

'How do they get away with it?'

'They keep moving the venue and only admit specially invited people. I think they're pretty careful and there's enough heavies around to deal with any conscientious objectors.'

I drove into the city and pulled into the forecourt of the Britannia Adelphi Hotel. 'We're not meeting anyone here, are we?' Hilary asked suspiciously. She was used to our nights out being interrupted by various business calls.

'No. I just wanted to go somewhere normal where there are ordinary people around and this is about the best you'll get at midnight in Liverpool.'

The lounge at the Adelphi resembles a state room in one of the old Cunard liners. We sat beneath the huge chandeliers and a waiter came over to take our order for drinks. It was a quiet night. A few salespersons, down for a conference, were gathered in one corner, otherwise the place was empty.

'Well, that was a different night out,' I said.

'I hope it was worth what you went for,' said Hilary.

'So do I. I'm going to see the Whitney Houston girl tomorrow.'

'Jim Burroughs won't be too pleased if you're interfering with his case. Have you seen him lately?'

'Yes, I saw him last night.' For some reason, I didn't feel like recounting all the recent events again. 'He was fine.'

'And did you take Maria to the theatre on Saturday?'

'No. I went on my own.'

'Oh.' She looked surprised. I was surprised too. It wasn't like Hilary to be jealous. There'd been plenty of other girls before Maria and they'd never worried her.

'It was *Annie Get Your Gun* and the cowgirls were bigger than the cows.'

'Just like that one we went to? Do you remember?'

'That tap dancing one, you mean? Willy Russell.'

'That's the one, *Stepping Out*, but it wasn't Willy Russell, it was Richard Harris. That amateur operatic society did it and the women in the chorus were colossal.'

We talked about plays and films but part of my mind was on Davinia and her amazing claim that Matt Scrufford was gay. At last, we finished our drinks and left for the flat.

'When are we going out again?' asked Hilary.

'We can go down the Masquerade Friday night, if you like? What time do you finish?'

'I can get down by eleven.'

'Fine.'

I was glad I'd changed the sheets after the night before. Hilary couldn't wait to get undressed and into bed. Now she was safe at home, she could allow herself to be aroused by the night's events. They could become sexual fantasy instead of horrific reality.

She turned to me as she unclipped her bra and pushed her boobs forward. What do you think, Johnny? Should I have them pierced?'

'And chained together so's you don't lose them,' I said, and took the left one in my mouth. For the first time, the evening's entertainment we'd witnessed was starting to have an aphrodisiac effect on me as well.

We didn't speak much more. Our lovemaking was frenetic and after about an hour, we both collapsed into a deep sleep for which I was grateful. It had been a hectic six days but the madness was only just beginning.

Chapter Ten

Rain was falling as I parked outside Everton's ground the following afternoon. In deference to Davinia's instructions, I'd left my call until after lunch. The commercial office was open and a few people were buying tickets and replica blue shirts.

I walked the couple of streets to the address Davinia had given me, apprehensive about what I'd find. I'd seen the commissionaire watching us when we were talking in the club and clocked that he'd seen her take my card. There could be people waiting for me.

Alternatively, it could be a false address or she could have left. I thought of my trip to Bennison's house in Freshfield. Davinia, too, might be lying in the bedroom, dead.

The street could almost have been a model village with the buildings looking like dolls' houses, a terraced row with identical bay windows and distinguishable only by their curtains and their exterior decoration. Most of them were painted in bright, primary colours and number 24 was no exception, being flamingo pink with a sun-yellow front door. What made the house stand out, though, was the matching jardinière net curtains in all the front windows, whiter than any in the street.

I rang the bell, which gave an Avon chime, and prepared for a long wait but the front door opened almost immediatly and Davinia stood there. She was almost unrecognisable from the night before. The long frizzy hair had gone. Instead, she had a curly mop cut short like a boy's. In faded-blue denims, a polo-necked sweater and trainers, she looked barely out of her teens.

'You found it then? You'd better come in.' Out of the club, her voice betrayed overtones of Scotland Road. 'I've only been up a few minutes.'

'A late night?'

'It always is. I got in after five.' She picked up a packet of cigarettes from a glass coffee table. 'Want one?'

I shook my head and watched her light up using a disposable lighter. She blew the smoke out ostentatiously, like a vampire expelling fresh air in disgust, and coughed a rattling cough.

'You look different.'

'The wig, you mean? You don't think I dress like a geisha girl all the time, do you?'

'No.' The dividing wall had been knocked down between the old front parlour and the living room, giving more light and space. A modern three-piece suite in white leather toned in with the thick-pile oatmeal carpet and the Ikea furniture. 'Nice room,' I commented.

She smiled in acknowledgement. 'Take a seat.' I could still see traces of Whitney Houston, even in her scruff.

I took the armchair beside a brass uplighter and she settled into the other one.

'It was Matt I wanted to ask you about. Have you known him long?'

'Only a couple of months. He came down to Stripes one night with one of the regulars. A guy called Colin Bennison. Do you know him?'

I was astounded. I hadn't figured on any relationship between Matt and his lecturer. 'I know him, yes. But I didn't know he and Matt were friends.'

'They seemed to be quite pally.'

'You say Colin was a regular. How long had he been coming to the club?'

'Oh, before I started there, which was last Christmas.

He's well into the S & M scene. Bondage boys and all that stuff.'

'Hang on. Last night, you told me you thought Matt was gay.'

'He was with Colin, wasn't he?'

'That doesn't make him gay. Colin was his tutor at university.'

'I know. Matthew wasn't the first of his boys he'd brought down.'

I wondered how people like Bennison ever got their jobs. You could imagine their careers advisers at school: 'Fancy young boys, do you, Hodge Minor? Then you ought to train for the priesthood or, if the exams are too much for you, try for housemaster at a boys' prep school with special responsibility for the Scouts at weekends.'

'And did he bring Matt more than once?'

She thought. 'Only a couple of times. To be honest, Matt wasn't really into all the whipping and stuff.'

'What was he into? I mean, you say he was gay, but did you see him with any boys ever?'

'No, I didn't, but I didn't see him with any girls either.'

'He was engaged.'

'So you said. I never saw her.'

'She's called Sarah. She was with him at the university.'

She finished the cigarette, stubbed it out in an ashtray and immediately lit another one, coughing again as she did so. 'He never mentioned her.'

'You talked to him then?'

'One night. Matthew arrived and Colin never turned up. Everyone has to have an escort at Stripes, male or female, whatever they fancy, so I was asked to look after him to encourage him to spend his money.'

That must have been the night Badger saw them, I thought. 'And did you?'

'He hadn't got any money. Colin was the one with the cash. Matthew told me he was at uni doing Geography and . . .' she stopped.

'Yes?'

'Don't laugh. I'm going to college doing my A level Geography.'

'Why should I laugh?' There were a lot of black girls like Davinia in Liverpool, and probably in other cities, attractive and intelligent who ended up in dead-end 'glamorous' jobs when they could have become accountants or lawyers given the right opportunity.

'I mentioned it to Matthew and he sort of offered to help me with the course which I thought was nice of him. I gave him my number but he never rang and I never heard from him again. Then I read about him in the paper. It was horrible.'

'How did you get to work at Stripes?'

'I really work behind the bar at one of their other clubs, have done since I left school.'

All along I'd had her down for twenty-five or six. Suddenly, I wasn't sure. School! 'How old are you, Davinia?'

'Twenty, and my name's Laura not Davinia. They gave me that name at the club.'

I guess it was her height that had fooled me but there was also a sense of worldliness about her, although I imagine a few visits to Stripes would take away most people's innocence.

'Stripes isn't a proper club,' she explained. 'They just hold these special evenings every so often in different premises and get all the weirdos in.'

'Rich weirdos by the look of them last night.'

'God, yes. I mean, they make a fortune on the Stripes nights. There's talk of blackmail too. Some of the people that go there wouldn't want everyone to know. But nobody tells them about the video cameras hidden round the place.'

'Sounds a charming setup. And do people really get hurt?'

'I'll say they do. A couple of times they've had to have doctors in pretty fast and I know they have a tame plastic surgeon lined up in case anybody gets really cut up.'

'And Bennison liked to watch all this?'

'He likes to see young boys get lashed. How he could afford it on his salary, I don't know.'

I had a good idea. Selling exam results must have been quite remunerative. 'Why do you think he brought Matt down to Stripes?'

'I don't know. Perhaps he was trying to seduce him.'

'Does it ever worry you, getting involved in all this?'

'Not really. It's just a job, isn't it?'

'You live here alone?'

'I sure do. That's the way I like it. I've been on my own since I was sixteen.'

'You've done well getting this house.'

'I'm not stupid. I know how to work the system.'

All the same, I didn't give much for her chances of passing her A level. She was too far drawn into the club scene. She'd made too much money and seen too many things. This furniture hadn't come cheap. 'So it seems.'

'I'm sorry, do you want a drink or anything?'

I shook my head. 'Did Matt make any enemies at the club?'

'With the staff, you mean? No, I'm sure he didn't. Why should he? As far as I know, I'm the only one he spoke to. And that was just on this one night.'

'What about Bennison? Had he upset anyone there?'

'I don't think so. He was a punter; the management encourage punters.'

'Why didn't he turn up the night you were with Matt?'

'Don't ask me. Perhaps he was ill.'

'What day was it?'

She thought for a moment. 'It was in Princes Drive. I think it was a Wednesday.'

The day before Matt disappeared. 'So you don't think Matt's death had anything to do with the club then?'

She looked serious. 'Look, I'm very sorry about Matt but I can't see any connection. You said you were a friend of his father?'

'We used to play in a group together in the sixties.'

'Oh, right.'

'Well, thanks for helping me, Laura.' I stood up to leave. 'Oh, just one thing. Have you ever come across a man called Sonny Loumarr in the clubs?'

'Never heard of him. A punter, is he?'

'More likely a bouncer.'

'Not in our clubs he isn't.'

'Right. Thanks for your time, then.'

She stood up to escort me out, barely two inches shorter than I. 'Do me a favour in return. Play me a record on your show and say it's for Winston.'

'Your boyfriend?'

'Sort of.' She smiled enigmatically. 'He owns the club.'

I walked back to the car in a state of confusion. The Stripes Club appeared to be a dead end as far as Matt's death was concerned. Colin Bennison likewise. So, who had set the heavies on to me? And why?

I drove out to Old Swan and stopped in Green Lane for a bacon sandwich and a cup of tea. It was barely two thirty and I was only twenty minutes' drive from Mally's. I thought I might go over and see if he had any news. This is what I told myself but I realised he'd probably be at work and that I'd be just as happy to see his wife again. Mal Two.

There was a red Vectra outside the house so I pulled

up on the opposite side of the road. I switched off the engine and was about to get out of the car when a man came down Mally's drive. His walk looked familiar. I waited as he turned into the street and straight away I knew who it was.

It was Sonny Loumarr's friend, the other man who'd attacked me at my flat. What had Jim Burroughs called him, Teddy Twigg? Quite unexpectedly, I had the chance to solve the greatest mystery.

I didn't wait to wonder what he was doing there. I jumped out of the car and ran across the road.

He'd just got into the driver's seat and didn't see me until I was alongside. Before he had time to start the engine, I wrenched open the door and pulled him into the gutter.

I held his throat and banged his head a couple of times against the car to unsettle him. 'Right,' I said. A rivulet of blood ran down the side of his face. He cut easily. 'I only want to know one thing. Who sent you?'

He didn't answer. I banged his head again, then, still holding his throat, I pulled at the belt on his trousers. 'How do you fancy an audition for lead role in *Evita*? If you don't answer me, you'll wish they'd refused you bail.'

This seemed to have the desired effect. 'All right, bastard, I'll tell you. You're crazy. It was fucking Mal King sent us, didn't he?'

I stopped dead. He might just as well have said the Queen Mother had sent him. Mally! I couldn't believe it. 'Mally sent you to kill me?'

'Not to kill you, to frighten you off. He didn't want you nosing round.'

'Why?'

'I don't fucking know, do I?'

'But it was his son that was killed.'

'I know nothing about that.'

'If you're lying . . .'

I banged his head once more to emphasise my point then stood back to allow him to scramble to his feet. 'I don't want to see you ever again, right? If I do, you're dead.'

He spat on the ground but got into the car and drove away with a squeal of tyres as if he was afraid I might change my mind and follow him.

I was working on automatic pilot. I couldn't take it in. Why should Mally want me warned off? I walked slowly up the drive. None of it made any sense. I rang the bell and Marilyn came to the door. She wore a clinging sweater and a skirt that stopped just above her knees. Her perfume was musky, heavy for the morning, but a very seductive odour. I think it was Oscar de la Renta.

'Hello, Johnny. Didn't expect to see you so soon. Come in.'

I accepted the invitation and followed her into the lounge. 'Mally not in?'

'No, he's at work. He's up in Manchester today, I think.'

'Who was the man who just left?'

She looked at me. 'I don't know. He wanted Mally. Why do you ask?'

'I'm sorry. I didn't mean to be nosy. It's just that I thought I knew him from somewhere. Have you seen him before?'

'No, I don't think so. I mean no, I haven't, but I think he's phoned. I recognise the voice.'

'When did he phone?'

'In the last couple of days. Hey, what is this?'

'Sorry. It's just I've had a bit of trouble and . . . it doesn't matter. Look, I just called to see how things were.'

'Would you like a cup of tea?'

'Love one.' I picked up a magazine and sat down to read it while she went to the kitchen. It was a recent issue of *Mojo*. Mally was obviously still into music. I was halfway through an article on the Rolling Stones when Marilyn came back with the tray. The chocolate fingers had returned and I took one to dip in my tea.

She joined me on the settee. 'I heard your programme the other night, when you asked for information about Matt? Did anybody get in touch?'

I hesitated. Until I had time to think things through, I didn't want to say anything that might get back to Mally. 'No, but I didn't really expect it.'

'I suppose not. It's so strange, though. We've not heard a thing from anyone.'

'Where's Matt's mother staying?'

'Maureen? Somewhere in Bootle with her mother. Near Walton Prison, I believe.' She said the words with some venom as if she thought Maureen would be better incarcerated there.

'You don't sound so keen on Maureen.'

'She's baggage.' I raised my eyebrows. 'You know, part of Mally's past that's always around. When we first got married, she was always on the phone and next thing we've got Matt living here. Don't misunderstand me, Matt was a lovely lad but Maureen sort of hovered in the background.'

'What about his second wife, Carol?'

'Oh, we never see her. She's well off the scene. But Maureen . . .'

'He used to visit her in the Isle of Man he said. Didn't this upset you?' I looked into her eyes and saw a lot of hurt. Behind her glamorous exterior, I felt she could be very vulnerable.

'What could I say? Matt was his son and he wanted to see him. I'd no reason to suspect there was anything more to it than that.'

'But you did?

'I know Mally.' There was a silence as we both took sips from our cups and pondered the implications. I felt a great urge to take her in my arms but I had enough women in my life and, besides, this was hardly the moment.

'When's the baby due?'

'Oh, not until next March, another six months.'

'Where's your little boy?'

'Gary? He goes to my mum's on a Thursday, over in West Derby.' I knew West Derby. The Cruzads once played at the Conservative Club there. 'It gives me a bit of a break.'

'You know, Mal, I remember Maureen's mother. When we were in the group we used to drop Maureen off sometimes after the gig. Her mum was a little woman with flat grey hair like a Brillo pad. God, she must be eighty if she's a day. Fancy her still being there.'

'It's the family house. Maureen's sister and her family live there now. They moved in after the father died.'

'That's right, her sister was called Sue, only she used to spell it S double O. She had dark hair and was very pretty, prettier than Maureen. Oggi used to say if she'd have been able to sing she could have joined the Vernons Girls.

Mal didn't remember the Vernons Girls.

'Why did Matt move in with you and not with his grandmother when he came to Liverpool?'

'He did live with them for a while when he first came but then he met Sarah and either they didn't approve of them living together or there wasn't room. Either way, Mally told him they could come here.'

'So Mally used to go and see him when he first came to Bootle then?'

'From time to time.' And as if sensing that was not enough; 'Mally's been devastated by the murder.' She started to cry. 'So have I, come to that. I liked Matt. He was quiet but very genuine.'

'What do you think of Sarah?'

Marilyn cleared her throat, took a gulp of tea and swallowed hard. 'A career girl. Don't get me wrong, she's very nice, probably would have been good for

Matt because she'd jog him along. She was the boss. Funny really.'

'What is?'

'Matt. Everyone says how nice he was, yet nobody will be that much affected now he's gone. Oh, I know everyone's upset and everything at the moment but Sarah will go back to university and get her degree and eventually marry someone else. Mally's got us, his new family. Maureen'll go back to the Isle of Man and get on with her life. Matt had been gone from there for over a year, don't forget. She's used to life without him. It's like taking a cup of water from a stream. The stream runs on as if nothing has happened. Oh dear, it sounds very cold-blooded but you know what I mean, don't you?'

I did. I like to think the world will stop turning when anything happens to me but Marilyn was probably nearer the mark. 'Life goes on' is one of the great all-time truths.

And yet . . . in Matt Scrufford's case, his death did mean a great deal to one person. The one who killed him.

For Bennison it could have meant saving himself from exposure as a fraud with the possible outcome of a prison sentence. Yet, if he was friendly with Matt, as Laura had said, it seemed unlikely that Matt would shop him. And there didn't seem to be anything at the Stripes Club that could lead to his murder. And where did Mally fit into all this? That was the big question now. Why had he paid to have me warned off?

'I'd better be going,' I said.

She stood up and walked with me to the front door. 'Any message for Mal?'

'Not really. I just thought I'd call while I was passing.'

'You're coming to the funeral tomorrow?'

'Yes, of course.'

'And you must come back here afterwards.'
'Are you sure? Won't it be just family?'
'No. I'd like you to come.'
'In that case, I can't refuse.' I smiled at her and our eyes met in one of those long moments that they talk about in romantic novels, that last only for seconds and yet seem to reach eternity. 'I'll see you tomorrow. Take care.'

I drove away, not sure where to go next, but my mind was soon made up for me. My mobile phone rang before I reached the end of the road. It was Geoffrey and he sounded upset.

Chapter Eleven

'Fuckin' tossers, sending stuff like this in the post.'

We were in the office at Aigburth Road. Geoffrey watched as I shook the contents of a small Jiffy bag on to the desk. I looked down at a clump of hair and a tiny round mirror on the back of which, over a motif of the Beatles, was the word 'NEXT' cut from a newspaper.

Geoffrey was oblivious to the similarity between this packet, the one Mally Scrufford received and the one with the fingernails so he didn't feel the same shiver of apprehension that I did.

'Remember the fellow that rang up about the nails the other day?'

'Yeah.'

'They were fingernails he meant and they came in a bag like this.'

Geoffrey whistled. 'Shit! Same bloke, then? Who is he?'

'That's what we don't know. Or, why.'

Geoffrey leant across the desk to feel the hair between his fingers. 'Seems real this, don't it? I wonder whose it is.'

'Or was.' I had my own ideas.

'You reckon he's been stiffed?'

'Could be.' I wasn't sure what colour Matt Scrufford's hair had been but Mally's had been this shade of reddish-brown when he was in The Cruzads.

'Is someone after you, boss? One of the tenants, is it?'

'Not that I know of.' And I'd sorted the Sonny Loumarr business so who was sending the envelopes? And why?

Geoffrey picked up the mirror. 'I don't get this. What's the point of the mirror?'

'I think I'm meant to look in it and say "you're next" but next for what I don't know.'

'And you're sure it's not someone from the flats?'

We've had trouble in the past. In the old days, when I first started in the property business, I'd had bedsits like rabbit warrens in nearly derelict houses. There'd been tenants like the Mad Axeman, the Glue-Sniffer, Crazy Dezi and Pigeon Ginger who'd caused a fair amount of aggro over the years but now I had upmarket flats with central heating, fitted kitchens and reasonably respectable occupants.

I considered. 'No. Can't see it, Geoff.' I thought it had to be something to do with Matt Scrufford, yet what?

'I suppose you're right.' He laughed. 'Not like the old Jermyn Street days.' I grimly recalled a lavatory bowl hanging through a kitchen ceiling and that was a house full of law students. They were probably all barristers and judges now. No wonder I have little regard for the country's legal system.

I replaced the hair and mirror in the Jiffy bag and put it in my pocket.

'Thanks for phoning, Geoff. Leave it with me; I've got a couple of ideas. I'll let you know how I get on.'

It was getting close to teatime and I had the show to do. I rang Jim Burroughs from the car.

'Ringing to confess, are you?'

'Piss off. Look, I need to see you, off the record, Jim. I might have something for you.'

'You doing the show tonight?'

'I'm on my way there now but I'm free after seven.'

'I've not eaten. Fancy a Chinese?'

'Why not?' We arranged to meet at eight in Chinatown.

It wasn't a bad show. I had a row with some prat on the phone-in about convicted rapists. He didn't agree with my views on their punishment. He thought they ought to be allowed to keep their balls. We argued about it and the discussion got a bit heated and I could see Ken getting agitated behind his glass window. You can't beat live radio for a good scrap.

'One day, someone will walk through those doors and stick a knife into you,' Ken said, as I came out of the studio. 'The way you wind those buggers up. How do you know they're not raving psychos?'

I laughed. 'Most of them probably are. They'd have to be to listen to the stuff I play.'

I was only joking, of course, but his remark made me wonder. Could my mystery correspondent be just some screwball listener whom I'd upset on the air? Maybe it was nothing at all to do with Matt Scrufford. After all, the fingernails had been sent before I knew he was dead.

I thought about this as I drove up Renshaw Street and past the bombed remains of St Luke's Church towards Great Georges Place.

Liverpool's Chinatown is nothing on the scale of the equivalent regions of Manchester or London. The area given the name occupies a mere couple of streets round Great Georges Place, not far from the Anglican cathedral.

Jim Burroughs was waiting for me by the stone lions that guard Nelson Street. I parked behind his Mondeo just down the road.

'I thought we'd go to the Hing Wah,' he said.

'Suits me.'

'Less far to walk.'

We went in and were shown to seats by the window. 'I'm getting too old for all this excitement,' said Jim. 'I should've taken my pension when I had the chance.'

'Why didn't you?'

'Chasing promotion, wasn't I? Fancied being Inspector, though now I've got it I wonder whether it was worth it.'

'Oh?'

'The job's not what it was, Johnny. Not worth a candle now. Do you know it takes an hour and a half of paperwork to book some asshole for riding a bicycle without lights?'

'It's the same everywhere, Jim. All jobs are crap nowadays.'

'You risk your life catching the bastards then the judges and magistrates let them off.'

'Why don't you jack it in? You'll get a decent pension and you won't have any trouble finding something else. How are the Chocolate Lavatory doing?'

He didn't want to talk about music. 'Jack it in? Wouldn't have time to write out my notice. And I'll bet you're going to add to my troubles.'

The waiter came to take the order.

'Are we having some wine?' Jim asked when we'd chosen. The waiter recommended an Italian white.

'Not a bad year,' said Jim, who could be very pompous on the subject. 'What do you think? It's a bit expensive.'

I checked the wine list. 'It's OK,' I said. 'We used to drink it all the time at the Betty Ford Clinic.'

'Oh, very amusing,' said Jim, humourlessly. 'If they ever bring *The Comedians* back, don't audition.' He ordered the wine. 'Right. You're not here for the gourmet experience. What have you got for me?'

There wasn't that much to tell him. I produced the two Jiffy bags and let him see the contents. 'The first arrived last Friday, posted to the radio station, and the other came today to my office. Are the bags the same as the one Mally Scrufford got?'

'You think there's a connection?'

'I think,' I said slowly, 'that these nail clippings and

the hair come from Matt Scrufford. I don't know why I think this. There is no reason for me to think it. I never even knew about Matt Scrufford until last Friday's *Post* and the nails were sent before then.'

'Yet you still think there's a connection?'

'Mmm.'

'What was the real reason for you getting involved in all this, Johnny?'

'I told you—'

'I know what you told me. You were bored, you'd sod all to do with your time, you knew Scrufford's old man, you wanted to be Sherlock fucking Holmes but I can't buy all that. There must be something else.'

'Believe what you like but there isn't anything. Look, can you check the nails and the hair and see if they were Matt's?'

'And you've no idea who might have sent them?'

'No, but someone rang up the office asking if I got the nails.'

'What did he sound like?'

'I didn't speak to him. Geoffrey, my office manager, did. He thought he meant the sort of nails you knock in walls but he said the guy sounded local.'

'If these items do belong to Scrufford, then that'll let our departed friend Bennison off the hook. He couldn't have sent the hair from the mortuary.'

'True.'

'That reminds me, you never made that statement to Sergeant Britton about your so-called mugging.'

'I decided it wasn't worth it. Like you say, nothing to charge them with really.' I kept quiet about my afternoon encounter with Teddy Twigg. 'How's Loumarr?'

'He'll live, luckily for you. And you still think that was tied in with the Scrufford thing too?'

It did, of course, involve Scrufford, but Mally not Matt, and I'd no idea if the two events were connected. That was something I wanted to sort out with Mally himself.

I took Ken's line. 'No, not any more. More likely some nutter I'd upset on the show.'

He seemed to accept this. 'Wouldn't surprise me, the crap you play. You'll be at the funeral tomorrow, I take it?'

'Yes. Will you?'

He nodded. 'Did you know that the murderer often attends the funeral of his victim?'

'Is that right?'

'So they say.'

'You'd better check the guest list then and take a pair of handcuffs just in case.' Perhaps he could borrow some from the Stripes Club. 'Are *you* getting anywhere with Matt's kidnapping?'

'Confidential police matters, Johnny. I'm not allowed to say.' He lit a Regal and blew the smoke out viciously. 'Are we fuck. Not a dicky bird. Case has gone dead.'

'But you're still investigating?'

'Insomuch as there've been three murders, two shootings, four armed robberies and three drugs raids to deal with since then.'

'And that's only this morning, yes, I see what you mean.'

'Basically, we're waiting for something to come up. We've interviewed everyone we know about, including your friend Mr Crook.'

'And you think Bennison's out of it?'

'Well, we've spoken to a few of his associates of the shirtlifting persuasion and can't find any hints of foul play. We don't even know that Scrufford did actually speak to him about his exam scam. He might not have known anyone was on to him until you opened your mouth on Saturday night. Then he went straight home and topped himself.'

'Am I supposed to feel guilty?' I didn't. I wasn't the one breaking the law but it meant we were no nearer to finding out about Matt's death. Perhaps it really had been a kidnap that went wrong but somehow I doubted it.

Jim changed the subject. 'How's Hilary?'

'Fine. I was out with her last night.' I didn't say where. We talked uncertainly about other things. He thought I knew more than I was telling him but I knew there was nothing that would help him so we steered round the subject like shadow boxers.

'See you at the church, then,' he said at last, as we drained the last cups of China tea. 'And keep your eyes open for the killer.'

There were no obvious murderers that I could see in St Peter's Church, Woolton the next morning. The place was pretty full and the whole choir was in attendance. John Lennon had been in this same choir over forty years ago.

I recognised Maureen with her family on the opposite side to Mally and Mal, who had with them a small child that I took to be their Gary.

Maureen looked old for her years. She was still noticeably thin, her greying hair was combed straight back into a bun and her cheeks were very pale. The black coat she wore was too tight, which didn't help. But then this was the funeral of her only son. I could hardly expect her to come looking like Naomi Campbell.

Sarah, surprisingly, was not with either family but in the company of young people whom I assumed were fellow students from the university. Jordan Crook was not among them. Neither was Laura, Matt's 'friend' from Stripes.

I took a pew near the back of the church. It was exactly a week since I was sitting in The Diner and first read about Matt's ears in the *Daily Post*. I was beginning to wish I'd picked up the *Daily Telegraph* instead. I felt I'd got myself involved in something that seemed to be spinning out of control.

The service began. The vicar was scarcely out of his twenties but the sermon was better than some I've heard and, though he may never have met Matt Scrufford, he'd obviously been well briefed and was able to offer a potted biography of Matt's life that held a certain ring of sincerity. But then, his father was, after all, one of his parishioners.

Attending church, for Mally, would be like joining the Rotary Club or the Masons, a reflection of his rising social status and a chance to develop his business contacts.

Personally, I've never been invited to join Rotary or the 'funny handshake' brigade but then, I take that as a compliment. Both of them are breeding grounds for corruption on a grand scale. It'd be like being eligible for the Veteran Aids Sufferers or Ex-Walton Inmates: societies for which you'd prefer not to have the credentials for membership. Better to be a social leper than a palmgreaser.

I don't go to church much either. Religion should be private. If I want to sing hymns, I can put *Songs of Praise* through the karaoke machine.

We finished up with 'The Lord is my Shepherd', which brought a few more tears, then it was out to the churchyard. I was glad I'd worn my parka over my charcoal suit as it was bitter out and wasn't there some old saying about the grave claiming its next victims from the waiting mourners?

I stood near the back with a group of sundry relatives and noticed Jim Burroughs and his sergeant hovering at the opposite end of the graveyard. The vicar was reading the prayers as Maureen and Mally threw soil on to the lowered coffin. Any minute I expected Vincent Price to appear with a raven on his shoulder.

Eventually, it was all finished. The family and close friends made for the hired limousines to be taken back to Mally's whilst the casual mourners and friends went back to their daily grinds. I followed the limos in the RAV4, glad I'd chosen the black. It matched the hearse.

The wake was a far cry from the usual boiled ham sandwich and cup of tea. In fact, it wasn't a wake at all, as wakes are supposed to be joyous occasions celebrating somebody's life and there was precious little to celebrate with the murderer still at large and, if Jim Burroughs was right, possibly in the room with us.

A catering firm was on hand to organise the spread and, by the number of people who were there, I could see why they hadn't held it at Maureen's sister's place. Even Mally's large house was packed.

'Thanks for coming, Johnny.' Mally came over to me and shook my hand, his lips tightly held in what he must have thought passed for an expression of gratitude. He wore a black two-piece suit in a shiny mohair material which was popular amongst the nouveaux riches back in the seventies. He'd put some weight on since the purchase. 'I appreciate it,' he added, and moved on to work the room.

He obviously hadn't been in touch with Teddy Twigg since the previous day.

I murmured something sympathetic and went across to talk to Sarah, who was with a couple of youths who turned out to be from university. She didn't seem delighted to see me.

I saw no point in subtlety. 'Have you heard about Colin Bennison?' I asked her.

She wasn't fazed. 'We were just talking about it, actually. What's your theory?' I hesitated and she carried on. 'Remorse for cheating the honourable exam system or was he frightened he'd been rumbled? Strange, isn't it? Just over a week ago, both he and Matt were alive. What's changed by them dying?'

Without warning, her voice cracked and she turned away. Her friends gathered round her and I moved across the room where Maureen and her sister were talking.

'Long time since The Cruzads, Mo.' She turned round at my voice. She looked strained and ill.

'Well, well, Johnny Ace. You've done all right since the group days. We listen to your show sometimes.'

'What's the reception like in the Isle of Man?'

'Comes over loud and clear.' She turned to her sister. 'You remember Johnny, don't you, Soo?'

She nodded. I said 'You never did join the Vernons Girls.'

'You what?'

'Oggi used to say you should have been in the Vernons Girls, don't you remember?'

She obviously didn't. She was still pretty though, and her hair was still dark. Just thirty years too late for the Spice Girls.

'Whatever happened to Oggi?' asked Maureen.

'No idea. I heard he went to Australia.'

'Frankie's doing well, I believe. Someone said he'd got a top management job with GEC. Lives in a big house in Birkdale near the footballers.'

'I've never heard from either of them for years. We lost touch after the group broke up. Come to that, I'd not heard from Mally till this week.' I hesitated, not sure how to phrase the words that had to be said. 'I'm really sorry about Matt, Mo.'

'It's terrible, Johnny. And for no reason. Why should anyone want to kill him? He'd never hurt anyone.'

'There must be something we don't know about, Mo.' But God knows what it was. I changed the subject. 'You've kept in touch with Mally then, despite everything?'

'You know what Mally's like, he's not someone it's easy to get rid of.' I remembered Mally's new wife's comment about his 'baggage'. 'He's always likely to turn up out of the blue as if nothing has happened.'

'You mean "nothing" like the divorce?'

'Yes. I mean, he left me to go with that tart but when

she ditched him and went off to London, he was round to mine in no time.'

'In the Isle of Man?'

'Yes, to my aunt's. We lived with her on the farm after I left Mally.'

'And he still came after he married Marilyn?'

Maureen looked sheepishly across the room towards the current Mrs Scrufford. 'He never wanted to lose touch with Matt.'

'Are you still living on the island?'

'Yes. I'm going back Tuesday.'

'Have you got a boyfriend there?'

'Not a regular one. I've got friends who take me out. How about you? Are you married?'

'No, I'm the same as you, I suppose. Friends I take out. And how's your mum?'

'Getting on. Can't knit like she used to, with her eyes.' We smiled in a quiet recognition of shared memories. After twenty-odd years, there was little else to say to each other. We'd moved on.

I needed to get Mally on his own and challenge him about Loumarr and Twigg but I knew it would have to wait. It was getting on for two o'clock and a few people were already leaving. I consumed some fresh salmon and salad and a glass of wine, then went over to where he was chatting to a group of expensively dressed businessmen.

I tapped him on the shoulder. 'I've got to be going now, Mally.'

He turned round. 'Oh, Johnny, right.' He excused himself from his friends and walked with me to the door. 'Sorry I've not had time to talk to you much. You know how it is. But thanks for your interest at this sad time. We must get together soon and have a drink.' The platitudes were uttered in a tone that suggested that a month or two after the Millennium would be soon enough.

I spoke sharply. 'How about tomorrow?'

'What?'

'It's Saturday; you won't be working. Shall we say ten o'clock at my place? I think you know where it is but here's my card anyway. I believe your friend Mr Loumarr is in hospital.' He looked startled but he took the card. 'And come on your own, Mally.'

He looked old again. His face had crumpled. I remembered the look from the old days. Mally lived by his wits and used his charm to extricate himself from potential disasters. When neither of them would work he was in trouble.

'OK,' was all he said. 'I'll be there.'

Chapter Twelve

I drove back to the flat from Mally's in time to catch the phone before the answerphone picked it up. It was Maria, saying she had two tickets for the opera at the Phil tomorrow night and would I like to go.

'It's *The Marriage of Figaro* with the Touring Opera Company. It's supposed to pretty good. I thought we could stay at mine afterwards then we're handy for Kaye's on Sunday.'

Perhaps she thought I was going to do a runner but I reassured her I wasn't and told her I'd enjoy it. I also thought it would be something to look forward to after the showdown with Mally.

I got changed out of my suit into jeans and a sweater, ready for the show. I paid a tribute to Matt on the air and remembered to play Laura's request for Winston at the Stripes Club, which I'd forgotten the night before. I thought Nazareth's 'Love Hurts' was appropriate and sent it with love from Davinia.

'Lionel rang for you,' said Ken, when I came out of the studio. 'Can you phone him back on his mobile?' He handed me a piece of paper with the number on.

Lionel's a comedian who used to live in one of my flats. In the sixties, he'd played in a band but he soon found his patter between numbers went down better than his singing so he eventually switched to comedy and hit pay dirt. He's been on my show a few times.

He's knocking fifty now but the gigs seem to come along as frequently as ever. With the judicious use of

Clairol hair colouring, he manages to look less than forty, which is very important in show business. Ask Joan Collins.

Lionel plays the nostalgia card and he's managed to establish himself as a Scouse personality like Mickey Finn and Billy Butler. Most of his act consists of amusing reminiscences about the 'good old days' rather than actual gags. I sometimes go and watch him if he's playing anywhere halfway decent and we have a drink and a chat.

'I'm doing an after-dinner at the Adelphi,' he said. 'A Round Table do.'

There's twice as much money in after-dinner speaking as in a stand-up act and usually a better class of venue.

'Don't tell me. Bread rolls flying all over the place and everyone well pissed before the dessert.'

Lionel laughed, a joyful, throaty sound that he used a lot in his act. 'Something like that. Anyway, it's only a half-hour spot and I'm not on until ten if you fancy coming down. I've got a message for you.'

'A message?' That was odd.

'I'll tell you when I see you.'

'Will there be any food going?' I'd not eaten since my fresh salmon and wine at the funeral party.

'Should be able to rustle up some sandwiches.'

'See you later, then.'

It was only a ten-minute walk to the Adelphi. The hotel was busier than when I'd been in on Wednesday night with Hilary, with a couple of company dos, a wedding reception and the Round Table dinner taking place, as well as Friday's night club in the basement.

I was about to ask at Reception which function room Lionel was in when he walked over. 'I've tasted the sandwiches,' he said, 'and there's more nourishment in a boil. Let's go and have a pizza downstairs.' He was in evening dress and looked suntanned.

The Pizza Coffee Shop was downstairs next door to

the Spindles Health Club. We sat in a corner beneath a row of wood carvings and tried to read the menu in the subdued lighting.

'I thought they fed you at these sort of dos?'

'They offer but I don't like eating with them before I have to speak to them. Makes me nervous.'

The pizzas were fine. Lionel ordered a bottle of red wine and I heard about his holiday in Malta over the garlic bread and cheese.

'Anyway,' I said at last, 'what's this about a message?'

'Met a bloke last night who said he knew you,' he said as he cleaned his plate. 'Wanted to get in touch with you. Said it was urgent.'

'Oh yeah? Who?'

'Fellow called Carlo.'

I thought hard. 'Doesn't ring a bell. What was he like?'

'Oh, about our age. Looked like a pirate; long black hair, bad teeth, swarthy complexion, a bit unkempt and he spoke like someone out of *Neighbours*.'

'A mental defective, you mean?'

Lionel laughed his hearty laugh. 'No, his accent, you pillock. He sounded Australian.'

'How did he know me?'

'Said he played in a group with you in the sixties.'

'I don't remember any Carlos.'

'He asked for your number.' Lionel saw my face and quickly reassured me. 'Don't worry, I didn't give it him but he wrote his address down and asked me to give it you. He isn't on the phone. I think he wants you to call round. Here.'

I read the crumpled piece of paper he handed me. It was a road on a council estate in Speke. 'Christ, you wouldn't fancy driving down there on a dark night. Where did you say you met him?'

'I was doing this charity gig at a pub down the road

from there. Never again, it was a nightmare. Half the cars in the car park were vandalised, windows smashed in, Mastick on the doors, that sort of thing; punch-ups all night in the pub. I was lucky, I took a taxi and had it waiting outside when I'd finished.'

'And this Carlo was in there?'

'They had a karaoke on and he got up to sing "Teenager in Love". He was terrible. Anyway, I did my spot and when I came off stage he came over, said he knew I'd been on your show and could I get a message to you.'

'Seems very odd. He could have rung the station.'

'I thought that but he insisted it was a personal matter.'

Immediately, the nails and the hair came to mind. 'Did he seem threatening?'

'No, just the opposite. He appeared downtrodden and defeated. Actually, more than that. He seemed nervous. Then again, he looked pretty smashed too.'

'And that's all he said?'

'Yes. No, wait a minute, he told me if you weren't going to come I had to say – let me get this right now – I had to say, "Remember June Tarbuck and the Peppermint Lounge".'

I nearly dropped my wine.

It was Oggi!

'Are you all right?' Lionel stared at me across the table. 'You've gone white.'

'Australian accent, you said?' It all fitted in. Oggi's real name was Carl Ogden and he was supposed have gone to Australia. Now he was back.

'You know who he is then?'

I nodded. 'Carl Ogden, our old bass player. We used to call him Oggi. We were in The Cruzads together. I played drums, a guy called Frankie Relphs played lead and Mally Scrufford sang. You'll know Mally. He did the clubs for years as Mal King, keyboard vocalist.'

'I know the name. So when did you last see Carlo?'

'When he left the group, way back in the seventies.' I'd not seen Mally since then either. What a remarkable coincidence that both of them should reappear in my life within a week of one another.

Or was it? A chill ran through me and I took a long slurp of the wine.

'Who was June Tarbuck?'

'This girl we picked up one night at the Peppermint Lounge, a real little raver she was. Couldn't have been more than seventeen. Mind you, we weren't much older ourselves. She was hanging round the stage with a couple of other girls and they followed us into the dressing room when we came offstage. Me and Frankie went with her mates, Lindsay and Lois I think they were called, and Oggi had June.'

'Biblically speaking?'

'That's why I remember it, because she was the first girl Oggi had been all the way with and he was grumbling afterwards because Tiffany's Dimensions had gone on next and Oggi complained he'd had trouble keeping up with the beat.'

'Where was Mal King when all this was happening?'

'Mally had gone to see the manager about some more bookings but when he came back, Oggi didn't stand a chance. It was always Mally the girls went for.'

'You mean, although she'd just been having it away with Oggi, she went with Mally?'

'Not immediately, but Mally took her home. However, it turned out she'd come with this bloke who went apeshit when he found she'd gone off with Mally. God knows what he wasn't going to do to him. He had this pair of knuckle-dusters he must have kept since the teddy boy days and he was a big bugger. We'd just packed up the gear when he came racing out to the van with a crowd of his mates. We had this old Commer that didn't start till the fourth attempt and we were terrified we'd never get away in time.'

'So what happened?'

'Mally got the van started when they were within ten feet of us. The guy picked up a rock from the car park and hurled it though the back window of the van. We were all covered in glass and Oggi's head was cut open. I'll never forget it. We were shitting ourselves.'

'Life on the road, eh?'

'Tell me about it. Anyway, Mally dropped us all off in turn, then took June to the back of Litherland Town Hall and had his way with her in the back of the van.'

'A bit draughty with the broken window.'

'I don't think he noticed. Anyway, he dropped her off at hers, somewhere in Aintree it was, near the racecourse, and never saw her or the boyfriend again. Come to think of it, we never played the Peppermint Lounge again. They said we were too bluesy.'

Lionel laughed. 'Those were the days, Johnny. It's not like that now. Today it's the girls who have their way with innocent boys not the other way round.' Lionel had daughters and spoke from experience. 'I'd be terrified if I was eighteen now.'

I poured another glass of wine. 'I wonder what Oggi wants?'

'Are you going to go and see him?'

'Might as well.' I spoke the words insouciantly but underneath my stomach was churning. First Mally, now Oggi. Behind Mally was a violent death. Oggi was nervous. I'd had the letters with the nails and the hair and the message 'next'.

Next for what?

We finished the meal. 'You won't be staying for the speech, will you, Johnny?' said Lionel.

'No, I'm word perfect on your speeches by now. Anyway, I'm meeting Hilary at the Masquerade.'

'Is that dive still going? You're the only person I know who's been there twice.'

Funny how the Masquerade has such a reputation.

Mind you, when you look around at the clientele, maybe it isn't so surprising.

Hilary was already there when I arrived, talking to Vince at the bar. 'You're late,' she said.

'I've been to a Round Table dinner.'

'You? But you hate all that.'

I explained about Lionel and ordered a myself Scrumpy Jack, a gin and tonic for Hilary and invited Vince to have his usual crème de menthe.

'You're so kind, Johnny.' He was wearing a shocking-pink shell suit with a big orange badge pinned on the front proclaiming 'I'm a Big Boy'.

'I thought shell suits went out of fashion in 1990,' I said.

He winked wickedly. 'Except for a select circle of people, dear.'

'Is Tommy not in tonight? I didn't see him at the door.'

'He's across there with his brother.'

I looked over the packed dance floor and saw them. Denis was the image of his twin except that he was almost bald whereas Tommy had retained the lustrous black hair, Brylcreemed back into a Tony Curtis, that he'd had since boyhood.

We went over. 'Don't see you in here much these days, Denis,' I said.

'All right, Johnny?' He shook my hand, crushing my fingers with his grip. 'Nah. Too busy running the gym, aren't I?'

'We're extending the premises at the gym,' explained Tommy. 'We're converting the warehouse next door into a leisure club with a big pool and jacuzzi, the works.'

Liverpool is full of disused warehouses waiting to be converted into dubious havens of leisure for upmarket gangsters.

'I'll have to come and see it when it's finished.'

'You and your good lady will be honorary members.'

'You don't happen to know a fellow called Sonny Loumarr, do you, Tommy?'

'Yeah, I know Sonny. Heavy for hire. Lives down the Dingle. Works the doors for Pony Taylor's mob.' Lance 'Pony' Taylor runs two nightclubs and a protection racket. He got his nickname because of his passion for gambling. 'He's been inside for GBH a couple of times. A hard man.'

'Not connected with the Stripes Club by any chance?'

'You still going on about those people?'

'We went the other night.'

'One of their special nights, was it? I've heard about them. What was it like?'

'Different,' said Hilary.

'He shouldn't be taking you to places like that,' said Tommy, giving Hilary a squeeze. 'I've heard if they get any gatecrashers, they eat them, is that true?'

'We stuck to the champagne,' I said.

Tommy turned to Denis. 'I can't see Loumarr with that outfit, can you?'

Denis shook his head. 'He'll work for anyone but they'd have their own boys. They're an out-of-town crowd, don't really mix with the local lads.'

'Keep away from them, Johnny,' warned Tommy.

'I'll make sure he does,' smiled Hilary. 'Now, are we going to have a dance or what?'

We squeezed on to the illuminated dance floor and Hilary wrapped her arms round me.

'How did you get on with "Whitney Houston"?' she asked, gyrating her pelvis against mine. I recognised the movement from my time at the back clinic when I had physio for a slipped disc. Trust a nurse to put it to more practical use.

'Oh, OK. She was a nice girl but she didn't know anything about Matt's death.'

'You're still playing detectives then?'

'Not any more. I've given up now. All my leads have turned into dead ends.'

'Good. You stick to doing what you do best.'

I slid my hand over her bottom.

'No time for that tonight,' she said. 'I'm on duty at six and I need to go home for at least four hours' sleep.'

I didn't mind. It suited me not to take her back to the flat with me. Mally was coming round at ten in the morning and I needed to speak to him alone.

But, as it happened, Mally wasn't my first visitor of the day.

Chapter Thirteen

I knew instinctively, when I saw the fire engines in the car park, that it was my flat they'd come to. The evening security guard, a tall, black African called Roger, ran over when he saw me get out of the taxi. It was gone one thirty.

'Sorry about this, Mr Ace. They think it was a petrol bomb through your letter box but it's all under control now.'

The chief fireman came down at that moment and confirmed the fire was out. 'The device didn't go off properly otherwise the whole place would have gone up.' He didn't say whether he meant my flat or the entire building.

'How did they get in?'

Roger looked embarrassed and murmured something about his 'evening brew'. I wasn't surprised. People can get into most places if they want to.

'You've not upset any of the Animal Rights people, have you, sir? This is one of their favourite tricks.'

'No. And I don't have a holiday cottage in Wales.'

'Ah yes. Those Welsh extremists also use these tactics, don't they? he smiled cheerfully. I didn't feel so happy.

'I'll come up with you and inspect the damage.'

Luckily, it wasn't too great as I'd shut all the inside doors, but the hallway was ruined and the smell of smoke permeated the whole flat.

'Good job you had a smoke alarm to alert your neighbours,' said the fire officer. 'Mind you, it'll all need decorating. I take it you're insured?' I said I was and we went through the paperwork before they all left.

'The police have been told,' he said, as a parting shot, 'but they were busy. You'll probably be hearing from them.'

They arrived half an hour later, two uniformed constables whom I'd not met before. We agreed it was arson, they'd spoken to the firemen, and I confirmed I'd no idea who'd do such a thing, as indeed I hadn't.

'They've probably mixed me up with this fellow in the next block,' I said. 'I believe he's in cancer research and I think those people experiment with puppies, don't they?'

The policemen weren't sure but were willing to consider it a possibility. It saved them questioning me any more.

I didn't get to sleep until three and then only fitfully. The smoke irritated my nostrils and my mind kept racing over recent events. Was this fire the 'next' referred to in the letter? Or would there be something more, and worse, to follow? And who was doing it?

At seven o'clock I gave up. I pulled on a jogging suit and went for a gentle trot round the Pier Head to clear my head. The air was clean and fresh, the buses had not had time to poison it with their carcinogenic diesel fumes.

I'm hoping to be still alive when the cities are free from traffic and fast, luxury trams run to every town and village in the country but, as I'll probably be 130 before it happens, I'm afraid I might miss it.

I was out about an hour, then I showered and dressed before making my usual cereal and egg mixture for breakfast, followed by Frank Cooper's Oxford marmalade on granary bread and a pot of Brooke Bond Choicest Blend.

Dead on ten o'clock, the doorbell rang and Mally's voice came over the Entryphone. I released the catch and waited for him to arrive at the door. He was panting.

'God, these steps would do for me,' he said. He didn't look well. I wondered if Marilyn had him insured.

'You're not fit,' I said. 'It's all that driving you do.'

I made him a fresh pot of tea and sat him down, dismissing the state of the hall as an accident. I guessed since I'd confronted him at Matt's funeral that he wouldn't have instigated this second attack. I remained standing. He declined the offer of toast. He was wearing a lime-green blouson with a cord collar, a pair of cavalry twills and a Viyella shirt in a light diarrhoea shade that matched his brogues. He could have stepped out of Greenwoods shop window. How sad, I thought, and to think he was once the lead singer in a trendy pop group!

I attacked from the start. 'To make it easy for you, Mally, I know you paid those two men to have me seen to, so we won't beat about the bush. What I want to know is, why?'

He didn't try to deny it. He must have spent the whole time since I 'invited' him round working out whether he could deny it or, if not, what excuse he could make.

In the end, he could do neither.

'I'm sorry, Johnny. I never meant them to hurt you.'

'You could have fooled me. Why else would they come with knives?'

'I just asked one of the doormen I knew from the old club circuit to find me a couple of boys and he put me on to them. I'd no idea they carried knives. Oh God, to be plain Mal King again and have no problems.'

I ignored his philosophising. 'You've not told me why you sent them.'

He hesitated. 'I didn't want you nosing around after Matt's death, so when you rang me for Sarah's address . . .'

'You hadn't anything to do with Matt's death?' I was shocked at the thought.

'No, no. Matt's murder is still a total mystery to me as it is to the police.'

'So why try to hush things up?'

This time he hesitated a bit longer. 'I'd heard you on the radio asking the public for information about Matt and I remembered what you're like when you get involved in something. You don't let go. I was frightened you'd find something out about me that I don't want Marilyn to know.'

'Go on.' I thought he was going to tell me he'd been having an affair with Maureen, something that was always on the cards, but I was wrong.

'It's Sarah.'

'What!'

'I've been seeing Sarah.'

'Your son's fiancée? I don't believe it.'

'I'm afraid it's true, Johnny.' He sighed. 'You know what I'm like with women . . . Can't resist an opportunity.'

He waited for me to sympathise but that was the last emotion I felt. I realised now that Loumarr and Twigg's visit occurred after I'd rung Mally for Sarah's address, later the same evening in fact. And Sarah would have already been expecting me when I called on her in Chiswick. 'I'm a friend of Matt's father,' I'd told her. No wonder my reception was so hostile. I remembered all the bullshit she gave me about them being faithful to each other.

'And Matt had no idea?'

'No. I don't say this as any defence but Matt wasn't that interested in, you know . . .' He struggled to find the right polite euphemism.

I thought of what Laura had said in Stripes. *Matthew wouldn't be engaged. He was gay.*

'Shagging, you mean, Mally? Well, I'm sure you more than made up for him.' A thought suddenly struck me. 'You realise that gives you a prime motive for killing him?'

'How do you mean?'

'Think about it. Let's say Matt finds out about you and

Sarah. He's furious and confronts you. There's a fight, Matt grabs some weapon and in the struggle, he receives a fatal blow. Or perhaps he falls and hits his head. Either way, you are now in the dock for manslaughter if not murder, because the police will say you killed him to stop him telling your wife.'

Mally looked shocked. 'I never thought of that.' Then he became angry. 'As if I'd kill my own son! What do you think I am?'

I didn't like to tell him. Sleeping with your son's fiancée would rate pretty high on most people's lists of despicable actions.

'Probably chief suspect if the police knew.'

'But the ears, the kidnapping?'

'What kidnapping? Everyone thought it was odd at the time; no note, no message. It was a decoy. You sent the ears to yourself and dumped the body in the dock.'

'How dare you!' Mally rushed at me with his fists flying. I stepped back and clipped him gently on the chin, just enough to knock him to the floor. I thought about hitting him again, retribution for the Sonny Loumarr attack, but in the end I couldn't be bothered.

'Now listen to me,' I said, as he shakily got to his feet. 'I don't think you killed him but if you start acting like that, I might change my mind. You'd better start thinking about your options.'

'What options?'

'If the police do find out about you and Sarah.'

'They won't now, unless . . .' He stopped and looked at me.

I finished the sentence for him. 'Unless I tell them, eh, Mally? And are you going to kill me too?'

But instead, he collapsed into an armchair. 'Johnny, I'm not up to all this. Look, I'll tell you how it happened.'

And he told me his version of the story. How Matt, when he started at John Moores, had come over from the Isle of Man eventually to stay with Mally and Mal. Then one night he brought Sarah home to go over some course work. They were just friends in those days but Sarah and Mally were immediately attracted and, shortly afterwards, started meeting secretly.

Mally encouraged Sarah to keep seeing Matt because it would give him more chance to be with her and it was on his suggestion they moved into the house at Woolton, by which time Matt had proposed to Sarah.

'Sarah accepted but she'd no intention of marrying him. You must understand, Johnny, that Matt and Sarah were not lovers. Sarah told Matt she wanted to be a virgin on her wedding night and Matt respected this.' He shook his head in wonderment that any man could be so stupid. 'Like I said, Matt wasn't over-interested in sex—'

I interrupted. 'How do you know that? I don't see that you had the right to make that assumption.'

'Once when I was telling him about the old days with the group, the things we got up to, I made some remark to the effect that he should be out there doing the same at his age and he said to me, "We're not all like you, you know." I was gobsmacked!'

I could imagine Mally being stunned by that. He assumed all men were exactly like him, what psychiatrists would probably call 'serial seducers', so it would come as a shock to find his own son actually respected women.

Of course, these same psychiatrists would see in Matt a classic pattern for homosexuality. An only child with an absent father, brought up by an over-protective mother and then his father coming back into his life and taunting him about his lack of sexuality.

Only I didn't think Matt was gay. There was no evidence he'd been with Bennison. Jordan Crook had said he was popular with girls. He was probably just a shy lad who was a bit frightened of women and tended to befriend them, rather than risk humiliation if his advances were rejected.

What Matt had needed, as Oscar Wilde would have

said, was the love of a bad woman. Or certainly an older, experienced woman. Instead he fell for a two-timing bitch like Sarah who had betrayed him in the most hideous way.

I hoped he had never found out.

'But I didn't kill him, Johnny, believe me. He never found out about me and Sarah and nobody else knows but you and you won't tell, will you?' He looked anxious.

'I can promise you I won't say a word.'

'Oh, thank you, Johnny.'

'Not for your sake, or hers. It's for Matt's memory I'd keep quiet. I wouldn't like him to be the subject of ridicule by his friends. Then, of course, there's your pregnant wife. What would it do to her?'

Mally looked even more guilty. 'Mall has no idea. She wouldn't understand.'

'Good God, man, would any woman?'

'I want to stay with Marilyn. She's the best wife I've had.'

'Look me in the eye, Mally, and tell me you've never once slept with Maureen since you married Mal. Go on.'

He looked away.

'I suppose you think I'm terrible,' he said.

'You don't realise the hurt and distress you cause people. Or, worse still, you do and don't care.' And here was a man who could sing Timi Yuro's 'Hurt' so sweetly, you'd swear it was an angel's voice.

There was silence.

'Look, this isn't getting us anywhere,' I said at last. 'I know now who attacked me so that's one mystery solved but I want some more answers and I want the truth. Have you ever sent me packets with either some nail clippings or a clump of hair?'

His surprised expression convinced me he hadn't and he shook his head. 'I didn't know where you lived till after you came to see me.'

'Where did you get my address?'

'From the radio station.'

I made a mental note to bollock somebody; I don't like my address being given out. He must have sensed my displeasure.

'It was someone I worked with on the clubs, Johnny. He wouldn't give it to just anybody.'

Then I told him about the Jiffy bags and the petrol bomb. 'I'm sure it's the same person who sent Matt's ears to you.'

'But who? And why? There's no motive.'

'There'll be a motive,' I said. 'It's just that we don't know it. Yet.' I paused and tried another tack. 'Have you heard from Oggi lately?'

'Oggi? Good Lord, no. Not for years. He's in Australia.'

'So you said the other day. Who told you?'

'I don't know. It was years ago, a few months after the group packed up. He'd had an offer of a job as a lifeguard on Bondi Beach, someone he knew over there.'

'Well, he's back.'

'Is he?'

'Living on a council estate in Speke.'

'You've seen him?'

'No, but I'm going round on Monday. Apparently, he wants to talk to me.'

'Shouldn't think you'll have much to say to him after all this time. He didn't say much when we knew him.' Mally had always thought himself socially superior to the rest of the group.

'I think there may be some connection between Matt's death and Oggi.'

He looked at me as if I'd announced my engagement to Camilla Parker Bowles.

'Don't be bloody stupid. I've had no contact with the man for over twenty years, before Matt was even born. What reasons have you got for saying that?'

'No rational ones. But it's odd that the three of us should suddenly find one another after all this time.'

'Hang on, there were four of us in The Cruzads. Where's Frankie in all this?'

'Ah. Well, I admit I've not heard from Frankie but—'

'There you are then,' said Mally triumphantly. 'Just coincidence.'

'Have you any better ideas?

He slumped back in his chair. 'No, Johnny, I haven't. If you want to know, I'm totally destroyed by all this. I've no idea what secrets there were in Matt's life that led to him being killed like that. All I know is, my son is dead and nothing will bring him back.'

If he knew of no secrets, neither did I, and I'd spent a week looking for them without success. I wasn't too worried about Mally's depressed state. I knew from the past his ability to turn defeat into victory and despair into profit. He'd survive. Besides, he'd got Marilyn. And Sarah! And Maureen! It was hard to feel too sorry for him.

He left shortly afterwards. I wondered how long he would last with Mal before someone else came along or she found out about his philandering.

The ones I felt most sorry for were little Gary and the new baby.

I raided the freezer for some lunch. Over the meal I read the *Daily Post*. Tranmere had beaten Portsmouth the night before. I'd always said John Aldridge should have signed for Everton instead of Tranmere. Even at his age he's more likely to score goals than most of the current team.

There was no Premiership football today because England had a World Cup qualifying game against Poland on Wednesday and the players were saving themselves, so I settled for a quiet afternoon watching a video.

I chose *The Third Man* for the umpteenth time. It's

the most atmospheric film I've seen. It has the effect of transporting me to post-war Vienna, a place that seemed infinitely preferable to 1990s Liverpool after a morning with Mally Scrufford.

Joseph Cotton was about to step on to the ferris wheel at Prater Park when the phone rang. I was inclined to let the answerphone take it but somehow I can never resist picking up a ringing phone. It was Jim Burroughs.

'About your little parcels, I've just had the results from Forensic.'

'That was quick.'

'They can be if you put a bit of pressure on. You were right about the nails. They were Matt Scrufford's.'

'Bloody Hell!' So now it was confirmed. Somehow, I was involved in this murder myself and had been before I'd even heard of the boy.

'But not the hair.'

'What?'

'The hair isn't his.'

'You're joking?'

'I'm not. Any ideas?'

'Have you done a DNA test?'

'It'd take two weeks for the results to come through. But we don't need to, we've got the corpse, haven't we? If you must know, I sent a man round to the chapel of rest last night to compare it and it's definitely not his.'

'I don't understand it. It doesn't make any sense.'

I told him about the petrol bomb.

'Is this connected with the Sonny Loumarr business?'

'No. I solved that one. That was someone I upset on the show but it's all sorted now.' No point in confusing him with the truth.

'Mmm.' He didn't sound convinced. 'But you've no idea who sent the petrol bomb?'

'No. Or the hair, or the nails. And I've no idea who killed Matt Scrufford or why. But I tell you what, Jim, I'm suddenly very frightened someone is going to kill me.'

Chapter Fourteen

I couldn't get into the film after that. I switched the TV off and went into town, finding some comfort from the noise and people in the crowded shops. I queued up for a cup of tea at C & A and bought a green jacket in the sale. Sales seem to last all year round these days. It's funny, I've been in C & A shops all over Europe and every one's the same. I could just as easily have been in Carlisle or Geneva or Vienna.

Thinking of Vienna, I went back to watch the rest of the film. It ended as always, with Harry Lime dead in the sewers. Sometimes I wished there was an alternative version and he could escape for a change.

I was glad I was spending the rest of the weekend with Maria. The Matt Scrufford business was getting on top of me and I needed the break. My visit to Oggi's on Monday would come soon enough.

I'd arranged to meet Maria at Casa Bella in Victoria Street at six, so we could have a bite to eat before the show. I packed an overnight bag and put on my new three-piece navy suit with the high-collared waistcoat, a kingfisher-blue shirt and a blue tie with bright-yellow sunflowers that Maria had bought me for my birthday.

She was already inside when I arrived, a glass of wine in her hand.

'I thought I'd order the wine,' she said. 'I know what you like.' She smiled in approval at my outfit. She, too, was in a navy suit with a pale-turquoise blouse and a silk scarf round her neck. It went well with her raven hair.

'There's a few in for so early on,' I said, glancing round the busy restaurant. The Casa Bella site used to be the main branch of the Irish Bank and holds a lot of people.

'Richard Williams' *Dream* is on at the Playhouse tonight as well.'

We discussed plays and opera. I'd never seen *The Marriage of Figaro* before although I like Mozart.

'You'll love *Figaro*,' Maria said. 'It's my favourite of his operas. I saw it in Vienna.'

'That's the third time Vienna's come up today.' I explained about the Orson Welles film and C & A.

'There's a word for that but I can't think what it is. Not coincidence, something else.'

'Serendipity.'

'I thought that was when you were looking for one thing and through your actions, something better came along by a lucky chance.'

'Could be that too.'

We chatted amiably over the meal, finishing in good time to catch a taxi to Hope Street.

The Philharmonic Hall had been refurbished and looked splendid but I was surprised at the state of the audience. Most of them were under thirty and dressed in T-shirts and jeans. I commented on this to Maria. She smiled mischievously.

'I suppose in your day everyone wore evening dress.'

'Hang on, I'm not that much older than you. The point is, I do feel the theatre is one place you can dress up to go.'

'Not any more, dear,' said Maria, taking my arm affectionately and leading me inside.

The opera was excellent and deserved the standing ovations. Obviously, despite their attire, the people appreciated good music.

We took a taxi back to mine and collected my car to drive to Maria's. She lives in a modern flat on The Serpentine out at Blundellsands and Crosby, overlooking the mouth of the Mersey estuary. At one time, from her lounge window, you would have seen all the great liners leaving for New York.

Now you see the gas and oil rigs out in the Irish sea. Perhaps this should be Liverpool's big hope for the future, to be another Dallas.

Maria's lounge is quite large and the white-painted walls add to the feeling of spaciousness. She has a couple of Hockney prints and the blues in them pick up the colour of the curtains, carpet and suite. It's a restful room and I always feel relaxed in it.

'Sit down,' said Maria, 'and I'll get the drinks. A good night, wasn't it?'

'Great.' I realised I hadn't given a thought to Matt Scrufford all evening. As if reading my mind, Maria asked me how things were going with the case.

'Pretty dreadful. I was going to say I was sorry I got involved but it turns out I was involved all along, even before I knew it.'

She brought two nightcaps over to the glass-topped coffee table and joined me on the sofa. 'How do you mean?'

I brought her up to date. I didn't go into detail about the Stripes Club and for some reason, I wasn't sure why, I didn't mention Hilary was with me.

She was disgusted with Mally's behaviour and horrified when I told her about the petrol bomb and the package with the lock of hair.

'You'll have to be careful, Johnny, seriously. I've got a feeling something terrible's going to happen.'

We went to bed and stayed there for most of the next morning. Maria made tea and bacon sandwiches. We listened to *Letter from America* and *The Archers* on the radio and made love in between.

At lunchtime, we took the back road out of Crosby, alongside the fields, towards Formby. Behind the stone farm cottages at Little Crosby, the local riding club was holding a pony show and lots of small girls on fat ponies were cantering round the fields. It was like a scene from a Thelwell cartoon with the twin goal posts of Hightown Rugby Club in the background.

I felt I was in another century.

We drove through Formby and stopped for a drink at The Grapes in Freshfield, Colin Bennison country. 'We played up there one Sunday with The Big Three,' I said, pointing to the building opposite the pub. 'It used to be an ice rink.'

'It's a gym and pool hall now,' said Maria, 'and you're getting nostalgic again.'

The Grapes was packed, mainly with teenagers, mostly girls. I noticed a couple of Liverpool footballers near the bar. Freshfield was another encalve of Premiership stars just like Birkdale. Loud chart music precluded conversation below a bellow.

We sat in the back bar over our drinks. After the petrol bomb and the unpleasantness with Mally, I was glad to have got away from things.

Maria's sister, Kaye, and her husband, Alex, lived on a small estate of mock-Tudor houses behind a riding school. Squirrels ran up and down the trees in the back garden. There are a lot of horses and squirrels in Formby.

Kaye was very like Maria, dark-haired and sallow-skinned, but she was older and plumper and looked more like Julie Walters than Cher. She had a bubbly sense of humour, which made up for her husband who was an accountant and had no humour at all.

Happily, at no time was it suggested that Maria and I were about to be betrothed so the visit turned out to be quite enjoyable. Kaye cooked a vegetable stew with herb dumplings followed by gooseberry pie and custard. We got through three bottles of wine and even Alex relaxed after his fourth glass.

We talked about jobs. Kaye worked for an estate agent in Formby. Alex told us he hated accountancy since self-assessment came in and wanted to give it up to be a market gardener. Kaye confided he couldn't grow a decent lawn so who did he think he was kidding?

Maria said the council were making so many cuts, some librarians might have to be redeployed.

'You could be on the bins by Christmas then,' laughed Kaye, but Maria didn't think it was funny.

'Don't laugh. It might happen.' She looked pensive. 'What I'd really like to do is open a small bookshop.'

'There's no money in those,' said Alex. 'The days of the independent retailer are finished. It's all the big chain stores and supermarkets now, even in the book trade. Publishers are owned by oil companies and run by accountants.'

'Like record companies,' I said.

'Oh, I know. But it's something I'd like to do. I mean, I like the library but a lot of the time now, my work is administrative. I'd like to be back working with books.'

The conversation flowed easily until we left at ten. I dropped Maria off at hers, then drove on back to the flat with some trepidation. One mugging and one petrol bomb had made me cautious but all was quiet and the flat was peaceful.

It was the calm before the storm.

Geoffrey rang first thing. 'I've had a couple of punters in over the weekend looking for a one-bedroom flat. That one in Percy Street is empty; do you want me to show it?'

Geoffrey's always pushing to do the lettings but I'm reluctant to allow him. Get the wrong people in and, whatever they say about landlord's rights, you're stuck with them for months and evicting them can be long-winded, expensive and unpleasant. I rely on gut instinct when I interview prospective tenants and it doesn't often let me down.

'What time are they coming?'

'Three.'

'That's OK. I'll do it. I've got to go to Speke this morning, I'll pick up the keys on the way.'

Armed with an A-Z, I waited till the rush-hour traffic had died down and drove out to Speke, calling in at the office on the way through. Geoffrey was on the phone, sorting out a problem with someone's gas fire. I took the Percy Street keys off the board and left him to it.

It was a long while since I'd been out to Speke and Halewood and the area shocked me. With the boarded-up shops, disused and overgrown factory sites, litter and graffiti, I could have been in Bosnia. Liverpool seems to have more derelict sites now than it did after the war.

Oggi's house was a semidetached on a council estate that would rank alongside anything that Moss Side in Manchester, St Paul's in Bristol or the Gorbals in Glasgow could offer.

The front door was bereft of paint; a pane of glass in the window was broken and a piece of cardboard inserted; old cans, bricks and plastic packets littered the front garden and the gate was hanging off its hinges.

A few kids were playing in the street next to some abandoned pushchairs. I wished I'd taken a taxi and wondered, as I walked up the path, whether I'd see my Toyota again.

It took a few knocks before someone stumbled down the stairs to open the door. I had to look twice to recognise the unshaven, lank-haired figure before me but it was indeed Oggi. He had on a grimy tie-dyed T-shirt which barely covered his large stomach never mind a pair of off-white Y-fronts.

He didn't recognise me.

'Johnny,' I said. 'Johnny Ace.'

'Shit, so it is. Johnny. I've been trying to get hold of you.'

'I know. That's why I'm here.'

I held my hand out to shake his but he just reached

out for my arm and pulled me inside. 'I've been trying to find you,' he repeated. I noticed he stooped slightly and his voice had a slight tremor. Whatever he was on, it wasn't doing him much good. He was forty-nine but I reckoned he'd have no trouble getting the pensioners' portions in the Dove and Olive up the road.

'Who is it?' came a voice from upstairs.

'It's Johnny,' he shouted up.

I looked round the room. It smelt of drying clothes that hadn't been washed first. Some of them were hanging on a white plastic maiden in front of an old gas fire. I used to have those fires like that in the flats at one time but they wouldn't pass today's Health and Safety regulations.

The carpet held an interesting collection of stains, unwashed crockery littered the table and there were cobwebs on the upper reaches of the woodchipped walls.

A woman came down the stairs and into the room. She wore a quilted dressing gown over a Snoopy nightshirt and fluffy slippers. Her hair was grey and straggly, her legs blotchy and she had a bunion on each foot.

'This is Johnny Ace, love. We used to play together in the sixties. Remember The Cruzads I told you about?'

She coughed, a consumptive croak. 'Give me a ciggy, Carl.' He handed one over. She lit it, coughed again and smiled at me. 'I'll put the kettle on?'

'Er, no thank you,' I said hurriedly. 'I've just had breakfast.' I could imagine the state of the kitchen.

'I'm glad you came,' he said, lighting up himself. 'We daren't fetch the police—'

'The police!' I echoed.

'With the drugs, like.' He said it matter-of-factly. 'I'm sorry. I'm not so good in the mornings. Come tonight I'll be singing "Sweet Little Sixteen" just like we did in the old days, eh?' He started to sing but broke into a coughing fit worse than his wife's.

So here was someone else frightened of the police because of drugs. How many more were there like this in the city? Plenty, I suspected. At least Jordan Crook only smoked cannabis.

'Let him sit down, Carl,' said his wife, and gesticulated to an old brown Dralon armchair. 'I'll move the papers.'

She gathered a pile of tabloids and magazines, put them on the table, allowing me access to the chair. They sat on a matching couch.

'We've been very frightened,' began Oggi's wife. 'Tell him, Carl.'

'There's someone after us,' he said dramatically.

'Perhaps it's Colombian drug dealers,' I ventured whimsically.

'No, no. Nothing to do with drugs. We take care of all that, know what I mean?' It sounded like dropsies to the Drug Squad but I didn't want to hear anything about that.

'They took Jenny,' he said.

'Jenny's our daughter.'

'But she got away from them.'

'Well, not really, Carl.'

'Hang on,' I said. 'Can we start at the beginning? In fact, start with Australia. What made you go halfway across the world?'

'I was promised this lifeguard's job in Sydney by a mate of mine who was over there,' said Oggi. 'There was nothing happening in Liverpool, with the group finishing, like. I was on the dole, so I thought I'd give it a try. I borrowed the fare and pissed off over there—'

'Only there wasn't a job,' interrupted his wife.

'But it was warmer than over here so I stayed anyway.'

Slowly, I got the story. He'd got a band together, played in local pubs, and for the next ten years made a living of sorts, augmenting his show business income by doing odd jobs like painting and decorating, labouring and working on the taxis.

Then he met Sharon, his wife, who also came from

Liverpool. She'd emigrated to Sydney with her first husband but they were now divorced. Sharon moved into Oggi's flat, got pregnant and they decided to marry and return to England.

They moved into Sharon's mother's council house in Speke and stayed on after the old lady died. Jenny was now ten.

Their financial situation hadn't improved with their change of location. Oggi was on disability pension for a nervous disorder and hadn't worked since their return. Sharon had worked on and off as a dinner lady at a nearby primary school but was now on Housing Benefit.

'Mind you,' he continued, 'there wouldn't be any jobs round here for me anyway. And if Ford ever pack in at Halewood they might as well shut Liverpool down. When I think back to the sixties and how we all thought we were really going to make it . . .'

I figure there are a lot of people like Oggi in Liverpool, casualities from the Merseybeat era. They gave up their apprenticeships and jobs to join a group, convinced they'd follow the Beatles to stardom, but only a very few of them made it and for many of the rest, it was too late to go back to pick up the pieces of a career. They became disillusioned and bitter.

'The drugs did for us,' Oggi said. 'We were on crack and coke and I did heroin for a long time. I'm off heroin now but I'm knackered.'

I didn't enquire how he was able to finance his coke habit but assumed, by his fear of the police, that he was doing some part-time dealing.

'What is it you're frightened of?' I asked.

He went over to a drawer in a teak sideboard and brought out a Jiffy bag. It was like the ones I'd received. 'Look in there.'

I opened it and took out a single piece of paper. It had the word 'NEXT' stuck on it, cut from a newspaper.

'There's more,' said Oggi. I felt inside and my fingers

caught on the jagged edges of nails. I shook them out. Ten toenail clippings.

'Two days after we got that,' said Sharon, 'Jenny didn't come home from school. We thought she was with friends but when it got to eight o'clock, we were really worried. Carl went round to all her friends and they hadn't seen her. Then, at ten o'clock, she ran in, crying.'

'But she was all right?'

'Sort of. She said this man had met her out of school with some story about being a friend of her dad's and he was waiting at the shops. We've always told her never to go with strangers but you know what kids are like, trusting, and she went.'

Oggi went on, 'He took her to a shop somewhere, gagged her and locked her in a room at the back. She managed to get out through a window and find her way home. She's pretty streetwise for ten.'

I thought she'd have to be, living where she did.

'She caught the first bus that came along with City Centre on the front that she knew would take her to town, then she got the Speke bus home.'

'And she was unharmed?'

'Oh, he hadn't done anything like that to her, and she wasn't hurt, except for one thing.'

'Yes?'

'They cut a chunk of her hair off.'

I went cold. 'What colour's her hair?'

'Auburn, why'

'Did she describe the man?'

'Not really. She said he was old like me. He was fat and he wore a baseball hat with Washington Redskins on.'

'What about the van?'

'Blue, but she doesn't know the make. Well, she wouldn't, would she? Not at ten.'

'And you haven't told the police?' I couldn't believe that their daughter's safety wouldn't come before anything else.

'Well, she's back now, isn't she? But I'm still worried. It's that letter and the nails.'

'We're frightened he'll have another go,' chipped in Sharon. 'Carl takes her to school and fetches her home every day now and we daren't let her out to play.'

'We've heard your show,' said Oggi, 'and we thought you'd maybe know what to do, for old times' sake, like. We don't know anyone else and, as I say, the police . . .'

'Leave it with me,' I said. 'I might be able to help you. I'll take the nails if I may.' More analysing for Jim Burroughs to do but I'd have given evens they were Matt Scrufford's.

Sharon looked at her husband desperately. 'She's had to have her hair cut short so's she won't look silly, hasn't she, Carl? And she's been having these terrible nightmares.'

I didn't tell them about my letters or the lock of hair, which I was sure was Jenny's. No sense in worrying them further.

'What are you going to do?' asked Oggi.

I wasn't sure. 'I've got some contacts,' I said. I needed to think it through but at some stage I knew Jim Burroughs would have to hear the story whether Oggi approved or not.

'Hey, great show you do, Johnny. Love the music. We should have made a record, you know.'

'Why did you call yourself Carlo?' I asked.

Sharon laughed. It was a sad little sound. 'That's who he was in Sydney, Carlo and the Pirates, like Johnny Kidd and the Pirates. Don't you think he looks a bit like one?'

'I wore an eyepatch like the guy in Dr Hook.'

'Lionel, you know, the comedian the other night, he said you looked like a pirate.' I couldn't see much resemblance myself. Admittedly his hair was still black, probably dyed, but there was little of a swashbuckling aura about him. And he didn't have a parrot on his shoulder.

'You're not on the phone, are you?' I asked. They shook their heads. 'Leave it with me. I'll call round in a few days. In the meantime, don't let Jenny out of your sight.' I thought about what had happened to Matt Scrufford. There was every chance Jenny Ogden could have met the same fate had she not escaped.

'Do you ever hear anything of Mally and Frankie?' asked Oggi, as he led me to the door.

I couldn't believe he'd not read anything in the paper about the kidnapping but he obviously hadn't.

'Funnily enough, I saw Mally last week. He's selling books for a living. Seems to be doing OK.' I took care not to mention Matt. 'I've not seen Frankie for twenty years, since the group broke up.'

But I had every intention of seeing Frankie Relphs again, and very soon.

Chapter Fifteen

I couldn't get back to town fast enough. Speke depressed me. The whole area was in decline. I'd not been there since I'd flown to the Isle of Man from the airport over six years ago. I'd been quite impressed with the new terminal and couldn't understand why they weren't going for the package holiday trade. Instead, they were bidding to get Manchester's second runway which I couldn't see happening.

I parked at Exchange Flags and walked over to Toffs Wine Bar for lunch. Toffs is in the heart of the City, so the clientele tends to be civil servants, accountants and bankers. I needed an antidote to the squalor of Oggi's house.

The place was pretty full but I found a seat opposite a lady who didn't mind me sharing her table and we ate our meals together without speaking.

When she'd finished, she took a folder from a brief-case by her side and started going over some papers. I figured her for a lawyer. I drank up my last glass of mineral water and started thinking about the morning's events.

Assuming that the hair sent to me was Jenny's, and I was sure it was, then the common factor here was The Cruzads. Oggi, Mally and I had all received these packages, in Mally's case with particularly horrifying contents. I'd had the petrol bomb. Oggi's daughter had been kidnapped like Matt.

The only thing missing was the motive. Why would

anybody want to do all this? There was no suggestion of personal gain. I remembered what Maria had said when we first discussed Matt's murder. *Could it have been a grudge killing?* But who would have a grudge against an unknown group that broke up twenty years ago? It could hardly be professional jealousy.

I was beaten. I knew, though, that my next step would have to be to contact Frankie. Had he received any of these packages? Or could it be Frankie that was sending them? I couldn't really believe Frankie had started a personal vendetta against his ex-colleagues after all this time, even if he had an imagined motive.

And I could think of nobody I'd upset to any extent that warranted torching my flat. I guessed the hair and the nails were meant to be some kind of warning but of what?

I checked my watch. I had twenty minutes to get to Percy Street. My lunch companion looked up from her papers as I rose from my seat and we nodded briefly to each other. British reserve, I thought. If it had been America, we'd have been close friends by the time the meal was over.

The traffic wasn't bad and I made it across town with time to spare. The houses in Percy Street are wonderful: dark stone terraces built way back in 1830 and very similar to the Georgian buildings in Edinburgh. I'm just amazed that, being in Liverpool, they've managed to escape the council's demolition hammer.

The house I own is divided into four flats. In 1959, Stuart Sutcliffe lived in a ground-floor flat down the road at number 7 where he did his paintings before he joined the Beatles.

I parked up on the kerbside and waited. A lad arrived dead on three. He wore a dark modern suit with a round collar, a bright yellow shirt and matching floral tie. Although obviously under twenty, he didn't look like a student.

'Mr Welles,' he introduced himself. 'I've come to see the flat.'

I escorted him into the house. 'Are you working, Mr Welles?'

'I work in town.'

'Whereabouts?'

'Near Church Street.'

I despaired. Why did people never answer questions properly? 'Who do you work for?' I persevered.

'Oh, McDonald's.' He sounded surprised I should want to know. 'Big Macs and that. At the drive-in down Edge lane.'

'Right.' I did my guided tour, he emitted a few grunts and finally said he'd let me know. He had a few others to look at.

We went back outside as a taxi drew up and a girl with long blonde hair got out. I did a double take as she turned towards me.

It was Sarah, Matt Scrufford's finacée. Mally's mistress.

She stopped dead when she saw me. 'What . . .?'

'Hello, Sarah.'

'Are you following me?' she said in accusing tones.

'As I am already here, it would seem more likely that you are following me.' I said it with a smile. No sense in escalating the tension between us.

'You can't be waiting to see this flat too?'

'No. I'm showing the flat.'

'You're the landlord?'

'Don't look so surprised. I've got to make a living somehow. Come on, I'll take you round.'

'I thought you were just a DJ.'

'I am a DJ but not, as you say, "just".' We went into the flat and through the hallway. 'Here's the kitchen, fully tiled, gas cooker, fridge freezer, central heating radiator.' I led her on to the bathroom. 'Anyway, what's wrong with being a DJ?'

'Nothing,' she said hurriedly. 'I just meant . . .' Her voice trailed away and she viewed the rest of the flat in silence.

'Well, thanks a lot,' she said, as we emerged into the street. 'Can I let you know?'

'Don't tell me, you've got others to look at.'

'No, this is the only one and I like it. I just don't know whether I'd want you as my landlord.'

I was taken aback. 'Nothing like being honest.'

'Quite.'

'Look, I think we ought to talk. I realise now why you were so – er,' I searched for a word, 'disconcerted when I came to Chiswick.' I paused. 'You see, I know about you and Mally.'

'Who told you?' she flashed angrily.

'Mally did. Don't worry, it won't go any further. No one else knows. But, forgetting about that for the moment, you've got to remember Matt's killer is still at large and he may kill again. I think all of us may be in danger and that includes you, Sarah.' For the first time, her defences slipped and she looked frightened.

'Look, let's go and have a cup of tea and talk about it. Jump in the car.' She hesitated but in the end she climbed into the passenger seat.

I took her to the Refectory at the Anglican cathedral. A few late-season tourists were wandering about and the gift shop was doing a brisk trade.

'I've never been in here before,' said Sarah. 'Isn't it big?'

'Biggest in the world. If religion ever goes out of fashion it would make a wonderful indoor football pitch.'

'Biggest in the world? You're kidding.'

'No. It's twice as big as St Paul's. It takes two lifts to reach the top of the tower and even then you've got over a hundred stairs to climb. The view's worth it, though; you can see right over Wales. Mind you, some Catholic cathedrals are bigger but this is the largest

Anglican one anywhere. And they do a nice cup of tea.'

We went through the gift shop to the Refectory and found an empty table beneath the stone arches. I brought over a pot of tea and home-made cake and we settled ourselves down. The atmosphere was decidedly more companionable than at our breakfast in Chiswick.

Through the window, we could look out over the sunken St James's cemetery with its catacombs and tunnels and across to Gambier Terrace where John Lennon and Stuart Sutcliffe had a flat together after Stuart left Percy Street. As a row of Classical houses, I reckoned it beat anything in Bath.

'Right,' said Sarah, as she finished her cake. 'What do you mean, I may be in danger? What have I done?'

'I've no idea, you tell me. What had Matt done? Nothing, as far as we know, and look what happened to him.'

'You said something in Chiswick about Colin Bennison. Had he anything to do with Matt's death because of that exam trouble?'

'He didn't kill Matt. In fact, it's probable that Matt never got to talk to him about his examination fiddle. From all accounts, they were quite friendly. Matt had been with him a couple of times of this Stripes Club.'

'You told me at Chiswick that he was with a girl there.'

'It turns out she was one of the hostesses.'

'Not my "rival" then!' Sarah could not resist the sarcasm. 'It figures he was friendly with Bennison, though. Bennison was supposed to be gay.'

'Hang on a minute, you said Bennison tried to grope you once.'

'I was lying, I'm afraid. I didn't want to let you have any idea that Matt might be that way inclined or you may have thought the engagement was a fake.'

'When it was really a good cover for your affair with his father?'

'Yes.' She said it without shame.

'And do you think Matt was "that way inclined", as you put it?'

'No, of course he wasn't. He was a romantic, was Matt, he liked being with girls.'

Jordan had said about Matt that women fancied him. But did he want them only as friends? He'd not tried to have his way with Laura and he'd accepted Sarah's rebuffs with remarkable equanimity. Not many boys nowadays would have gone along with all that 'wait till we're married' stuff.

'Yet you weren't surprised when I told you he was friendly with Bennison.'

'I didn't mean he was gay. He was just one of those aesthetic type of boys that attract gays. You know, slim, quietly spoken, gentle.' She became defiant again. 'Look, I was really fond of him, you know . . .'

Having an affair with his father didn't seem the best way of showing it but I refrained from saying so.

'. . . in a sisterly way, that is. We were best friends.'

'But not brotherly from his point of view. He asked you to marry him.'

'I know. But I did tell him I didn't want to.'

'What reason did you give him?'

She looked sheepish. 'I said I was too young and I had my career to think of.'

'Not that you didn't fancy him and he was wasting his time? And still you got engaged to him.'

'He wanted it. He said it gave him hope.'

'A bit like putting a deposit on a house and then being gazumped.'

'Well, he never knew that, did he?' she snapped. 'You could say I made his last days happy.'

'Good job he never found out. He might have thrown his lot in with Bennison and decided he was better off with boys.'

'That's a terrible thing to say.'

'It also, of course, gives you a motive for killing him. He would have been very bitter if he'd found out about you and Mally.'

'How dare you!'

'That's what Mally said when I suggested the same thing to him.'

'You told Mally you thought he'd kill his own son? I don't believe this.'

'No. I told him that the police might think it, just as they might about you. Don't you see, Sarah, you two are potential suspects? You could have killed him to prevent him telling Mally's wife about you both. In the meantime, the real killer is out there and we could all be victims.'

'That's what you said before, but why should anyone want to kill us?'

'I don't know.' I told her about the letters that Oggi and I had received. She choked when I revealed that the nail clippings sent to me had been identified as Matt's.

'Oh, my God. How terrible.'

'And on Friday night, after the funeral, someone put a petrol bomb through my front door. There seems to be some kind of tie-in with The Cruzads. I haven't been able to figure it out yet but I'm working on it, believe me.'

'What about the police?'

'As yet, they don't know about Oggi and his little girl. They're still treating Matt's death as a botched kidnap but, from what I can gather, it's on a back burner anyway.'

'So what are you going to do?' Her tone had mellowed again. I poured us each another cup of tea.

'I'm going to find Frankie. He's the only other member of the group. Maybe he's had threats too.'

'Where does he live?'

'I'm not sure but Maureen said he's got a place in Birkdale.'

'He's still in the area then?'

'So it seems, although I've not heard from him since the group broke up. But I'll find him, don't worry. And what about you? Are you going to carry on seeing Mally?'

'I don't know. I'm confused. As you see, I'm looking for a flat on my own.'

'Well, you can hardly stay on by yourself with Mally and Marilyn, can you?' Mind you, after all I've seen as a landlord, I shouldn't be shocked at anything people do. Sarah didn't act as though she'd feel too embarrassed or guilty at sharing a house with her lover and his unknowing and pregnant wife.

'Doesn't it worry you that she's having a baby?'

She shrugged her shoulders and murmured something about it being Marilyn's problem. Women certainly were becoming harder these days. I couldn't see Dora Copperfield surviving easily in the 1990s.

I didn't like Sarah's attitude but I had the consolation of knowing that Mally tired pretty quickly of his women so she would undoubtedly have her hook slung sooner or later.

'Can I have the flat, then?' I was surprised but business is business.

'If you've got £300 deposit plus £300 rent, you can move in today.'

'I'll write you a cheque.' Obviously her parents were supplementing her grant. She opened her handbag and smiled. 'You'll be able to keep an eye on me now.' I had to admit she was attractive, especially as I recalled her shapely figure beneath her T-shirt in Chiswick. I could understand what Mally saw in her although Mally was the type of man who'd have a blind nun on a zimmer if she inadvertently gave him encouragement.

'There you are.' She handed me the completed cheque. 'You don't need my bank card, do you?'

'If it bounces, I know where you live. Come to the car and we can do the paperwork and I'll give you the keys.'

I gave her a lift back to Percy Street. 'What about moving your stuff?'

'Mally's sorting that.' She held out her hand. 'He'll be surprised when I tell him who my landlord is. Look, thanks for giving me the flat. I'm sorry I was rude at times but it's all been pretty stressful, hasn't it?'

'I know. Things couldn't be much worse.'

But I was wrong.

They could.

Chapter Sixteen

It had been a long time since I last visited the little semi near Walton Prison but I actually recalled the occasion quite clearly.

Mally had been driving the red Transit van we had by then, with 'THE CRUZADS' painted on the outside. We'd dropped off Oggi in the Dingle, Maureen got out here and mine was the next stop, in Litherland. The gear was kept in a shed at the bottom of Frankie's garden. Frankie lived in a big detached house in West Derby, not far from the legendary Casbah Club in the cellar of Pete Best's house.

After unloading all the equipment, Mally would go back to Mo's for his supper, and whatever else, before going back to his own home in Seaforth.

Now here I was, pulling up outside, over thirty years later, and the house didn't look any different.

Inside, though, it had changed tremendously. Soo answered the door and invited me in. The old parlour and living room had been knocked into one large bright room. Central heating had replaced the coal fire, the clothes rack on the kitchen ceiling had gone, the large Bakelite black-and-white TV I remembered having pride of place on the sideboard had been superceded by a twenty-five-inch Panasonic with matching video recorder, and fitted carpets hid the remnants of the old linoleum.

An old lady sat in a chair by the fireplace, where a vase of flowers under the chimney acted as a focal point for the room. 'Who is it?' she asked, squinting at me through thick-lensed spectacles.

Maureen came in from the kitchen. 'It's Johnny Ace, Mam. You remember Johnny from The Cruzads.' She spoke in a raised voice.

'Of course I do. I don't like your programme on the wireless. You play some very funny records.'

'At least you listen,' I said, and went over to kiss her cheek.

'You played funny music in that group too.'

'You're looking well, Mrs Stanistreet. Not a day older.'

'What's he saying?' Her gaze returned to the television screen.

Maureen had to shout. 'He said you look well, Mam. She's a bit deaf,' she explained to me. She had more colour than at the funeral and the loose-fitting floral dress suited her. 'I don't see you for years then it's twice in less than a week.'

'It was the seventies when I was last here,' I said.

'You had a lot more hair then,' said her sister.

'Thanks, Soo.'

'Is this just a social visit, then?' asked Maureen.

'Partly. I wanted to catch you before you left.'

'You're lucky. I'm flying back to the Isle of Man tomorrow. I don't think I ever want to come back to the mainland again. I've lost my only son. There's too many painful memories.' She took a tissue out of her pocket and wiped her eyes.

'You said you knew where Frankie was living and I need to get hold of him urgently.'

'I haven't got his address, Johnny, I know it's in Birkdale somewhere and I only know that 'cos I read it in the *Echo*.'

'When was that?'

'Oh, over twelve months ago. It was when Matt first came to the university and we were sorting out his stuff for him to stay here with Soo. Before he went to Mally's.'

'What was the article about?'

'The collapse of the property market. It had pictures of people whose houses had dropped in value since the crash. One of them was Frankie, standing outside this huge place that looked more like a castle. It said he lived in the millionaire footballer belt in Southport and the house had been worth over half a million at the height of the boom, but now he'd be lucky to get £200,000 for it.'

'That was last year,' I said. 'If he hangs on, he'll get his half-million again.' I have every faith in property as an investment.

'You've not done badly, all of you, have you?' said Maureen. 'The old Cruzads. You with your radio show, Johnny, and Mally and Frankie with their big houses.'

'You've not seen Oggi,' I said.

'I thought you said he was in Australia.'

'He's back. I went to see him this morning. He's living in a council house in Speke, half out of his mind with drugs.'

'Poor Oggi. And he was the good-looking one, too.'

'Thanks.'

'You know what I mean. He looked the part, did Oggi, a bit like Rod Stewart but more sexy. Even in their stage gear, I always thought Frankie and Mally looked more like businessmen in fancy dress than pop stars.'

'I won't ask what I was like.'

'Did you ever see Bela Lugosi in *Dracula*?' She managed a half-smile.

'I asked for that.'

'Do you think they'll ever find Matt's killer, Johnny?' She was serious again.

'I'm sure they will,' I said. Or I will if they don't, I thought.

'I can't think of any reason why anyone should kill Matt.'

‘Can you think of any reason why they would want to kill Mally?’

‘Mally? You mean, they might have killed Matt by mistake for Mally?’

‘No. I don’t mean that. I think they intended to kill your son. But all this is somehow connected with The Cruzads, something that happened in the past, before Matt was born.’

‘How do you mean, in the past? Something Mally’s done? Or the rest of you? And Matt’s had to pay for it.’ She looked troubled and I wished I’d said nothing. ‘And that’s why you asked if Mally had any enemies?’

‘Has he?’

‘Probably. He’s the sort of man to make enemies. Women he’s discarded, men he’s cheated, husbands he’s cuckolded, I’m sure you’d find plenty if you looked.’

‘You’re not bitter, though. You still have him round.’

‘I’m bitter sometimes but then I think, what does it all matter? I’ve got my life now. And he can be quite charming, you know.’

I wondered if she’d think Mally was so charming if she knew about him and Sarah.

I was running late. I said my goodbyes once again to Maureen and promised to contact her if I had any news. She gave me her number in the Isle of Man.

I broke the speed limit all the way to the radio station.

I wanted to play ‘Kelly from the Isle of Man’ for Mo but I hadn’t got a copy so instead I dedicated Harry Belafonte’s ‘Island in the Sun’ to her, which was a lousy choice because most days when I’d been in the Isle of Man, it had rained.

On the off chance they’d be listening, I also played a record for Oggi’s daughter, Little Richard’s ‘Jenny Jenny Jenny’. Little Richard is over sixty now and is recording children’s songs. So much for the wild men of rock’n’roll. At least Jerry Lee’s still hell-raising.

I drove straight back to the flat after the show. I needed

a quiet evening at home to work out some sort of plan of campaign.

Frankie shouldn't be too hard to trace, I decided. The library would have the back copy of the *Echo* with the article in it. After I'd eaten, I rang Maria and asked her if she could find it for me.

'I need it in the morning,' I said.

'I'll photocopy it and fax it to you,' she promised. We talked for half an hour and I went through my day with her. Maria was very concerned about Oggi's little girl.

'I told you something awful was going to happen,' she said, 'but look, there's a pattern here. Have you noticed it's the children that suffer? Mally gets the packages but it's Matt who's murdered. Same with Oggi – he gets the nails but his daughter's kidnapped. She was lucky to get away, Johnny. I'm sure she'd have met the same fate as Matt.'

'It doesn't bear thinking about,' I said. 'But where does this leave me? I've had the nails, and the hair which I'm sure is Jenny's.'

'Seems a safe bet. But you've no children. Has Frankie got a family?'

'I don't know.'

'Because, if he has, they could be in danger.'

'The big question is, why should the children be a target?'

'It's got to be revenge, hasn't it?' said Maria. 'They haven't asked for money, just kidnapped the children.'

'So far. You're right though, they've had every opportunity to go for any of us. It would have been easier to abduct Mally than a fit young guy like Matt, and Oggi's walking around like a zombie half the time. It'd take him a day to realise he'd been kidnapped. So, yes, it must be just the kids they're after.'

'You know, we keep saying "they" but it strikes me that it's more likely to be some lone madman.'

'Madman?'

'Only a psycho would do this, surely. You've got to think, Johnny, is there anybody at all in the past that The Cruzads have upset so much that they'd want to get back at you all so long afterwards?'

'And in such a way.'

'And the other question is, why now? What's happened in the last few weeks to set it all off when he could have done this any time in the last thirty years?'

I thought about it for a moment but nothing at all sprang to mind.

'Maybe Frankie will have the answer.'

'I'm going to see him tomorrow. But I need the photo to find his house.'

'I'm in work at nine. I'll get it to you as soon as I can.'

'By the way,' I said. 'I enjoyed yesterday.'

'I'm glad.' She sounded pleased. 'After all the fuss you made.' But she said it with a smile in her voice. 'When will I see you or shouldn't I ask?'

'How about dinner tomorrow night, after the show?

'I'll pick you up at the station if you like, then you'll be able to drink. Where should we go?'

'I'll book a table at The Moat House for eight and you can come back to mine of you like. Handy for work.'

'Fine. I'll bring my overnight bag.'

After I'd put the phone down I pondered on whether I'd really phoned because I wanted the article or because I wanted an excuse to ring Maria. After all, I could have gone to the library myself. On the other hand, did I need an excuse to ring her anyway? And why was it Maria rather than Hilary I wanted to talk with?

Probably, I reasoned, because Maria was the person I tended to discuss the case with. She had the ability to analyse things, sift out the dross and get to the heart of the matter.

And I enjoyed her company.

If Maria was right, it was Frankie's children, if he

had any, who were most at peril and Maria had been right so far.

Would I be in time to prevent a further disaster?

Maria was true to her word. By nine thirty, I had the faxed article on my desk. It was pretty much as Mo had described it.

> Businessman Frank Relphs, 48, pictured outside his half-million-pound Southport home near the Royal Birkdale gold course. The area is known as 'Royal Football' because of the number of Premiership soccer stars residing in one square mile including ex-Liverpool manager Kenny Dalglish, who lives just opposite. Frank admits that, due to the recession, he will accept offers of £250,000 for this luxury Georgian home.

I could see what Mo meant about it being like a castle. The builder had erected a balustrade along the top of the frontage, obscuring the roof and creating the impression that the Sheriff of Nottingham and his men might be hiding behind, ready to fire their arrows at any advancing outlaws.

I wouldn't have given a quarter of a million for it but then, I prefer Tudor to Georgian and, being a lifelong Everton supporter, I'm not sure I'd want to be surrounded by Liverpool footballers.

Southport lies twenty miles down the road from Liverpool, past Crosby and Formby and in the opposite direction to Speke. The journey took me forty-five minutes in the morning traffic.

The area known as Birkdale Park starts after Hillside Station as the road passes first the Royal Birkdale golf course then open heathland leading down to sandhills and the sea.

I took a left after the Round House, a famous local

landmark, and cruised along streets of splendid Victorian mansions mixed with newly built palatial residences until I came upon a short road of half a dozen detached houses, all with the squared Georgian windows and balustrades I'd seen in the *Echo* picture.

I pulled up outside the first house and walked up to the front door. There was no reply. I tried the second with the same result. Obviously an area of working wives. I was luckier with the third, a cleaner answered the door but she didn't work for Mr Relphs and didn't know the neighbours.

At the fourth attempt I had some success. An elegant lady of late middle age, wearing enough jewellery to have sunk the *Titanic*, informed me that the Relphses lived two doors down but they would be out until lunchtime.

'Mr Relphs usually comes in around one; he works from home most afternoons. Mrs Relphs picks the children up from school on her way home from work at four. She's a teacher.'

'Have they many children?'

'Just the two, both girls, nine and ten.'

I shuddered at the possibilities this presented. 'I used to be in business with him years ago,' I explained, 'so I thought I'd look him up whilst I was in the area. What's he doing nowadays?'

'I'm not sure. Something to do with computers, I think. He was with GEC at one time. My husband used to be there. They once had 15,000 people in East Lancashire Road but now there's only 600 left.'

'Your husband get out in time, did he?'

'He died,' she said matter-of-factly, and I could think of no suitable reply.

I drove the extra two miles into Southport. I had a couple of hours to kill so I parked on the Promenade and took a walk round the sea front. I'd not been down there for years and I was horrified.

Peter Pan's Pool, once a children's amusement park,

was now a heap of rubble; the Sea Bathing Lake was razed to the ground, the rusting Marine Drive Bridge was closed as unsafe and the pier was looking none too safe either.

I decided to chance my luck on it. Halfway down, an old man sitting in Victorian shelter engaged me in conversation.

'Pretty grim, isn't it?' he said. 'Be careful you don't fall off. The sea's out, of course, so instead of drowning you'll be poisoned by the mud. Dirtiest beach in Britain this, next to Blackpool.' He said it proudly, as if there should be some award. 'Nothing up there when you reach the end, just a few folk fishing. When I was a lad, boats used to go all over the country from the end of that pier.'

'I'll walk back then if there's nothing there.'

'It's no better down South, you know. You want to go to Hastings. Full of down-and-outs.'

I was glad to reach the bustle of Lord Street, which had managed to retain some of its genteel Edwardian atmosphere with elegant shops beneath ornate glass verandahs down one side of the road and gardens and fountains along the other.

I went into Boothroyds, one of the old-fashioned sort of department stores. If they had Sloanes in Southport, in the absence of a Harvey Nichols, they would shop at Boothroyds. I had a pot of tea and toasted teacake in the crowded restaurant. Most of the patrons were fully paid-up members of the blue rinse brigade. All that was missing was a string quartet. It was very 1930s and a far cry from Speke.

Southport over the years had never decided whether to be a seaside resort or a shopping centre, but now events seemed to have made its mind up for it.

By the time I got back to Birkdale, Frankie had returned. I clocked the white Mercedes in his drive as I pulled up and parked alongside it. Frankie must have been watching from the window because, as I climbed the four steps to the front door, it opened and he stood in the porch.

'Johnny Ace, I don't believe it, after all these years.'

We shook hands, looked each other up and down and made appropriate noises about how young and well the other was looking.

In his case, it was true. He was lean and suntanned, he'd kept most of his dark brown hair and he had the fluid movement of a man who kept himself fit. He wore a pair of grey slacks and a navy blazer.

'Come on in, have you had any lunch? I'm just rustling something up if you'd care to join me.' I followed him through a wide hallway to the kitchen.

It struck me how his language and manners had changed since we were The Cruzads. Mally too. No slang or swearing or horseplay. I guess that's upward social mobility for you. Or is it just maturity? I seem to have missed out on both so I can't be sure. Maybe it's the company I keep. I couldn't see Mally or Frankie down the Masquerade.

Frankie produced two salmon pancakes and took them over to the oven. 'Karen made these – a wonderful cook, my wife. I don't think you've met her, have you?' I said I hadn't. 'It was after the group broke up. I got a job at GEC on the computer side and Karen was on one of my courses. We've been married eighteen years now.'

'Any children?' No need to let him know I'd been questioning the neighbours.

'Two, Sammi and Nikki, nine and ten.' He pulled out a wallet and showed me a picture of two smiling girls with long red hair in matching blue school uniforms. 'They're at school at the moment, the same school Karen teaches at, which is quite handy.' And a lot safer in the circumstances, I thought.

'Would you like a beer while we're waiting?'

'Have you any cider?'

He hadn't so I settled for a beer. He opened the fridge and produced a couple of cans. While he was opening them and finding some glasses, I looked around the room.

The kitchen ran the width of the house and overlooked a vast expanse of garden way below.

'Split level,' said Frankie, reading my thoughts. 'We're on the first floor at the back of the house.'

'Big garden,' I said. 'You could hold the Badminton Horse Trials in that.'

'Keeps the gardener busy though I think a goat could be cheaper.'

We took our beers through to a conservatory off the dining room, furnished with the obligatory cane and cushions.

'So what brings you to see me after all this time?' said Frankie. 'I'm not on your Christmas-card list and I don't owe you money. You've not come to reform the group have you?' He didn't look like he relished the prospect.

'Have you read about Mally's son in the papers?' He must have caught my tone because he suddenly became serious.

'It was Mally's boy, was it? I thought it might be when I saw the name but I wasn't sure. What a terrible thing. They haven't caught the fellow either, have they? Didn't the police say it was a kidnap attempt?'

'They did but it wasn't. Listen, Frankie, I saw Oggi yesterday.'

'Oggi? I thought he'd emigrated to New Zealand.'

'Australia, but he's back and living in Speke with his wife and their ten-year-old daughter. Last week, his daughter, Jenny, was kidnapped. She managed to escape but not before they'd cut off some of her hair.'

The colour drained from Frankie's face.

'There's worse. The week before last, I received an envelope in the post containing some fingernails. I took them to the police. They were Matt Scrufford's nails. Oggi received a similar package with what are probably Matt's toenails. Shortly afterwards, the same person sent me a lock of hair. I think it could be Oggi's daughter's. I've also had a petrol bomb put through my letter box.'

I looked hard at him.

'What have you had, Frankie?'

Chapter Seventeen

'I might have known it was no coincidence you coming here.' Frankie took a sip of beer and I noticed his hands were shaking slightly.

'Go on.'

'Yesterday, we got a letter. Hang on, I'll show it to you.' He left the room and returned a minute later with a brown envelope which he handed to me to open. Inside was an old picture of The Cruzads in their early days, cut out of a copy of *Mersey Beat*.

'I remember this,' I said. 'It was down by the Pier Head, one Sunday morning. Look, you can see the ferry in the background. Doesn't Oggi look young?'

'We all look young. We couldn't have been more than eighteen when this was taken. But do you notice anything?' I looked closely. Frankie's head had been circled with a blue biro. 'Turn over.'

On the other side was the word 'NEXT' printed in the same ink.

'What do you make of it?' asked Frankie.

'What did you?'

'I don't know. It came quite out of the blue. I'd never thought about the group for years. I mean, I hear your show, of course, but it's been so long, I never connect it with The Cruzads. After all, you started on the radio long after we broke up. Then this thing about Mally was in the paper and, even then, I read it and forgot about it. Hang it all, I wasn't even sure it was him. There must be other Scruffords about somewhere.'

'The way Mally put it about, there's probably hundreds,' I said.

'And then this photo came and I didn't know what to think. Well, that's not true, the first thing I did think of was the kidnapping but I told myself I was being fanciful and I put it away.'

'Did you show it your wife?'

'No. I didn't want her worried unnecessarily.' He took another drink. 'After what you've told me, I'll certainly discuss it with her now.'

'It seems to be the children who are in danger. I haven't got any but you have two and that's why I came here today. I think you should send them away until this thing is cleared up.'

'For God's sake, Johnny. What do you think's going to happen to them?'

I chose my words carefully. 'They could be murdered.' Frankie looked ashen. 'I think Jenny Ogden would have been killed had she not got away from this man and quite possibly she would have been dismembered first like Matt Scrufford.'

It wasn't something either of us wanted to dwell on. 'But why should anyone want to do these things?'

'I've no idea why. Money isn't the motive. No attempt was made to extract money from Mally, and Oggi hasn't a penny to his name. As for me, all I've had is the letters which I suppose I should take as threats or warnings.'

'What do the police say about it all?'

'They don't know about Oggi yet so they don't know the link.'

'What is the link?'

'The group, of course, The Cruzads. All four of us have had communications from this person. He's killed Matt and abducted Jenny. He means business, make no mistake.'

'How can we stop him?'

'Like I said, hide the children somewhere safe for starters. Then we go and look for him, hunt him down.'

'Shouldn't the police be doing that?'

'They haven't done particularly well so far. No, the answer to all this lies somewhere in the past, the group's past. That's where the motive will be. We've upset somebody pretty badly, that's for sure.'

'We?'

'One of us or all of us. I have a suggestion. We should all get together, say tomorrow night at my place as it's the most central.' I gave him my address. 'And then we'll take it from there.'

He put my card in his wallet and sat back silently in his chair, doubtless contemplating his children minus various limbs.

'Are those pancakes ready yet?' I asked.

He jumped up. 'God, I'd forgotten,' and we went back into the kitchen for lunch.

'You've done well for yourself,' I said, after we'd eaten. 'Nice house.'

'I was lucky. Computers were the right thing to be in.'

'So what exactly do you do now?'

'Consultancy and programming mainly. In the mornings I go out and find the business and in the afternoons I do the work.'

'Sounds reasonable. You do nothing in show business then?'

'Oh, every now and then I get my Fender out and play a few of the old numbers but nothing public. What about you? Apart from your show, of course.'

'I doodle out a few tunes on the piano but I haven't played drums since the group finished. Do you remember the last booking we ever did and that woman in the pink dress with the slit up the side fell on top of Mally?'

He laughed and we exchanged reminiscences about the playing days. 'This is what we have to do,' I said. 'Go back in time in our heads and search for something that may explain all this trouble.'

'If we do catch this maniac, Johnny, what are we going to do with him? Turn him over to the police?'

I thought for a moment. 'Eventually,' I said.

I left shortly afterwards. I wanted to set up the reunion of The Cruzads, which meant driving to Speke as Oggi wasn't on the phone.

I called in the flat on the way through to pick up any messages. Hilary was on the answerphone. 'Haven't seen you since Friday, babe. How do you fancy a movie tomorrow? Call me.' Tomorrow was the meeting and I had too much to think about at the moment to arrange an alternative date. I decided I'd ring her later.

Mally wasn't at home so I left a message on his answerphone for him to call me on my mobile.

The journey to Oggi's hadn't improved any since the day before but at least I had a meal with Maria to look forward to later.

Mothers in small cars picking up their children outside school gates slowed the journey down considerably and Jenny was already home from her school when I reached Oggi's house.

She was a cute child with freckles and curly auburn hair. I'm not good at colours but it looked pretty much like the hair in the Jiffy bag.

She didn't seem to have suffered any lasting disturbance by her experience, at least not that I could tell, and chatted to me quite happily once her mother told her who I was. Not all children will have a conversation with an adult they've not met before.

'You played a record for me,' she said.

'That's right, "Jenny Jenny Jenny".'

'When are you going to play me another one?'

'Shush, Jenny,' said her mother. 'You don't ask questions like that.'

'That's OK. What would you like?'

'Boyzone. They're my favourites, I've got them on my wall.' I could understand she'd prefer Boyzone to Little Richard and promised to play her their new single.

'Come and get your tea now, Jen. *Neighbours*'ll be on soon and I've got your favourite fish fingers.'

I thought of Laura alias Davinia. She was another clever girl who'd never reached her potential. Sadly, I could see Jenny ending up at Stripes too.

'Do you want a cup of tea?' Sharon asked me, and I didn't like to refuse again.

As they left the room, Oggi came in. This time he was dressed, in a pair of stained chinos and one of those blue check work shirts that you see on building sites or in country music videos. His trainers were ripped and dirty.

I'd always thought drug-dealing was a well-paid occupation. Maybe Oggi was just not very good at it.

'Have you found anything out?' he asked eagerly.

'I got hold of Frankie.' I told him about the photo.

'So they're after him as well.' He lit up a cigarette and allowed the smoke to drift under my nose.

'I want us all to get together,' I said. 'You, me, Mally and Frankie.'

'Yeah, sure. When?' He seemed a bit slow tonight and I found myself pausing between sentences to make sure everything had sunk in.

'Tomorrow night, eight o'clock at my place.' I gave him a card with the address. 'And in the meantime, I want you to think back about anything that might have happened with the group that could have led to all this.'

'Yeah,' said Oggi again. 'Yeah, I will.' Then, 'Frankie all right, is he?'

'Fine. He's living in Southport. He's got two little girls.'

'Is he playing at all?'

'No. He's into computers these days.'

'Can't be doing with them things. They keep sending

me the wrong gas bills. I wouldn't mind playing again,' he said, his mind suddenly changing tack. I made no comment. I didn't want to encourage him. 'Are they all right?'

'Who?'

'Those girls of Frankie's.'

'Oh, yes. So far.'

'I'm very worried, Johnny. It's Jenny. I'm very worried.' He stubbed out his half-smoked cigarette into a full ashtray. 'I might go down the karaoke tonight. I usually do 'Teenager in Love', do you remember that? Marty Wilde,' he said.

'Dion and the Belmonts,' I corrected automatically. 'Theirs was the original.'

Sharon came in with a mug of tea liberally laced with milk. I'd neglected to mention I liked it strong but I forced it down my throat.

'We're having a meeting of the group tomorrow night,' I told her. 'Hopefully, we'll get a lead as to who's doing all this.'

She nodded. 'Good. I knew you'd help us.'

Her faith was touching. I wished I had as much myself.

'I've given him the address,' I said to Sharon. 'Eight o'clock. Make sure he's there.'

Oggi smiled and waved as I walked to the door. Sharon opened it for me and followed me to the car. 'He might seem like he's not with us all the time but he's there really,' she said, 'and he's very worried about our little girl. So don't let us down, will you?'

'I won't,' I promised, 'don't worry.'

I played Boyzone on the programme for Jenny. I had a short phone-in about whether famous footballers should play for England if they are alleged wife-beaters. Most people thought they should.

'If a footballer can score a hat trick for England tomorrow, he can do a *Brookside* and bury his missus under the bloody patio for all I care,' said one caller.

This brought a switchboard-blocking number of protesting calls and the excitement continued at a high level until I quietened things down by playing Pat Campbell's 'The Deal', the greatest or most awful all-talking record ever, depending on your point of view.

Even Ken mentioned it after the show. 'That was a terrible record you played. I don't know how you get away with it. We're going to have more complaints. And you should have cut that bloke off about burying women under patios. Couldn't you tell he was a nutter? Mind you, they have to be nutters to listen to some of the crap you play. Hey, you can't lend us a fiver till Saturday, can you, Johnny?'

I smiled and handed it over. 'I'm leaving my car in the car park tonight, Ken,' I said. 'I'm being picked up.'

I took the mail out of my pigeonhole at Reception as I went out. Maria was parked outside the entrance in her maroon Primera.

'Dead on time,' she smiled, and kissed me as I sat beside her. 'Still the Moat House?'

'Yes.' As she drove, I sorted through my mail, relieved there were no Jiffy bags.

We took our seats in the Brasserie, ordered our meals and set about a bottle of Chablis. 'Had a good day?' asked Maria.

I gave her a résume of my visits to Frankie and Oggi.

'It's the best chance you have of solving it,' she said, 'getting you all together. Somebody might just remember an incident that happened years ago that will lead to this maniac, and once you know who he is . . .'

'We'll have to find him.'

'I don't think that will be a problem. After all, he found all of you easily enough.'

'That's true. And my packages went to three different addresses, the station, my office and my flat so he's kept a close track on me.'

'Precisely. Shows how easy it is.' She paused. 'What will you do when you find him?'

'Frankie asked me that. I don't know. I feel I'd want to do something, by way of retribution.'

'Wouldn't it be better to leave it to the law?'

'I've not much faith in the law. What will he get? Ten years in jail, colour TV in his cell? He'll study for a degree, join the prison squash team and he'll be free to kill again in seven years if he behaves himself? Not much of a punishment to my mind, or a deterrent.'

'What would you prefer, hanging?'

'Not necessarily, the electric chair would do fine,'

The starters arrived and we concentrated on the food. I had the melon boat, Maria had the prawn cocktail.

'Penny for them,' said Maria when we'd finished eating.

'I was just thinking about the group. In the seventies when we were getting a fair bit of work in the Mecca dance halls and the clubs, we were all much on a level, not tremendously well off but doing all right.'

'And?'

'Now there's this unbridgeable gulf between Oggi and the rest of us and I wonder why that is.'

'I'd say the gulf was already there, in Oggi's head. Success is up to the individual concerned. The propensity for success or failure is in us all, we just need the will to go for it. Most people are too lazy to try.'

'But some people get more knock-backs than others.'

'True, but it's all about attitude, isn't it? That's what counts in the long run, how people react to the knocks.'

I could see her point. Mally would be successful because he'd charm his way into anything and trample on anyone who'd stand in his way. Frankie would succeed through being efficient at what he did. But Oggi just couldn't cope with setbacks and he'd take the easy option instead of fighting back.

I didn't know about me.

The main course came.

'Why don't you leave the Primera here and we'll get a taxi?' I said.

'You're right. Half a litre of that Chablis would turn any policeman's bag green.'

'I thought it was brown but I'm colour blind.'

The porter phoned us a taxi, which was outside within minutes and got us home just as quickly.

'That was a dreadful record you played on the radio tonight,' she said, 'that talking one. I was listening to it in the car.'

'The listeners love it,' I lied. 'It's always being requested.'

'Come to think of it, you play a lot of records I never hear anywhere else.'

'The secret of my success,' I smiled, and kissed her.

I felt more relaxed than for ages. At last, I felt, something positive was going to be done. Instead of being on the defensive we were going to attack.

Now we would be the hunters.

Who would we catch?

Chapter Eighteen

Maria woke me up with a breakfast tray and paper.

'Don't expect this all the time,' she said.

'What time is it?'

'Eight thirty.'

'I must have overslept.'

Maria was dressed for the library. Blue pencil skirt to her calves, white blouse and hair up in a bun. And she still managed to look like Cher. 'I've got to go,' she said. 'I've got to be in work for nine. Good luck tonight at the Big Reunion. Ring me and let me know how you get on.'

I glanced at the paper. 'God, it's the football tonight and I'll miss it with them coming round.'

'Never mind, you can always video it.' Maria's interest in football is minimal. Lionel used to tell a gag about a woman who thought Glasgow Rangers were a group of Scottish park keepers and I felt it summed up Maria's comprehension of the game.

Hilary, on the other hand, is a Manchester United fan, something I've never been able to wean her off.

Thinking of Hilary reminded me of her message. I waited till Maria had left and rang her.

'What time do you call this? I've been in bed two hours.'

I could never work out Hilary's complicated shifts at the hospital so I've given up trying, especially as she's constantly changing them. 'I got your message,' I said, ignoring her rebuke 'but I didn't ring you last night because I thought you'd be asleep.'

A slight hiss came down the phone. 'There's a good film on at the Edge Lane Multiplex this week. Do you fancy going?'

'I do, but not tonight.'

'Oh, I forgot, it's the England match, isn't it? You'll be watching that.'

'No.'

'No?'

She sounded amazed and I had to explain to her The Cruzads were coming round. 'Anyway, I'll be able to video the match.'

'You're not going to start the group again like Jim Burroughs? Tell me you're not.'

'I'm not.'

'It must be something special for you to miss the football.'

'It's a long story, Hil. When I see you I'll explain it all but how about the movies tomorrow?'

'Make it Friday, Johnny.' I wondered if she'd arranged to see Barry on Thursday but said nothing.

'Friday's fine. I'll pick you up after the show.' A bleeping noise came on the line. 'Hil, I'm getting Call Waiting, I'll see you Friday.'

I've noticed that you can sit by a phone for hours and it never rings but you pick it up to make a call and somebody's trying to get through to you within seconds. This time it was Mally.

'Got your message,' he said. 'What is it?' He'd probably hoped he'd heard the last of me for another twenty years.

'I want you to come round to my place tonight. Believe it or not, I've managed to get hold of Frankie. He's living out at Birkdale. Oggi's coming as well so we'll have the whole group together.'

'Why?'

'Because I think Matt's death is tied up with something that happened long ago with The Cruzads.'

'Why do I have to come? It won't bring Matt back.'

I gritted my teeth and tried to be patient. 'You might be interested in bringing his killer to justice,' I said sarcastically.

'I'll think about it.'

'Mally, Oggi has a daughter ten years old. Last week, someone picked her up off the street, locked her in a house, cut her hair off and sent it to me in a Jiffy bag. She managed to escape. Frankie has had a threatening letter and he has two small daughters. This person is going to kill again.'

'OK, I'll come. What time?' He sounded contrite.

'Eight o'clock.'

'I'll be there.'

I had a quiet day. After breakfast, I drove up to Livingstone Drive on my way to the office and called on Badger. He answered the door in silk pyjamas and a matching dressing gown that reminded me of Colin Bennison's final attire.

'Come on in, man, I don't owe you no money, do I?'

'For once, no. I was just passing. Thought I'd let you know I went to the Stripes Club the other night.'

'And?'

'Nothing, really. It turns out Matt Scrufford was just a casual visitor. The girl he was with was one of the hostesses, a girl they call Davinia.'

'Is that who she is? You wanna be careful there, man. Davinia is Winston Bond's lady. He owns the club and he's not a nice man to cross.' I recalled what Tommy McKale had said about the Stripes crowd.

'It's all right Badger, I wasn't thinking of asking her out.'

'And how did you like the entertainment?'

I shuddered. 'Not quite to my taste,' and described the 'game' we'd seen.

'If you think that's bad, you should have been there the

night I went. They tied a rope round this poor bastard's dick and hung him from—'

I squirmed. 'I think I'd rather not know.'

'Suit yourself. So is your little mystery solved?'

'Not really. If anything, it's more complicated than ever.'

'Well, if you need any more help . . .'

I thanked him and drove over to Aigburth Road to the office. 'Sorry I never made it yesterday,' I said to Geoffrey. 'I had to go to Southport. Anything happening?'

'All taken care of, boss. Just a few letters to deal with.'

I spent the afternoon at home. I was fidgety. Somehow, I felt I was on the verge of discovering something and I couldn't concentrate on anything else. I was glad when it was time to leave for the station.

I played a record for Oggi on the show, 'Boys on the Dole' by Neville Wanker and the Punters, one of the best records from the punk era with Tim Rose on lead guitar. I thought it appropriate.

As soon as the show was over, I walked back to the flat feeling excited yet apprehensive.

In a few hours' time, I could know the name of the murderer!

Oggi was the first to arrive. I'd just had time to switch on the video to record the football and watch a few minutes of the pre-match build-up over a tuna sandwich and Scrumpy Jack.

'I'm a bit early,' he said, 'but you never know with the buses.' I gave him a can of beer and a glass and he joined me in the lounge. I switched off the TV.

Frankie arrived shortly afterwards. I explained about the hall and he looked shocked, but, if anything, he was even more shocked to see Oggi, who was dressed in a grey sweatshirt emblazoned with the logo of the

Rock On Tommy Bar at Magalluf, jeans with a tear at the knee and a bright-orange anorak. This was in contrast to Frankie's maroon jacket, black trousers and white open-necked shirt. They shook hands almost self-consciously.

'Been a long time,' murmured Oggi.

'You've been in Australia, I believe. Any good?'

Oggi shrugged. 'All right. Bit hot in the summer.'

I left them to it and went to fetch two more cans of beer from the fridge. Mally arrived as I was bringing in the glasses, wearing yet another mohair suit, this time in brown. He must have bought a job lot.

'Just in time,' I said, and handed him a drink.

He shook hands with Oggi and Frankie. Twenty years ago, I thought, we'd have slapped each others hands, embraced and generally larked about. And they say age doesn't change you.

'Still in the computer game?' Mally asked Frankie.

'Yes. More money in it than playing guitar, eh?' said Frankie as if seeking to justify giving up the group.

The breakup had been a mutual decision. We'd finished a summer season at a holiday camp and none of us could face going back on the circuit, setting up the gear in a different venue every night, travelling all over the country playing to dickheads, never sure if there'd be a fight and the gear would get smashed and our heads kicked in. And knowing we'd never have a hit record if we kept at it till we were eighty.

We'd been on the road for over fifteen years and what had started out as a starry-eyed adventure, playing The Cavern and hoping to be the next Beatles, had become a chore.

Also, after we'd paid our expenses and petrol, we weren't earning a fortune. Mally had worked out he'd make twice as much money as a solo act, Frankie was already doing computer work on the side whilst Oggi had been offered a job with a building firm.

'What about you, Johnny?' Frankie had said. 'If we pack in, what'll you do?'

I hadn't really thought about it till then. I'd been the one most interested in music so becoming a DJ was, I suppose, a natural progression. I had the contacts and discos were the up-and-coming thing. But I never thought it would last, which is why I started investing in property. Yet, here I was, over twenty years later, still a DJ with my own radio show.

'We should have made it,' Oggi was saying bitterly. 'When I think of some of the talentless bastards that did.'

All failed pop stars say that, as if talent has anything to do with success. Talent is just what keeps you up there when you've already made it. The rest is down to luck and perseverance. But I didn't try to explain this to Oggi.

'We had a good run,' said Frankie philosophically. 'What was it, twelve years?'

'More.'

'Getting paid for something you enjoy doing seems like a fair deal to me.'

'If I'd have known what I could've made, I'd have gone solo from the start,' said Mally, whose main motivation had always been money. Closely followed by sex.

'You'd have missed all the fun and camaraderie of being in a group,' I said, but Mally didn't look as though this would have unduly bothered him.

'If only we'd signed up with Epstein,' said Oggi. 'All Eppy's groups did well. Look what he did for Billy J. Kramer and if he could do it for him he could have done it for us.'

'Except that he never offered to,' pointed out Frankie. 'He must have seen us play.'

'And we should have recorded "Do You Love Me?" I had that record by The Contours before Faron did and he went and let sodding Brian Poole nick it from him.'

It was easy to see why Oggi had been a failure. His

conversation was littered with 'if onlys' and 'should haves'. It was sad. Maureen was right, too, he did have the looks to be a pop star. Once.

'It was me who told you to do that song,' said Mally, 'but you couldn't master the bass riff. If you'd have been a half-decent fucking guitarist—'

'Hang on a minute,' I interrupted. 'Let's not start a punch-up before we've even got one drink down us.' Now I remembered the arguments and fights in the final months of the band and I wondered how we'd lasted so long. Only a masochist would want to resurrect The Cruzads.

Or a group of middle-aged men bound together by a dreadful knowledge, knowing a monster was out there threatening to kill their children and aware that, in one terrible case, he had already succeeded.

Chapter Nineteen

'Let's sit down, fellas, and talk about what we've come here for.' My reminder of the situation quietened them as effectively as a blast of tear gas. They took their seats and waited for me to speak. I went through the whole thing from the beginning, showing how each one of us was inextricably involved.

'So, the conclusion we must come to is that whoever is doing this has a grudge against The Cruzads, and by that I mean all of us, not just Mally.'

'OK. That's fine, but how are we going to find out who it is?' said Frankie. 'Shouldn't we be phoning the police right now to protect our families?'

I admitted that we might end up doing just that. 'On the other hand, remember, the police have not been able to solve Matt's murder and they've not found out who sent me the packages. He might be a psycho, this guy, but he's cunning.'

'So if the police can't catch him, what makes you think we can?'

'Only that I think the clue to his identity lies somewhere in The Cruzads' past, someone we've upset.'

The mood was too sombre for the obvious gags as we silently contemplated our lives in the sixties and seventies.

'I wouldn't know where to start,' said Mally, at last. 'I mean, is it something that happened in the sixties in Liverpool or in the seventies when we were playing all over the place?'

'It's probably the earlier period, I would think,' decided Frankie, sensibly. 'The envelopes were posted here and both kidnaps took place here.'

'Right, let's take it as that then for the moment. We started in 1962, didn't we?'

'When I was sixteen,' said Oggi.

'There was that fight at Garston Baths,' suggested Frankie, 'when we were on with Bilbo Baggins Band and that police dog got kicked to death.'

Oggi contradicted him. 'That wasn't at Garston Baths, it was at the Riverside. And I thought it was Steve Day and the Drifters who were playing.'

I could see we were going to have problems with our long-term memories.

'Wherever it was, how did it affect us?' I asked.

'Don't you remember, that bloke with the club foot went berserk and broke your snare drum and you knocked him senseless against the back of the stage?'

'Oh yes.' I nodded. 'Didn't he make a big crack in the wall?'

'Yes, with his head. He might have taken a dislike to you.'

'No,' I said. 'You wouldn't carry that around with you all this time. Besides, he probably didn't know who hit him, he was so pissed.'

'God, we got to some hovels,' sighed Mally. 'I couldn't do it now.'

'Some of those clubs round Upper Parliament Street were good fun,' I recalled. 'That Christmas we spent at the Nigeria, I thought that was a great weekend.'

'We didn't upset any of the gangsters or the protection mobs, did we?' asked Oggi.

'We wouldn't be here now if we had.'

'That's true.'

'I wonder,' began Frankie. 'Were there any pregnant girls whose fathers were after us?'

'Ask Mally, that's his department,' I replied.

Mally shot me a fierce glare. 'If there were, they'd all be pensioners now.'

'The man that picked up our Jenny was about fifty,' said Oggi, 'and fat.'

'So he'd have been about our age at the time. Someone in another group perhaps?'

'That narrows it down to about fifteen hundred,' Mally commented bitterly.

'It's better than half a million but I know what you mean.'

'And he needn't have been in a group,' Frankie added. 'He could have been a punter.'

'So we're back where we started.'

There was silence. I went to fetch some more beers.

'I can't see this leading anywhere,' said Mally. 'Who the hell is going to hold a grudge this long then suddenly start out on a mission of revenge?'

'You might be tempted to think that,' I pointed out, 'but what other reason have you got for Matt being killed? There was no ransom note; it wasn't a kidnap.'

'It must have been something to do with Matt, not me. Matt upset somebody.'

'In that case, why have we all been getting these threats including Matt's nails? No, Mally. I'm certain Matt was an innocent victim.' I'd checked all that out. 'The person they wanted to get at was really you. Just as, if they'd harmed Jenny, it would have been to get at Oggi. I thought we'd agreed all that.'

Frankie looked disturbed as this was spelt out to him 'Look, I reckon we're gonna have to get the police in here.'

'They won't give you a twenty-four-hour guard,' I told him. 'They don't have the resources. It'll still be up to you to keep an eye on your kids. Did you send them away like I suggested?'

'Karen's taking them to her mother's tomorrow. She lives in Conwy.'

'Good.'

'I've thought of something,' said Oggi, suddenly. 'Do you remember when we won that competition to be on *Ready Steady Go*?'

' 'Course we do, it was the only time we've been on the telly.'

'That group that came second said it was a fix.'

'We knew it was a fix, they'd booked the hotel for us the week before.'

'So, they'd have reason to be pissed off with us. They were better than us.'

'They were not, they were crap,' said Mally. 'What were they called?'

'The Albert Memorial.'

'That's it. What happened to them?'

'They broke up and joined other bands.'

'What about The Joy Riders?' asked Frankie. 'They said we'd pinched that song their lead singer wrote . . . What was it?'

' "Best Say It Sooner". No, it wouldn't be them. I mean, we never recorded it or nothing. We only played it on stage.'

'And there was Vic and the Alsatians,' I reminded them. 'When they had all their equipment pinched, that Vic Grierson swore blind we'd nicked it.'

Suddenly it seemed that there were loads of people who hated The Cruzads.

'I never realised we had so many enemies,' said Frankie.

Oggi snorted. 'Vic Grierson was a pillock. He'd accuse anyone. Just 'cos we were on the same bill that night at that broken-down old social club they used to play at. Anyway, it was their doormen that took their stuff. They did time for it.'

'What about the seventies?' asked Mally. 'We seem to be getting nowhere with the Merseybeat scene.'

'The seventies,' mused Frankie. 'Do you remember those clothes we wore?'

'I used to wear lipstick and put glitter on my face,' said Oggi, 'and my hair was round my shoulders in ringlets.'

'I wore a silver lame jump suit,' I said. 'Wasn't half hot playing the drums in that.'

'And you used to wear those green patent platform shoes,' grinned Mally.

'That's right, and you had yellow ones to go with those yellow flares with the moons painted on them. I can remember you singing 'Blockbuster' in those at Nantwich Civic Hall and those girls on the front row threatening to throw their knickers at you.'

Oggi and Mally broke into a chorus of the old Sweet number. It helped relieve the tension that had built up.

Oggi laughed. 'Bring back Glam Rock, eh?'

'I wonder why he's waited till now,' said Frankie, and immediately the mood changed back again.

'What?'

'Forget *why* he's doing it for a minute and ask yourself why he's doing it *now*, at this time. Why not last year or ten years ago? What's set him off? Have any of us done anything different or unusual in the last three months that might have triggered something in his brain?'

'I wondered that,' I said. 'But nothing has changed with me. I'm just doing the radio show and the houses as always.'

'And I'm working in the same job I've had for the past eight years,' said Mally. 'How about you, Frankie?'

'Same. All my clients are regulars I've had for ages.'

We all looked at Oggi. 'Search me,' he shrugged. 'I don't see no one 'cept from round our way.'

'It's just that he's waited an awful long time,' continued Frankie, 'and I feel there must be a reason.'

'Probably there is but how can we know it? Let's face it, we're stymied.'

'There's one other avenue,' I said. 'One person has actually seen this man and that's Oggi's daughter. I think it might be an idea if we tried to get her to give us a clearer picture of what he was like. It's what the police would do.'

'I don't want no police coming round to ours.'

'Precisely, but you'd let me talk to her, wouldn't you?'

'I suppose so.'

'Right. At least we'll be doing something. Otherwise, it's just a case of keeping our eyes open and trying to remember any incident in The Cruzads' past to account for all this.'

'In the meantime, our kids are in danger,' Frankie reminded us.

'I think we could all be in danger,' I said quietly. 'Even you, Mally. He might want to wipe out the whole lot of us with our families. That's why we need to get him before he gets us.'

There was a general shuffling of feet and nervous glances were exchanged.

'I think that's about all we can do tonight,' I said. 'Let's go home and think hard. I suggest we exchange phone numbers so we can keep in regular contact. Oggi, is there no number we can reach you at?' He shook his head. 'OK, I'll just have to call round if I need you. Should I give you a lift home now and perhaps I'll be able to speak to Jenny tonight if she's not in bed?'

'She doesn't go to bed till after ten. She's a nightbird.'

'Then let's go.'

We all went downstairs to the car park, said our goodbyes, and Oggi jumped into the RAV4 alongside me. We talked as I drove to Speke. He seemed more coherent than the day before.

'How long have you been dealing, Oggi?' I asked him. Nothing like being direct.

'Seems funny to be Oggi again. Everyone calls me Carl now.'

'Or Carlo,' I reminded him. 'So how long?'

'Since I came back really. Well, there was nothing else

going for me, no work, and if you live on this estate and don't do drugs they think you're a snout and you're liable to get your house torched.'

'Aren't you frightened you'll get caught?'

'All the time. The drug squad are always around but they're after the big boys not small fry like me.'

'Doesn't it worry you that Jenny is growing up amongst all this?'

'I suppose so but what can I do about it?' he mumbled resignedly, his familiar acceptance of defeat showing itself again.

Jenny was still up when we arrived. She was full of *Brookside*, which she'd been watching with her mother. They were doing a storyline about incest which I wasn't sure a child of ten should be watching but who was I to say?

Nowadays, magazines read by twelve-year-old girls offer advice on improving their oral sex technique, teenagers drink lemonade that's stronger than premium beer and there's enough sickening violence on TV to satisfy even members of the Stripes Club.

I sometimes felt that kids of ten would be better with Enid Blyton and Ovaltine but, not being a father myself, I was hardly qualified to proffer my opinion. Maria would probably say I was living in the past again.

'Jenny, love, Johnny wants to talk to you about the man that took you away.'

'I just want you to try and help me paint a picture of him.'

I can't draw to save my life but I hoped that turning it into a game might encourage her to remember things. Sharon brought me a pencil and a sheet of lined writing paper.

'He was old,' Jenny said. 'like you and Daddy.' I consoled myself with the fact that people of twenty look ancient to a ten-year-old. 'And fat.'

'Where was he fat?'

'His tummy, it stuck out like he was pregnant.'

'What about his hair?'

'He had a cap on.'

'That's right, I remember. Washington Redskins. But could you see any of his hair under the hat?'

She thought. 'A lump of hair at the back.'

I drew a man with a fat stomach and a round head. What about his nose?'

She almost smiled. 'Big and red like my dad when he's been drinking.'

'What else was he wearing besides the cap?'

'I don't know.'

'Was it a raincoat?' I drew a long coat.

'It was shorter, I could see his knees.'

'An anorak then?' She nodded. 'And his trousers? You said you saw his knees.'

She pulled a face. 'Just jeans, I think.'

'Shoes?'

'You don't wear shoes with jeans,' said Jenny scornfully. 'You wear trainers.'

'And he did?'

'Yes.'

I sketched the man the best I could and handed it to Jenny. 'Well? Is that anything like him?' It was hardly Identikit standard but it was vaguely recognisable as a human being.

'I suppose so.' I felt she was trying to be kind. 'But hundreds of people look like that, don't they? You ought to be asking me if he had any distinguishing features.' I stared at her, quite taken aback. 'You'll never make a detective, Johnny. Don't you ever watch *The Bill*? They always ask that.'

I confessed I didn't. 'I watch Inspector Frost, though; he's brilliant.'

'Yes, I like him. I like David Jason but I didn't like him in *The Larkins* 'cos him and his wife with the big boobies were doing it all the time.'

So much for childhood innocence. I wondered if there were any virgins left in Speke over the age of twelve.

'Right, the features then. What were they?'

'He had tattoos on the backs of his hands.' I was impressed.

'Both of them?'

'Yes.'

'What design?'

'I don't know. Some sort of dogs, I think. I didn't see properly.'

It was a good clue. Not many people have the backs of their hands tattooed. I thanked Jenny and turned to her parents.

'She's a clever girl that. You want to get her into a decent school.'

'Round here?' said Oggi. 'You must be joking.'

'Make sure you don't let her out of your sight,' I reminded them. 'He might come after her again.'

'Don't worry,' said Sharon. 'We will.'

I set off back home and gave some thought to the evening's events. We knew a bit more of what the man looked like but we were a long way from an identity parade. I felt I'd reached an impasse and I couldn't see the way forward. For the sake of Frankie and his wife, should I ring Jim Burroughs and tell him about Jenny's kidnapping and the threats to Frankie?

I was too late.

My mobile rang as I drove past the Pier Head. It was Frankie and he sounded hysterical.

'He's got Sammi,' he said. 'Get down here.'

So much for childhood [illegible]. I wonder if there were any [illegible] left in [illegible] over the age of twelve.

[illegible] there. What were they?

[illegible]

Both of them?

Yes.

What exactly?

I don't know. Some sort of illegal [illegible]. He didn't [illegible] properly.

[illegible] but many people [illegible] of [illegible] I [illegible]

[illegible]

[illegible] school.

[illegible] you [illegible]

[illegible]

[illegible]

[illegible]

[illegible]

[illegible]

[illegible] Both of them [illegible]

[illegible]

Chapter Twenty

I raced down the dock road, straight past my flat, and out to Birkdale, doing sixty most of the way. I was lucky. There are no speed cameras yet on the lower dock road.

I arrived at Frankie's house to find a police car already outside. That wasn't good news. Jim Burroughs was not going to be pleased that I'd not informed him of recent events and it wouldn't take long for this case to land on his desk once the Scrufford connection was known.

It was Frankie who let me in. We stood together in the hall.

'Any sign of her?' I said.

He shook his head. 'Nothing.' He was shaking.

'What happened?'

'Karen went to pick them up from Brownies. She arrived just as Nikki was coming out. Nikki said Sammi had just gone over to one of their friend's cars to collect a comic so she waited a few minutes until she realised something was wrong.'

'What then?'

'She parked the car, locked Nikki inside and went to look for this friend but there was no sign of the car or of Sammi.' Frankie swayed and I thought he was going to pass out but he carried on. 'Karen drove to this friend's house, a girl called Anya. Anya's mother said she'd waited a few minutes in the car for Sammi but when she didn't show up she assumed Karen had taken her home so she went home herself.'

'Why didn't Sammi walk with Anya to her car?'

'According to Anya, she wanted to go to the toilet so Anya ran on ahead to get the comic from the car for her, but she never came.'

'So someone was waiting for her as she left the toilet?'

'Seems like it. I don't know if you know Emmanuel Church, Johnny, but it's on a main road. The hall's alongside the church and you can drive right up to the door so, God knows, you'd think it would be safe enough.'

'It only takes a second,' I said, 'and if someone's really determined . . .'

He looked defeated. 'Do you think he'll kill her?'

'No,' I replied, but my words lacked conviction. Matt Scrufford had died within twenty-four hours. I didn't dare imagine what might be posted to Frankie in a Jiffy bag. 'At least, not yet – but we've got to find her quickly.'

I'd never met Sammi Relphs but looking around her middle-class, comfortable home, I couldn't imagine her being as streetwise and resilient as little Jenny Ogden.

'Where's the police?'

'Upstairs with Nikki. One's a policewoman. I rang for them as soon as Karen got home. Then I called you.'

'Have you told them about Matt Scrufford and the threat in the post?'

He sighed wearily. 'Not yet. I was more concerned about finding Sammi and they wanted all the details of what happened. Look, we can't stand in the hall all night. Come in and meet Karen.'

I followed him into the lounge and was impressed. A red and gold suite with two three-seater settees was positioned around a white reproduction Adam fireplace with a real coal fire burning in the hearth. A cut-glass decanter with six matching glasses stood on a silver tray on a mahogany sideboard, the carpet was soft and thick, and gilt-framed Victorian landscape paintings that looked genuine hung on the walls. Everything in the room spoke of a quiet wealth.

Karen Relphs was dressed in a blouse and calf-length skirt and Windsmoor jacket, looking very much the professional lady who had kept herself in trim to look less than her forty-five years. Except that now she looked haggard and frightened and her face was stained with tears.

'This is Johnny Ace, love. My wife, Karen.'

She looked up at me, tried to smile and shook my hand.

'I'm very sorry about this,' I said inadequately.

She held on to her husband's arm. 'It'll be my fault if anything happens to her. I should never have let her go in the first place.' She began to sob again.

It's odd how people are affected by events. It might have been expected that being a teacher, Karen would best be able to deal with a crisis but instead it was Frankie who was the rock that she needed to support her.

Frankie put his arm around her shoulders. 'You couldn't keep her locked up, love.'

'Where's your other daughter?' I asked.

'We've put her to bed,' Frankie said. 'There's a policewoman up there with her.'

'Surely they don't think he'll come here?'

'She's just reassuring her and going over her story,' answered Karen. 'Nikki's hysterical. She and Sammi are very close, like twins really. There's only thirteen months between them. I've given her a sedative so we're just hoping she'll get to sleep.'

Frankie and Karen didn't look like they would get any themselves. I checked my watch. It was after midnight.

'What have the police done?'

'I've given them a photo of Sammi. They've sent someone to the church hall to check she's not locked in and they're going to question the parents and children who were at Brownies and anyone else they can find who was at the church.'

'I asked everyone who was still there if they'd seen her,' said Karen, 'or if they'd seen any man acting furtively but nobody had.'

'But he needn't have been acting furtively,' I said. 'He'd just look like any father waiting to pick up his daughter. How many kids were there in the hall?'

'Oh, over thirty.'

'And not all the parents would know one another.'

'No. That's true. And then there were the bellringers coming out from the church next door.'

'And not every car would be able to drive straight up to the church hall if they all arrived at once?'

Karen agreed. 'Yet he'd have to have grabbed her to carry her off surely, and someone would have seen him.'

'Where would you park if the space outside the hall was full?'

'You'd have to drive round to the back of the church where there are some spaces. Otherwise, out of the side gates and on to the road round the corner.' Frankie tried to give me a picture of the geography of the area.

'Where were Karen and Anya?'

'Karen was round the corner in Emmanuel Road, Anya was in the car park.'

'So he was probably standing outside the hall with the other parents waiting for Sammi to come out. When she came out on her own, he'd have followed her as she walked behind the church and seized his chance.'

'What if she hadn't gone that way or had stayed with Nikki?'

'He'd have waited for another opportunity. He's probably been stalking both of them for some time. If he's waited thirty years to do all this, another few weeks wouldn't make much difference to him.'

'Sammi's the youngest. Nikki might have been able to cope better.' Now Frankie started to cry.

I felt helpless. For the last fortnight I'd amused myself,

if I could call it that, by trying to track down Matt Scrufford's killer. Four of us had spent this very evening looking for someone who had a motive. Not only were we no nearer a solution but now another of our children's lives was in danger.

I didn't know if Jim Burroughs could do any better but the police had all the resources that we didn't and time was against us.

The two police officers came back down the stairs, and we went out into the hall. The police were both from the Southport station and I didn't know either of them.

'There's a few things I should tell you about this case,' I said.

'Oh, really?' The man answered. He seemed to regard himself as superior to the girl, despite them both being constables. I guess that's the way it is in the police force. For every woman Superintendent there's a hundred sexually harassed, down-trodden WPCs stuck on the beat.

'And who are you?' he said. Neither of them looked old enough to have finished A levels.

'Johnny Ace. I'm a friend of Frankie's.'

'So what do you know about his daughter's disappearance?'

'Nothing, but I do know it's connected with a recent murder in Liverpool.' I explained to him about the Matt Scrufford case and the threats that Oggi and I and Frankie had received. 'Detective Inspector Burroughs is in charge of the case. I suggest you liaise with him. Tell him I'm here if you like.'

He looked hard at me as if he didn't want to be seen taking instructions but finally went to his car to phone.

Karen said, 'I'm going to make us a cup of tea. It'll give me something to do.'

Frankie and I went back into the lounge and the policewoman came with us. 'Nikki's asleep now,' she said. 'I'd keep an eye on her, though, in case she wakes up.'

'Thank you for all your help, Johnny,' said Karen when

she brought the tea in. She started to cry again. 'Sammi would have been in Conwy later today, alive and safe.'

'She'll be alive now, don't worry.'

The phone rang and Frankie went into the hall to answer it. 'Johnny, it's for you,' he shouted. He lowered his voice to a whisper as I came in. 'It's Detective Inspector Burroughs. He doesn't sound too happy.'

I took the receiver from him. 'Johnny Ace.'

'I don't know what the fuck you're playing at but I want you at the police station at ten o'clock this morning and you'd better have some answers for me.'

The police station at St Ann Street isn't the most impressive of buildings, the outside resembling a Lego concoction in brick and concrete. I walked up the steps to the reception as the clock approached five to ten. No sense in upsetting Jim Burroughs by being late.

I hadn't slept much. I'd only left Frankie's at two and I woke at seven. The fate of little Sammi Relphs was on my mind. There had been no news.

I went over to The Diner for some breakfast. The story had caught the late editions of the *Daily Post* and the front page had a picture of nine-year-old Sammi in her school uniform with the headline 'Brownie Abducted'.

An older man in a dark suit and regimental tie asked if he could join me at my table. 'Terrible business that little girl,' he said, indicating the paper. He placed his coffee down and started to undo three packets of sugar. 'They want putting away for life, these paedophiles.'

I murmured sounds of agreement. Personally, I'd have had them shot but I didn't feel the inclination for a long moral discussion at that moment and retreated behind the paper.

I turned to the football pages. England had beaten Poland 2–1. Yet again I'd videoed something I knew I'd end up never watching. I finished my meal in silence and walked to the police station.

The uniformed constable on the desk showed me through to Jim Burroughs' office. 'The inspector won't be long, sir. Have a seat.'

He was twenty minutes. I wondered if he'd kept me waiting as a punishment or to soften me up. Either way, he didn't apologise but strode to the other side of his large desk and sat himself in a leather swivel chair.

'I want to know every single thing about this whole business that you haven't told me,' he said. 'Then I want you to get out of here and stop interfering in police business that doesn't concern you. Have I made myself clear?'

I thought it did concern me but wisely didn't say so. Instead, I filled him in with the missing details he wanted.

'There's nothing I haven't told you already, apart from Oggi.'

'That's the same Oggi that used to play in The Cruzads with you, I take it?'

'That's him. Carl Ogden.'

'Didn't he go to Australia?'

'He came back.' I told him about the letter with the toenails and the abduction of Jenny, the whole story in fact, except for the possibility that Oggi was the local representative for the drug mafia.

'You're telling me this child was abducted nearly a week ago and her parents didn't deem it important enough to inform the police?'

'She came back. They didn't want to bother you.' Even I had to admit it sounded a lame excuse.

'And you've known for three days. I suppose you didn't want to bother me either?'

'I think that lock of hair might be hers,' I said, trying to gloss over things, 'and the toenails are probably Matt's. I've brought them for you to check.' I handed him the package.

'You're probably right. Unless there are more missing people I've yet to be told about.'

'No, no more. Not that I know of, anyway. Look, Jim, all four of us have had these letters, warnings, call them what you will. It must be connected with The Cruzads and as we've not been together for twenty years, it's got to be tied up with something that happened in the past.'

Jim Burroughs glared from across the desk. 'And it's taken you all this time to work that out, has it? I wouldn't waste your time going on a murder weekend.'

I said nothing.

'I don't want you meddling in this business any more, do you hear? Or I'll have you for obstructing the police. Do I make myself clear?'

'Have you had any leads on Matt Scrufford?'

'Not a thing.'

'But you'll agree, it's got to be the same person.'

'Look, I said I don't want you interfering.'

'Jim, I could be the next victim. I've already had a petrol bomb through my letter box. I might want police protection.'

'If you are the next victim, try and write his name in your blood before you expire. Now, if you don't mind, I'm going to pay a visit to your friend Oggi in Speke and find out if there's anything you've missed out of your little story.'

I took this as my cue to leave. I hoped Oggi wouldn't be too annoyed at me for telling the police about Jenny but, after Sammi's abduction, he should be grateful. I wondered if he knew about that yet.

I walked back into town, not sure what to do next. Did Mally know about Sammi, I wondered, and stopped off at a phone box to ring him. Marilyn answered.

'He's out working,' she said. 'He's up in Barrow-in-Furness today. Johnny, have you seen in the paper about Frankie's little girl?'

I told her that was why I'd rung.

'It's happening all over again, just like Matt. I'm

frightened, Johnny. What if he comes after Gary? He might not stop at one.'

I was beginning to be apprehensive myself. It seemed the killer could go anywhere, any time, undetected. Soon I'd be looking over my shoulder.

I rang off and dialled the library. 'Can you do lunch?' I asked Maria.

'Oh, I'm sorry, Johnny,' she said. 'I'm at a book selection meeting and won't be out before four. Listen, I've seen the paper about Frankie's daughter. It's terrible. I'll come over to yours when I finish about six, if you like.'

'I'll be doing the show.'

'I forgot about that.'

'Tell you what, I'll drop a key off at the library and you can let yourself in.'

I wondered afterwards why I'd done that. Even Hilary didn't have a key to my flat. I'd been seeing Maria for less than three months yet she had become part of my life without me really noticing it. I had to ask myself if I wanted this. The answer, I supposed, was yes. Or was it just that she was there for me at a difficult time?

Whatever it was, I left the key with the girl at the Local History desk. I bought a salmon and salad bap at one of the sandwich bars in Dale Street and ate it as I walked down to the Pier Head.

I still had four hours to kill before the show but I couldn't settle so I decided to drive up to the McKales' gym in Toxteth.

From the outside, the building resembled a warehouse. I entered a door beneath a sign saying 'Boxers' and walked up a flight of stone steps to the first floor.

The whole floor was taken up with rows of weights, punch-bags, rowing machines and other advanced gymnasium equipment. I spotted Tommy McKale on the weights.

'What brings you up here? Come for a workout?' He

stayed on the floor, his arms moving up and down like pistons.

I shuddered. 'Walking's the only exercise I want.'

He lowered the weights and stood up. 'Then it must be conversation you're after, so come and have a drink.'

He led me through to the bar. A peroxide blonde was serving and chatting to a noisy group of men in tracksuits or shorts, most of them in their twenties and thirties. Tommy went behind the bar himself and brought out a cider and a glass of mineral water.

'Let's go into the office. It's quieter.'

His office was plastered with photos of celebrities who had appeared in his club at one time or another. I recognised many famous faces.

'They weren't at the Masquerade,' he said, following my gaze. 'They were taken when I had the cabaret club in the seventies.'

'I remember it,' I said, 'Cleopatra's Palace. It was fitted out like an Egyptian temple.' The Cruzads had never played there but I'd been as a punter and seen a few big names.

'We had them all at Cleo's – Tom Jones, Engelbert, Lovelace Watkins, P. J. Proby.' He sighed. 'That sort of entertainment's gone now.'

'Yet it was so popular. There was The Wooky Hollow and The Shakespeare and Allinsons as well as Cleo's, all serving food and booking top-class acts. I'm sure there'd be a market for that today.'

'No. That time has gone. There aren't enough good acts and the ones that would pull the crowds have priced themselves out of the market. However good he is, how many times do the public want to see Tony Christie?'

'I see your point.'

'Which is why he works abroad all the time and why I'm running the Masquerade.

'What happened to Cleo's in the end?'

'It burnt down, a mystery fire.'

'That's right, I remember now.' Tommy didn't seem keen to discuss the origins of the conflagration. Too many nightclubs in Liverpool had met similar ends over the years. He moved the conversation on.

'How's that little girlfriend of yours?' He meant Hilary.

'Fine. I'll probably be down the club with her tomorrow night, after we've been to the movies.'

'And the show going OK?'

'Yes, fine.'

'So what's your problem? You're not in trouble with those fellas at the Stripes you were on about?'

'No, not them, but I have got a problem.' I sketched out the bare bones of what I called the Matt Scrufford Case. Tommy listened carefully without interrupting.

'You certainly have got a problem,' he said when I'd finished. 'The main part of any battle is knowing your enemy. Without that, you're fucked.'

'If I could find out who he is, would you be able to help me find him?'

'No problem. The sort of asshole who'd do all this is bound to have form. The boys would know him and he couldn't hide from them for long. Remember Archie Bushell?'

I did. Archie Bushell had incurred the displeasure of some rather unpleasant people, friends of the McKales, and probably these same 'boys'. They commandeered two taxi cabs and chased him through the city suburbs until they finally ran him to earth in Wavertree, holed up in the outside toilet of a terraced house. They broke the door down and chopped his feet off. The taxi drivers were never located and the prosecution were unable to get the case to court.

'I'll get you a name, Tommy,' I promised. How I was going to do it I didn't know but I felt more reassured having Tommy McKale's boys on my side than I did with Jim Burroughs' men.

'I read about that kid in the paper,' Tommy said. 'Me

and the boys would regard it as an honour and pleasure to assist you. Just let us know who we're looking for.'

I said I would. He insisted on showing me round the new extension to his premises, the jacuzzi that held a dozen people, the whirlpool bath, the swimming pool and the saunas. Denis was talking to some workmen in his office and waved convivially.

'I'll see you tomorrow, Johnny. Try and have something for me,' said Tommy as we parted.

I drove back to the flat. There were no messages on the answerphone. I wondered how Oggi had fared with Jim Burroughs.

I rang Frankie. There had been no word. 'I had an idea, Johnny. If I offered a reward for information, we might get something that could lead us to this maniac. Could you mention it on your show.'

'Have you discussed it with the police?'

'No. I'm not sure they'd go along with it but I think it's worth a try, don't you? Say £5,000.'

'I think a thousand for starters,' I said. 'No sense in throwing it away. If you're sure, Frankie, I'll do it.'

He said he was sure.

I did as he asked. If anybody had any information leading to the safe return of the kidnapped girl, Sammi Relphs, a thousand pounds reward was being offered by her father. Would they please contact me at the radio station?

It was a sombre show. My heart wasn't in the music which was very unusual for me. I played the Everly Brothers' 'Ebony Eyes' and Etta James' 'All I Could Do was Cry' and felt like crying myself.

'The police want you to ring,' said Ken, as I came out of the studio. 'They probably want to lock you up for making everybody so miserable. Haven't you any happy records?'

I rang the number he gave me. It was Jim Burroughs' private line.

'What's all this crap about a reward?'

'Frankie asked me to do it. I assumed you knew,' I said innocently.

'Did I fuck? Do you know what you've done? You've opened the floodgates for a load of opportunist nutters to ring up claiming they're holding the girl and for an extra ten grand they'll release her.'

'Frankie'd pay that to get Sammi back.'

'Except they won't have the kid, will they? The real nutter doesn't want money. It just fucks everything up for us because we have to check them all out just in case.'

'But the real nutter might be tempted if he thinks there's enough in it for him. You once said you thought it was a kidnap but the police scared him off.'

'The front page of every paper in the country must scare him even more.'

'Did you see Oggi?' I dared to ask.

'You didn't tell me he was doing drugs. That's not my concern, though; I leave all that to the drug squad. Yes, I saw him. Nothing much to help us with really other than the kid's description of her assailant. No, we'll just have to wait till tomorrow and see what the post brings.'

He rang off and I pondered his parting shot. I just hoped Karen Relphs wasn't the one who answered the door to the mailman.

Chapter Twenty-One

I had a pleasant surprise when I got back to the flat. Maria had a couple of Indian meals going and the table was set for two with melon on the plates and a bottle of wine in the ice bucket that Hilary had bought me the Christmas before last.

'They're only ready-made from the supermarket,' she said, 'but they looked appetising.'

They were fine and I was very impressed at how she'd found her way round the kitchen. We ate the meal in companiable silence, then moved over to the settee with our glasses of wine.

'I'm sorry I didn't ring you last night but I didn't get in till after two.' I ran through with her The Cruzads' meeting and the trip to Oggi's and, finally, the dreadful scenes at Frankie's.

'Everything we feared,' she said at last. 'That poor family.'

'I had to go to see Jim Burroughs this morning. He wasn't very happy. Told me to stay out of it.'

'How stupid! You're in it whether you like it or not.'

'That's what I said.' I recounted my visit to Tommy McKale.

'I'd feel a lot happier with him guarding me than the police,' said Maria. 'He sounds capable.'

'Just what I said.' I refilled our glasses.

'I heard about the reward,' she said. 'I listened to your show while I prepared dinner. You're going to have to play some more cheerful records, you know, or all your listeners will be switching over to the shipping forecast for light relief.'

'So my producer tells me. The reward was Frankie's idea. The police aren't thrilled about it.'

'Have you heard from any of the others today?'

'No. Oggi's not on the phone. I rang Mally but his wife said he was working in Barrow. He's a sales rep.' I sighed. 'Jim Burroughs said we have to wait for tomorrow's post.'

'How insensitive.'

'I suppose he's right, though I dread to think what that'll bring.'

Maria stood up and went over to her shopping bag by the door. 'I don't know about you but I think the best thing we can do is forget about the whole thing for one night and relax a bit. I rented this on the way here, I hope you haven't seen it.'

It was a video of *Sleepless in Seattle*. I had seen it but I didn't tell Maria I had and I was more than happy to watch it again, if only for Jimmy Durante's singing.

'Shall we watch it in bed?' she said. 'It'll save us getting up again when it's over. I'll just clear the dishes.'

'Leave them. I've got all tomorrow to tidy up. Come on.' I led her to the bedroom.

'I haven't brought a nightie,' she said.

'Borrow one of my T-shirts.'

I opened the wardrobe door for her and she chose the navy-blue *Crazy For You* one, a memento from the Gershwin musical. 'It'll match my underwear,' she smiled.

I enjoyed the film even more the second time round, or maybe it was Maria's company. I remembered the first time I'd seen it, at the Multiplex, with Eileen who worked at Barclays Bank in town. I took Eileen out a few times but I don't see her any more. Tomorrow night I'd be at the Multiplex with Hilary.

Eileen had cried when Meg Ryan finally found Tom

Hanks on top of the Empire State Building. Maria didn't cry. She just squeezed my hand and kissed me.

After the film had finished, we made love and went to sleep, relaxed, at last, and contented, all thoughts of The Cruzads temporarily forgotten.

It wouldn't last.

'This is beginning to be a habit,' said Maria, appearing at my beside with a tray.

'What time is it?' I struggled to a sitting position.

'Eight o'clock. Move over, I'm having mine with you.' I saw there were two mugs of tea on the tray and a plate of toast and marmalade. 'I used the Frank Cooper, was that right?'

I kissed her. 'Perfect.'

'I was going to go out for a paper but if anything had happened it would be too late for today's edition, wouldn't it?'

'Yes.' We munched our toast.

'I wish I didn't have to go to work today,' said Maria

'There's a lot to be said for not working.' I didn't think Oggi would agree with me. It's all right not working when you have an income.

'I've left your key on the table, by the way,' she said. 'I don't want you to think I'm trying to move in.' She drank the last of her tea. 'What are you doing today?'

I had to be careful. I couldn't take her out this evening because I was seeing Hilary. Suddenly, I was seeing an awful lot of Maria.

'I thought I might go down to Oggi's this morning. But I'll ring Frankie before I go, see if he's heard anything.'

I didn't get the chance. He called me. Maria had gone to work and I'd promised to let her know if I had any news. I left it at that. I washed up the dishes and I'd just come out of the shower when the phone rang.

'Nothing,' Frankie said. 'No letter, no phone call, nothing.'

'You know what the post is like,' I said. 'You'll probably get something tomorrow, or maybe in the lunchtime post.' But I was surprised and concerned. The waiting was the worst of it.

I rang Mally but Marilyn said he was still up in the Lakes; he'd stayed overnight. 'He'll be back late this evening,' she said. 'Is there any message?' I told her I'd ring on Saturday.

I decided to go to Oggi's and make sure everything was all right there after Jim Burroughs' visit but when I went down to the car park I received the first shock of the day.

All four tyres of the RAV4 had been slashed!

I went over to the security office. Roger was on duty. He was suitably horrified when I told him and could only think it had been done under cover of darkness.

'What about security lights?'

'There are shadows, Mr Ace, especially since a couple of the lights have been vandalised recently.'

'And I thought we had closed-circuit TV cameras here.' I pointed to the small flickering black-and-white screen on his desk showing different areas of the car park in turn. 'Do you ever look at those?'

He admitted he might take his eyes away occasionally, to make a cup of tea or go to the toilet or glance at the paper.

'There'll be a film in the camera, though, won't there?'

They'd run out of film.

'So we won't have a picture of who did this?' Another piece of luck for the killer although I realised he'd probably paid someone else to slash my tyres rather than risk doing it himself.

I went back to the flat and rang the Toyota garage to pick up the car and replace the tyres. They offered me a replacement but I decided to walk to the bus station and catch the 82 to Speke

I sat upstairs. It was years since I'd been on a bus and

what struck me most was the graffiti and the torn seats. Also, the windows were so dirty I could hardly see out of them.

We'd not travelled more than two stops before an old lady with two carrier bags clambered up the stairs and sat down beside me.

'I hope you don't mind me sitting here,' she said, indicating the many empty seats, 'but I don't like sitting on my own in case someone grabs me, do you?' She was about seventy, with a faint moustache and a humped back.

'It's never happened to me yet,' I said.

'I've just been to the library,' she continued, pointing to the books in one of the bags. 'I like a nice detective story and the girls in the library are ever so helpful at finding them for me but they're all lesbians nowadays, have you noticed?'

'The librarians I know aren't lesbians.'

'No, the detectives. Give me the Toff any day. Do you like the Toff?'

'Before my time, I think.'

'And the Saint. I used to love him in the pictures. George Sanders. He looked just like my husband. He's dead now.'

'Oh, I'm sorry.'

'They're all dead, Stewart Granger, Errol Flynn . . .' She looked at me. 'And what do you do for a living then?'

'Er . . .' Saying you have a radio show is worse than admitting to being a doctor and nobody likes landlords. 'I work for the council,' I said.

'My husband worked for them. He was a clerk.' She pronounced it the American way to rhyme with jerk. 'But he couldn't work indoors because of his breathing condition so they moved him on to the bins.'

'Has he been dead long?'

'Dead? He isn't dead.'

'I thought—'

'He went into hospital. Broke his leg falling into the tip. That's where he met this other woman, she was in the next ward having a hysterectomy with a previous marriage. He told the doctors to tell me he was dead but he's living with her in Warrington, just down the road from the artificial leg factory.'

'So you're on my own then?'

'I'm on my own now,' she repeated. 'With Roland, my deerhound. He's cheaper than a burglar alarm but he affects my asthma so he has to sleep in the spare bedroom.'

She proceeded to regale me with details of her other major illnesses of the last fifty years before, thankfully, she alighted from the vehicle at Garston. 'Nice to talk to you,' she said. 'I hope your knee gets better.'

No wonder they say Liverpool's full of comedians.

I left the bus myself a few stops later and walked through the council estate to Oggi's. A few small kids were playing with old tyres.

'Carl's out,' said Sharon, coming to the door in the same dressing gown and slippers she'd worn on my last visit but the Snoopy T-shirt had been superceded by a winceyette nightdress. 'He's gone into town on the bus.' She stepped back to let me in.

'I came to see if you'd heard about Frankie's little girl.'

'We have. It was on television last night. It's terrible, isn't it? Carl was going to ring you this morning when he got to town. None of the phones work round here. Have they found her yet?

'No. We've heard nothing. Is Jenny OK?'

'She's at school. Carl took her on his way.'

'How did you get on with the police yesterday?'

'Oh, all right. He was quite nice, that Inspector. Carl remembered him from when he played in the Chocolate Lavatory. He had a word with Jenny but she couldn't tell him anything she hadn't told you.'

'No trouble about the drugs?'

'Carl's not a bad person, you know. He just finds it difficult to cope sometimes. He's never really come to terms with not being able make a living as a musician any more.'

'I suppose being in a group is like being a footballer,' I said. 'One minute you're playing for Everton, then you're forty and you find yourself in the Sunday League.'

'Carl never got to play for Everton, Johnny. He was always Sunday League.'

'No, that's not strictly true, Sharon. We were fully pro for over ten years with The Cruzads.' I struggled to continue the analogy with football teams. 'You could say he at least reached Tranmere Rovers level.'

'It's all the same in the end though, isn't it? He ended up a mess. But he's off all that dope and stuff now. I just want to see him get a job, if only for Jenny's sake. I want her to be able to be proud of her dad.'

'Being proud of him is nothing to do with having a job,' I said. Would Matt Scrufford be proud of his rich, successful father if he knew about Mally and Sarah? 'It's about being the person he is. I think Jenny has every reason to be proud of Carl.'

'You're very kind to us, Johnny.' Sharon put her hand on my arm and I noticed a tear in her eye. 'He looks up to you a lot, does Carl. Thanks for helping us.'

'You just take care of that daughter of yours,' I said. 'I'll be in touch. Ring me if you need me.'

I took the bus back to town. Happily I had the seat to myself. I picked up a *Daily Post* and walked back to the flat. The Toyota was back in my parking space with four new tyres.

I made myself some lunch and read the paper. Sammi's kidnapping was headline news but the article said nothing I didn't know already. The police had come up with a drawing of the man they wanted to question. It bore little resemblence to the sketch I'd done for Jenny and it could have been anybody.

I rang Frankie again. He'd heard nothing. I thought of ringing Jim Burroughs but decided it wouldn't be wise.

I left early for the station and Ken greeted me with a handful of message sheets. 'All people claiming this reward,' he said. 'More idiots.'

I sat in the staff room and went through them. Ken was right. Very few of them looked genuine but there were about six that I thought the police ought to see, just in case.

I made a point of playing happier records on the show including two surfing songs by the Beach Boys, and Jan and Dean, the new single by Cast, currently my favourite Liverpool band, and Tim McGraw's 'I Like It I Love It' for line dance and country fans. Ken seemed pleased when I came out of the studio. 'Not as suicidal as usual,' was all he said.

Hilary was waiting for me at the main entrance to the hospital. 'Would you rather go and see *Psycho*?' she said. 'It's on at the Phil.'

I nearly said I'd been to the Phil on Saturday to the opera but stopped myself, which was odd. Usually I told Hilary about other women I took out.

'I've seen it years ago, and I didn't like it then.'

'That's fine. Let's go and see *Independence Day*.'

In the end, I didn't like that either. We came out and went for a pizza next door to the Multiplex.

After the meal, we drove down to the Masquerade Club. Tommy McKale was on the door as usual. 'All right, Johnny? Hello, love,' he said to Hilary. 'Had any luck with your madman yet?'

'Not yet, but I'm still looking,' I replied. 'You're busy tonight.' I didn't want to discuss the case at the moment.

'We've got a new DJ for Saturdays. He's like that fellow on Radio One that upsets everyone, what's his name?'

'Chris Evans,' said Hilary.

'That's him.'

'Is he good?'

'No, he's an arrogant, foul-mouthed yob but the punters seem to like him. I put him on last week and look at it.' He indicated the long queue of people waiting to pay, most of them in their teens and early twenties. 'That's because he plays all this Britpop and Boyzone stuff instead of rave and reggae. Brings in the kids, which is what I want.'

I thought of little Jenny Ogden and the Boyzone poster on her wall. Not long before she'd be coming to clubs like this. I didn't think Frankie's girls would be Masquerade people but you could never be sure of anything with kids. I knew if I'd have had a daughter, I wouldn't have wanted her in the Masquerade.

'I never thought of this as a disco, Tommy.'

' 'Course it's not. It's what it's always been, a drinking club for gangsters, queers, perverts and show business personalities like yourself.' He patted me on the shoulder. 'And that is why the young people come here. It gives them an edge of danger, like mixing with the Krays in London nightclubs in the sixties. And the perverts like good-looking young girls, and boys, to ogle so everyone's happy.'

'I suppose so.'

'Furthermore, the kids drink these new alcoholic fruit juices. Most of them are stronger than premium beers but because they taste like Ribena or whatever, they don't realise they're getting drunk, so they keep drinking more and more. And the mark-up's twice that of spirits.'

The mark-ups at the Masquerade have always been rather spurious at the best of times. It's the only club I know where they change foreign currency at the door and the prices often bear little relation to the money extracted from the customer.

'Come on, Johnny, let's try one,' laughed Hilary. 'We can get smashed on lemonade.' She bounced happily to the bar where Vince was mixing one of his exotic cocktails.

'Hello, sweetie, be with you in a minute. I'm just giving this young lady an Orgasm.' I noticed he'd had a ring put through his belly button to match the one in his ear.

'We want two of those alcopop lemonades,' said Hilary when he'd finished.

'What you ought to have first, lovely, is a Tequila Slammer, to set you up for it.' He poured out a glass of tequila, took Hilary's wrist and put a small amount of salt on the back of her hand then placed a coaster on the glass and handed it to her.

'Now, you lick all the salt off your hand, slam the glass on the top of the bar, take off the coaster and drink it down in one. When you've finished it you immediately bite on this lemon.' He cut a wedge of lemon and laid it next to the glass.

A few interested people round the bar watched as Hilary went through this ritual and they cheered as she downed the drink and, breathless, sucked the piece of lemon.

'Now for the lemonade,' said Vince, fetching two bottles from the shelf. 'You've been playing some very gloomy records this week, Johnny. Your piles been bothering you, have they?'

A couple of the watchers giggled and Hilary laughed.

'The ointment isn't working,' she grinned.

One of the features that had always appealed to me about Hilary was what I called her irreverent cheerfulness. Tonight, I found it wearing. Perhaps I was getting old. Or perhaps the Matt Scrufford affair was getting me down.

Hilary led me to the dance floor and we gyrated to Pulp and Blur and Oasis. I noticed that most of the worn-out bulbs that made up the illuminated dance floor had been replaced so it glowed more brightly. The cracks in the glass were still there, reminders of previous altercations in the club.

Tommy McKale was right about the alcopops. I didn't

like the sweetness of them but Hilary persuaded me to try the orange, cola, lime, blackcurrant and ginger flavours and by one o'clock I felt a lot happier and Hilary was well away.

'Let's go back to the flat,' she said. 'I'm hungry.' We took a taxi. Tommy said he'd keep an eye on my car.

Hilary had her clothes off before I'd properly locked the door. 'Come on,' she said, 'you're slow,' and tugged off my sweater and slacks. Then she went to her handbag and produced a vibrator that looked like a scale model of the Eiffel Tower only black.

'This is in case you've got brewer's droop from your fruit juice,' she laughed, switching the batteries on and pushing it slowly inside her.

Surprisingly, the drink hadn't affected me in that way and by now I was as excited as she was. The torpor of the early part of the evening had left me.

'Tell you what,' she said, 'let's look in the fridge. I fancy some real fruit.' The vibrator was cast aside and she ran into the kitchen where she found some out-of-season strawberries from Greece that I'd bought in Safeway's. 'Got any cream? Oh yes, here it is.'

She carried them to the bedroom and dragged me behind her, still in my boxers. We ended up sprawled on the bed. She took a couple of the strawberries and inserted them where the vibrator had been.

I put my face against her belly and thrust my tongue in search of the strawberries. I remembered someone I knew dislocated his jaw doing this. He ended up, very embarrassed, at the hospital, dribbling and unable to shut his mouth and having to explain to an Indian lady doctor that he'd done it trying to cough when he was sneezing. I was careful not to open my mouth too wide.

'Oooooh, that's lovely,' moaned Hilary. 'Put some cream on them.' Most of the cream ran through my lips and on to the sheets.

Eventually, we changed positions and Hilary took a

turn at licking cream from various bits of me. I've never found sex as exciting with anyone else as with Hilary.

'Remember the Stripes Club?' she said, squeezing her boobs together for me to suck. We made love violently until we eventually fell asleep, hot, sticky and exhausted.

The ringing of the telephone beside the bed woke me.

It was Frankie.

'For God's sake, where've you been? I've been calling you.'

I yawned, not quite aware where I was. 'Sorry, I had a late night, I only just woke up. What time is it?' My head was throbbing.

'Johnny. You've got to come down. We've had the Jiffy bag. The police are here now.'

Suddenly I was wide awake and a wave of nausea hit me in the stomach. 'What was in it?'

His voice broke. 'Sammi's finger!'

Chapter Twenty-Two

I put the phone down and checked my watch. It was ten o'clock. Suddenly, I was stone-cold sober. I strode into the lounge and checked the answerphone. Four messages were registered. I played them back.

The first was Mally returning my call. That was at nine thirty. Three minutes later, someone rang off without leaving a message. I checked the display and Frankie's number came up. Jim Burroughs was next, ringing from Frankie's, asking me to get down there and the fourth was the call I'd collected, our conversation recorded on the tape.

I quickly rang Mally and told him the awful news. 'I'm going to see Frankie now. Will you be in later?'

'I've got to see a client in Widnes but I'll be back around six.' I wondered if the 'client' was Sarah.

'I'll come round at quarter past.'

I ran back into the bedroom. Hilary was still sleeping. I took a shower and threw on a clean pair of slacks and sweat shirt before waking her.

'Look, sweetheart, something's come up. I've got to race off. Make yourself some breakfast. You can let yourself out, can't you?'

'What about you? Have you had something to eat?'

'No time, I'll explain later.'

'When will I see you?'

'I'll phone you tomorrow. Bye.'

I ran down the stairs, leapt into the car and roared off down the dock road, just like on Wednesday night, only this time the Saturday morning traffic through Waterloo and Crosby was heavy and the journey took longer.

Frankie was waiting at the door. He was still in dressing gown and pyjamas. 'No note or anything.' His face was grey and he was breathing very shallowly. I was worried he would have a heart attack.

'The police are here, we've had the press round, but nobody can *do* anything.'

'What have you done with the finger?'

'We put it in the freezer. I thought they might be able to sew it on again if . . .' his voice faltered, 'if we ever get her back alive.'

'Of course you will. There's too much publicity now. He daren't kill her.' The publicity hadn't stopped him amputating her finger, though.

'Why, Johnny, why is he doing it?'

'That's what we were trying to work out on Wednesday night.'

'I can't think of anything at all.' He looked a beaten man.

'Where's Karen?'

'In the sitting room. Your mate's with her – Inspector Burroughs, is it? I seem to know him from somewhere.'

'Jim Burroughs. He played in a group in the sixties, the Chocolate Lavatory. We were on with them a couple of times at the Four Winds.'

'I think I remember. They played a lot of Coasters numbers and they were bloody awful.'

'That's them.'

'He's better off in the police.'

'Don't be too sure. They're thinking of getting together again to do a Merseycats show.'

'I hope he's a better detective than he is a musician.'

We were making conversation, something to fill the silence because there was nothing constructive to say. All the same, his words filled me with disquiet. How good a detective was Burroughs? He was the one leading the whole investigation from the day, over three weeks ago, that Matt Scrufford was abducted, and so far he'd found out nothing.

I read once that the police are only as good as their informers and without tip-offs, nobody would get arrested. If this maniac worked alone, did that mean they might never catch him?

I went through to talk to Karen. She was sitting by the table, silently weeping. Jim Burroughs came over and intercepted me.

'I'm not hopeful we'll find her alive,' he murmured in a low voice. 'It's like the ears all over again. No ransom note, no motive. Obviously the same person, the envelopes match.'

'We knew it was going to happen,' I said, 'and we were powerless to stop it.'

'Have you come up with anything?'

I thought of reminding him how he'd told me to stay out of it but this was not a time to score points. We needed to help one another all we could. But there was nothing I could tell him.

'I'm putting a guard on this house and on Carl Ogden's,' he said.

'What about Mally? He's got another child, a two-year-old.'

'You think he'd target them a second time?'

'Anything's possible. Better to be safe than sorry.'

'I'll organise it. And you'd better watch yourself. You've no kids; he might go for you instead.'

I told him about my slashed tyres. 'We might have had a picture of him if the cameras had been working properly.'

'He's stalking you all, isn't he? He seems to have access to your movements and the places you visit. He must have been planning this for months.'

'Thirty years,' I said.

I stayed for an hour or so to try to comfort Frankie

and Karen. Jim Burroughs left but a policewoman stayed behind. Sammi's sister, Nikki, had been picked up by Karen's mother and taken safely to Conwy. Her mother wanted the whole family to go but Frankie had to wait at home for news of Sammi, and Karen insisted on staying with him.

I drove back home. Hilary had left. The breakfast dishes were in the sink and a red cross for a kiss was scrawled in lipstick on the bedroom mirror. The sheets were crumpled on the bed, still sticky from the night before and the cream was starting to go sour.

I spent the next hour washing up and tidying the place. I shoved the sheets in the washing machine and put clean ones on the bed. Then I got same lunch and sat down in the lounge to try to unwind.

I realised how impotent the police must have felt after Mally had received Matt's ears, waiting for a ransom note that never came, then finally finding the body. Was history going to repeat itself?

I knew I should ring Maria but I wanted to get the night with Hilary out of my mind first. Why, I don't know.

I finished the meal and wondered what to do next. Mally wouldn't be in till six. I picked up the paper. Already, the kidnap had been relegated to the middle pages. After the finger, it would be back on the front tomorrow.

The police, the paper said, were following a number of leads, although I couldn't imagine what they were. It also said that DI Burroughs was expecting an early result but I knew it was all bullshit, meant to reassure the public and frighten the criminal. I doubted it would do either.

I turned to the back page and realised that Everton were playing at home this afternoon, against West Ham United. That would kill a couple of hours, I thought, and I could go straight over to Mally's from Goodison Park.

The phone rang whilst I was fetching my parka from the cloakroom.

'If you've nothing planned, do you fancy coming round to my place for a meal tonight?' I was strangely pleased to hear Maria's voice.

'I'm going over to Mally's after the match but I should be free around eight. How does that sound?'

'Sounds great. I take it there's been no news or I'd have heard from you.'

I nearly said 'I was going to ring you' but it sounded false. Instead, I told her about the finger. 'I just got back from Frankie's a few minutes ago. They're both distraught.'

'And no note or anything again?'

'Nothing.'

'And is the other little girl all right?'

'They've taken her to Karen's mother's.'

'Oh God. You must be careful, Johnny. He's dangerous and he could be after you next.'

It was getting to me now. I looked over my shoulder as I walked across the car park and all the way to Goodison I kept glancing in the driving mirror in the expectation of being followed.

I parked in one of the side streets off Walton Road and took a route past Laura's house to the ground. A blue Bentley was parked outside so I assumed the Stripes' owner was visiting. I wondered what would happen to any kid who vandalised his car.

There was a good crowd for the match, perhaps encouraged by England's win over Poland. Everton managed to secure a 2–1 victory but the School of Science days seemed to be gone for good and I wasn't overly optimistic about a place in Europe.

I drove round the back of the city to Woolton, passing Hilary's hospital and the Everyman. It wasn't the best route with the Saturday shopping crowds but I was curious about something.

I drove up Catherine Street and took a right into Percy Street. Sure enough, there was Mally's car outside Sarah's flat.

I didn't stop. I carried on up Upper Parliament Street and down Smithdown Road through Mossley Hill and reached Mally's house well before six.

Marilyn let me in. 'Hi! He's not back yet. Come in and I'll make you a cup of tea, or would you like a real drink seeing it's so late?'

'Tea'll be fine, thanks.' I could smell the aroma of meat cooking in the kitchen, ready for Mally when he deigned to leave his mistress.

Marilyn looked more desirable than ever. Her blonde hair had been cut like Rachel's in *Friends* and it made her look far younger than thirty. Her top was low-cut and her skirt midway to her knees.

I followed her into the kitchen without being asked but she didn't stop me. 'He's never in these days, is he?' I couldn't resist stirring it.

'He works hard,' she said.

And plays hard, I thought. There was no way I would ever have told Marilyn about Mally's philanderings but I didn't feel that my knowledge of them gave me a moral right to seduce his wife, much as I might fancy her.

I also felt that to do so would be disloyal to Maria, despite my little speech about being free to see who I wanted.

'Has Maureen gone back now?' There seemed no harm in flirting.

'Hopefully.' She grinned and I smiled back conspiratorially and our eyes exchanged knowing glances. 'Good riddance to bad rubbish. Oh, I shouldn't say that, should I, with her losing her son?'

'He was your son, too, in a way. I think that makes it OK.' Saying that reminded me of her own child. 'Where's Gary?'

'Up in the playroom.' Some degree of alarm in my tone

must have registered because she asked if anything was the matter.

'No, but I think you ought to keep a careful eye on him. This maniac is still out there. After Sammi's finger, anything is possible.'

'Sammi's what?'

'Finger. Didn't Mally tell you? I rang him this morning . . .' I couldn't believe he hadn't mentioned it, if only to alert her to the possible danger to Gary.

'He never mentioned anything. What's happened?'

I brought her up to date. She sat down. 'How absolutely terrible. That poor couple. Who the hell is doing this, and why?'

'It's something to do with The Cruzads. One of us has upset this person enough for him to seek revenge thirty years later.'

'That'll be Mally, then,' she said automatically.

'What!'

'I don't know what the other two in the group are like, of course, but Mally is the sort of person who can hurt people most cruelly without ever knowing it. Or, maybe, without caring.' I wondered if she meant herself and how many times he'd hurt her. Knowledge of Sarah might not come as too awful a shock.

As for what she said about the other members of the group, well, Oggi had never had any malice in him. He might be a scally but he wasn't the type to hurt people. Frankie had always been rather serious and respectable.

Marilyn was right. Mally was a man you'd never entirely trust. He'd let us down more than once on gigs and he had a reputation round the clubs when he went solo for not always turning up or sending another act in his place.

'Do you know anyone he's upset?'

Her laugh was hollow. 'Loads, but not thirty years ago.'

'And it must have been when he was in the band because we are being targeted too.'

'Sounds like Mally. Letting someone else suffer on his behalf.'

'Why do you stay with him?' I asked suddenly.

She thought for a minute. 'Do you think people ever know the motives for their actions? I could say I love him, and I do, but sometimes I despise him, and that happens more often than it used to. On the other hand, I have a nice house and he buys me anything I want – I can't say he's not generous. Then there's the children.' She patted her stomach. 'But one day I might meet someone who's nice to me as well, then, who knows?'

Again, something passed between us, call it an empathy, a fusion of spirits. It didn't last more than a second because Mally chose that moment to return.

'Sorry I'm late, Johnny,' he barged in the room and clasped my shoulder. 'Had a deal to tie up. Hello, love, dinner ready?' He kissed her perfunctorily on the cheek and moved over to the dresser to look over his post. He wore a suit, obviously to keep up the pretence of being at business.

She stood up. 'I've just put the kettle on to make Johnny a cup of tea.'

'Fine. I'll have one too. Any news on the kid yet?'

'You never told me about that little girl's finger,' said Marilyn accusingly.

'What? Oh no, didn't want to worry you.' It sounded almost plausible. 'They've not found this maniac yet then?'

'No.' I told him about my slashed tyres and how the security cameras should have filmed the perpetrator, if indeed it was him.

'Oggi's daughter's the only one who's seen him in the flesh and all she could say about him was he's old and fat and has tattoos on the backs of his hands.'

The crash startled us both. Mal dropped the teapot she was holding as Mally fainted clean away across the table, breaking two plates and cracking his head on the table leg.

I rushed round to him and loosened his collar. His cheeks were white and his pulse rapid. 'Get some brandy,' I said. I suppose I should have said aspirin in case it was a heart attack but who thinks straight in an emergency?

Marilyn rushed over with the glass and I lifted his head up as she forced a little of the spirit through his lips. He spluttered and started to come round. We sat him upright. He looked like a man who had seen his Maker.

'Take it easy,' I said, as he started to speak.

He pushed my arm away. 'I know,' he said. He gripped my wrist tightly. 'Oh God. I know who the murderer is!'

Chapter Twenty-Three

'It was the tattoos, don't you see? Nobody had mentioned those to me before. It has to be him. I never saw anybody else with tattoos there. He had a snarling bulldog on the back of each hand.'

We'd helped Mally into a chair and Mal had made strong tea for us all. Mally sipped his and started his story.

'His name is Jed Fulger although you may remember him better, Johnny, as the drummer in Froggie and the Hoppers.'

'I remember the group's name; I never knew him, though.'

'You will. Do you remember a night we played the Peppermint Lounge and you, Oggi and Frankie took these girls backstage?'

'Oggi and I were talking about that the other day. June Tarbuck his was called and you ended up taking her home.'

'That's the one. Oggi would remember her, wouldn't he? She was the first woman he'd ever screwed.'

'And those teds came after us and threw a brick through the van window. We were lucky to escape with our lives. Oggi's head was streaming with blood where the brick hit him.'

'It was Jed Fulger who threw the brick. June Tarbuck was his fiancée.'

'And the rest of them were the Hoppers?'

'No. He didn't go around much with the Hoppers

except on their gigs. He had his own gang of thugs, the Seaforth Slaves they called themselves and brutal bastards they were too. I know because they used to hang out round the Star of the Sea in Seaforth, not far from our house.'

'But they didn't know you?'

'They did after that night. We had our name on the van, remember? But I was careful to keep out of their way. They never knew where I lived and I made sure we never played anywhere where his group was playing, although it didn't last long as he was done for GBH shortly afterwards and ended up being detained at Her Majesty's pleasure.'

'Certified?'

'Oh, totally crazy. Nearly killed the poor bastard he attacked. Apparently it took five coppers to drag him off.'

'But if it was him, why's he waited till now?'

'Don't you see, he must have been released from Broadmoor or wherever they were keeping him?'

'But hang on, she went with you and Oggi willingly, didn't she?'

'Course she did. Christ, her mates were having it away with you and Frankie at the same time. It was hardly mass rape. She knew what she'd come for.'

I glanced up at Marilyn. She didn't looked thrilled at these disclosures. Mally must have sensed it too.

'We were young boys, love. We formed a group because we liked music, and suddenly all these girls were offering themselves. What normal boy would refuse it offered on a plate?'

'You weren't with us in the dressing room, though, Mally, so why you?'

'I took her home, didn't I? He saw me leaving with her and he'd brought her, which naturally upset him. Whether he knew she'd been with Oggi earlier, I don't know, but I think he must have guessed. He probably thought we'd all had her.'

'Which is why he's after all of us now.' It seemed a reasonable assumption. 'I remember you dropped us all off first.'

'That's right, then I went and parked round the back of Litherland Town Hall with her.'

Litherland Town Hall was where the Beatles made their famous triumphant return from Germany at one of Brian Kelly's dances in December 1960. Now it had a new claim to fame.

'She couldn't get my pants off quick enough.'

'Or hers, no doubt,' said Marilyn acidly.

'Then what happened?'

'Nothing. I screwed her and took her home and never saw her again.'

'But, Mally, you've had other women over the years that have been married, engaged or had steady boyfriends who had equal reason to attack you, so what makes you think he's the one?'

'The tattoos for a start but the girl really. After we'd done it she was terrified. She said if Jed found out that she'd done it with me he'd kill me. Said I must never go near her again and I should watch out for him because he was a sadist and he was crazy. She said she'd once seen him slash a lad's face with a broken glass in a pub. Apparently, the lad had smiled at her, that's all. It put the fear of God into me, I can tell you.'

'But he knew we were The Cruzads, he could easily have found us. We were advertised in the *Echo* and *Mersey Beat* all the time.'

'Ah, but don't forget, he was in a group too so the odds were he was out playing himself.'

'But he can't be sure you did it with her? Or Oggi come to that?'

'I bet he forced her to confess. After all, he knew I'd taken her home. Besides, what about her two friends that you and Frankie had in the dressing room? They could easily have told him.'

I tried to recall their faces but I couldn't bring them to mind. Somehow I felt ashamed about that.

'But that sort of girl's likely to go with anyone. Christ, she'd had two fellows in one night, and that's when she's out with her fiancé! How many more did she have when he was staying in washing his hair?'

'Johnny's got a point.' Marilyn entered the conversation.

'Then, perhaps he's murdered other people as well that we don't know about.'

I tried to absorb all this new information. It did give us the motive we'd been looking for and, if Jed Fulger had been locked up for thirty years, that would explain the time lapse.

I found it awesome that somebody could sustain a campaign of hate for so long and said so.

'But if he was crazy . . .' said Marilyn.

'It must have been festering in his mind all the time he was in his cell.' I shivered at the thought.

'So what are we going to do?' asked Mally.

'The police,' I said. There was no question about it. Sammi Relphs might still be alive.

I rang the police station. Jim Burroughs was out. I told them it was urgent, to do with the Sammi Relphs kidnapping and could they try and contact him.

'DS Skidmore's in charge of that case now, sir, Serious Crime Squad. I'll put you through to him.'

A voice younger and more educated than Jim Burroughs' came on the line. I explained who I was. He'd read all about me in the case notes. He didn't say he listened to my show.

'So, what can I do for you, Mr Ace?'

'We think the man you're looking for might be a Jed Fulger who has probably recently been released from prison for GBH.' I gave him a shortened account of Mally's theory. 'It fits in with the vendetta against the group and, if he's been locked up for the past thirty years, it explains why he hasn't come after us before.'

'Have you any idea where he lives?'

'He lived in Seaforth thirty years ago but he could be anywhere now.'

'We'll check him out. Thank you for ringing us. Where can I get hold of you if I need you?'

I gave him my mobile phone number.

'From what we know of him, Superintendent, he's crazy and dangerous.'

'I think that's already obvious,' he said drily. 'Have you any photographs of him?'

'Not me. There's bound to be some of him with his group in the old issues of *Mersey Beat* though.' I thought of Jim Burroughs. He'd collected a fair bit of memorabilia over the years dating back to his Chocolate Lavatory days. 'You could try Detective Inspector Burroughs, he might well have something from that era.'

The two Mals looked at me as I put the phone down. 'So that's it, is it? We just sit back and wait?' Mally seemed concerned at the prospect.

'What else can we do?'

'Nothing, I suppose. Realising it's him has made me nervous.' It also began to make him angry. 'The bastard! To think my son was killed for this.'

The sins of the fathers . . . I thought and looked across at Marilyn and I knew she was thinking the same. I felt it hadn't been an edifying experience for her, hearing her husband's debauchery recounted out loud. Mind you, I hadn't come out of it too well either.

'Isn't it Buddhism that says ultimately we have to answer for every one of our actions in life?' she said.

'Could be. It seems a fair system whoever invented it.'

'But answerable to whom?' cried Mally, who was slowly working himself into a rage. 'Not to that asshole so he can come and make judgements on me. If I got my hands on him, I'd break his fucking neck—'

'I'll get the dinner out,' interrupted Mal diplomatically. 'Will you stay for something to eat, Johnny?'

I looked at my watch. 'No thanks, Mal. I'm supposed to be having a meal at eight in Crosby and it's nearly half-past seven now. I'll have to go.'

'Keep in touch,' said Mally, calming down. 'I want to know what's happening. Leave me your mobile number, I lost it.'

'Don't forget to keep an eye on Gary,' I said, 'for two reasons. One, it might not be Jed Fulger after all, and two, whilst the police are looking for him, he is still probably stalking us.'

I set off for Maria's. I switched on the car radio to listen to the end of David Mellor's football phone-in on Five Live but I couldn't concentrate and turned it off again.

I was thinking about Mally and his anger at Jed Fulger. *I'd break his fucking neck.* I'd had the letters with the nails and the hair, I'd had a petrol bomb put through my letter box and my car tyres slashed. No serious harm although, in different circumstances, I supposed I could have been burnt alive in my bed or had all my possessions destroyed.

I reckoned Oggi's little girl was lucky to be alive because Fulger already killed once. In the end, all she'd lost was a lock of hair but who knows what traumas she might suffer later. And if I'd had kids . . .

Even if Sammi Relphs was rescued, she'd had a finger amputated and, like Jenny, would probably have nightmares for years to come. *If* she was rescued . . .

All because one promiscuous teenager was unfaithful to her fiancé thirty years ago.

When I thought about it, I got very angry too. I could see no justification for Fulger to bear any resentment against any of us. OK, Oggi and Mally had both had sex with his fiancée but she was willing, even initiated it. They didn't know she was engaged to Fulger. To them she was just a seventeen-year-old girl, out with her mates, who'd happily gone with both of them without protest.

But Fulger didn't even punish the people who'd upset him. He went for their children which, to my mind, was inexcusable and for that reason alone I went along with Mally. If it was up to me, I'd break his neck as well.

I pulled up outside Maria's, really wound up.

'You're late.' Maria greeted me with a smile and a kiss. 'Good job I know you and timed the meal for half-past. Sit down and I'll get us a glass of wine.'

'Something's happened,' I said.

She saw my face. 'Hang on, I'll get the wine and then I can sit down while you tell me. Have they caught him? Is Frankie's daughter safe?'

We sat on the settee and I went over the events at Mally's without mentioning myself and Frankie's part in the proceedings at the Peppermint Lounge. I'd seen enough of Marilyn's face as Mally's catalogue of licentiousness was revealed to know when to show some discretion.

'It's horrible to think of someone storing up all that revenge. It's just to be hoped they catch him in time.'

'It's not in time, is it?' I said bitterly. 'She's already lost her finger.'

'But she may still be alive.'

'I've just thought,' I said, 'I ought to ring Frankie and tell him about Fulger. Oggi's not on the phone but Frankie ought to know what's happening.'

'You ring him while I finish preparing the meal.'

Frankie didn't remember Froggie and the Hoppers at all but he remembered the night at the Peppermint Lounge and the altercation in the car park and found it hard to come to terms with the fact that the events of that one night had led to his daughter's life being in danger.

'He's a psycho,' I said. 'He's been storing this up for years.'

'I can't accept that. How can you be a hundred per cent sure you're right?'

'I can't,' I admitted. 'But it's the only thing we've got.'

There was still no news about Sammi. Frankie said Karen was distraught. He didn't sound so good himself.

I'd hardly put the phone down before my mobile rang. 'I've just had my Superintendent on,' said Jim Burroughs, 'and he's told me about Jed Fulger. Did you know this guy?'

'I remember his group, don't you?'

'Funnily enough I do. We played with them once at Blair Hall in Walton, you know, above the Co-op. Halfway throught the night, there was a big punch-up when they were onstage and some clown threw a chair and split the skin on his bass drum. He dropped his drumsticks, went into the audience after this idiot and bloody near killed him.'

'Sounds par for the course. He nearly did the same to someone who dared to smile at his girlfriend.'

'Is she the same girl that your mates were—'

'The same one.'

'Have you no idea where Fulger might be?'

'That's your job. I've stopped being a detective, remember. And how come you're not running the show any more?'

'They brought the Serious Crime Squad in, didn't they? High-level stuff. I'm still involved in the case, of course.'

'Jim, you should have a picture of Froggie and the Hoppers in one of your scrapbooks, shouldn't you? You might be able to get one in the Sundays if you're quick.'

'I don't think I have. They were hardly in the Searchers' or Beatles' class. I suppose there could be one in an old *Mersey Beat* perhaps, I'll check when I get in tonight. We're a bit late for tomorrow's paper now, anyway. In the meantime, we've put out an all-stations alert for

Fulger. He was let out of Ashworth Hospital a few months back.'

'I suppose it's all part of the government's plan to close the mental hospitals. So long as all the nutters remember to take their tablets we can sleep safely in our beds.'

He didn't disagree.

'They'll be letting Hindley and Brady out next.' The Moors Murderers are in Ashworth too. 'No news on Sammi?'

'Not a word. If you come up with anything, I want to know straight away, right?'

Maria was putting out dishes of prawn and avocado when I got rid of him. 'I'm switching this phone off,' I said. 'I want to relax.'

'So you should,' she said, and we sat down to eat. The meal was delicious. Maria had cooked swordfish steaks in a pineapple sauce with spinach, carrots and sauté potatoes. For sweet we had tipsy pudding with brandy sauce.

'Do you want to stay?' she said when we'd finished.

'I haven't brought my pyjamas.'

'Don't worry. I've got a T-shirt you can borrow.'

'As long as we can watch *Match of the Day* in bed. Everton's goals will be on.'

I enjoyed the evening more than the strawberries and cream of the previous night. I don't know whether to put this down to age. Or Maria's company. Or because the football was good. And if it was the football, then I suppose we're back to age again. Or perhaps I'm not too keen on strawberries.

I didn't ponder on it too long. Maria put down the book she'd been reading and threw her arms around me. 'Isn't that football match over yet?' she said.

I picked up the remote control and switched off the TV. 'It is now.'

I could have stayed the weekend at Maria's but felt I

ought to go and see Oggi next morning. There was no news again from Frankie. Sammi was still missing.

I left after breakfast and drove over to Speke. The family were still in bed but after I'd knocked for a few minutes, Oggi came down to let me in.

'All I remember about them,' he said, after I told him about Froggie and the Hoppers, 'is the bass player used to go out with a friend of my sister's. In fact, they got married though I don't know if they're still together.'

'What was her name?'

'Pamela Murray but her married name would be Tushingham.'

'Where do they live?'

'Why? You're not thinking of going, are you?'

'I might.'

'Well, I don't know where they live but I believe she works on the checkout at that supermarket in Belle Vale, before you come to the road junction.'

'What does she look like?'

'Bloody hell, Johnny. She'll be over forty now, she's had five kids and she's on her feet in that shop all the hours God sends. She'll look like shit.'

'And you look tired,' I told him.

'We haven't been sleeping. Jenny's still been waking up in the night, screaming. Sharon's taking her to the doctor's tomorrow.'

I left him taking his *News of the World* upstairs and told him to ring me every day on my mobile. Then I set off for Belle Vale.

I'd made a decision. Never mind the police. I was going to track down Jed Fulger. I wanted to get to him before them and, if I did, he might not live to regret it.

Chapter Twenty-Four

I found the supermarket. It was one of those Eight Till Late places and it was full of couch potatoes in their jogging pants and anoraks, stocking up on newspapers, cans of lager and frozen meals for an afternoon in front of the telly. Nobody ever seems to dress up on a Sunday any more. There wasn't a tie to be seen in the place.

I asked the Asian girl on the checkout where Pamela Tushingham was and she said she'd be down in a minute.

I read over the headlines in the papers until she arrived. The tabloids continued their tradition of reporting the soaps as if they were news. I sometimes think if Bill Clinton was assassinated by IRA sympathisers, disclosures about *EastEnders* storylines would keep him off the headlines.

Sammi's finger made the inside pages. The police were looking for released mental patient Jed Fulger. There was no photograph.

None of them had latched on to The Cruzads connection and nobody yet had majored on a serial killer story or a revenge campaign, but they did mention the Matt Scrufford case.

A woman came through the staff room door and the Asian girl pointed to me. She walked over. Oggi was wrong, she didn't look like shit. She had a pleated skirt and a blouse beneath her nylon uniform and her hair was still blonde and styled in soft waves. The skirt was short enough to show she had shapely legs.

'Can I help you?' she said.

'I hope so. Are you Pamela Tushingham?'

'Yes.'

'Married to Harvey who used to play with Frankie and the Hoppers?'

She laughed. 'That was a long time ago. I'm surprised anybody remembers.'

'I'm Johnny Ace. I used to play in a group called The Cruzads.'

She screwed up her face and an attractive dimple appeared in her left cheek. 'I think I remember them vaguely. But you're the one on the radio, aren't you?'

'That's right.'

'We often listen to your programme. My husband likes the music you play. Nobody plays a lot of that old stuff nowadays, not on Atlantic 252 that my kids listen to.'

'I'm trying to find the drummer who used to play in Froggie and the Hoppers, Jed Fulger.'

'Oh God, I've seen it in the paper. He's something to do with that kidnapping, isn't he? That little girl?'

'Have you any idea where he might be?'

'I haven't. Harvey's the one you need to talk to about the group.'

'Whereabouts do you live?'

She gave me an address in Childwall, off Queens Drive, a nice middle-class suburban area. I must have looked surprised because she answered my unspoken question.

'I work here because it gets me out of the house and I like meeting people. I used to live in Belle Vale before we were married and I still know a lot of the folk round here.'

'What does Harvey do?'

'He's got his own business. He sells second-hand Skodas. He does quite well. They're cheap and reliable little cars, which is what people want if they haven't got much money.'

'Will he be in if I go round now?'

'It's Sunday and there's football on Sky so he'll be in.'

He was, although I was too early for the football. The house was a neat semi with a carefully tended lawn bordered by late flowering bedding plants. An M reg. Skoda stood outside. It looked like new.

Harvey answered the door. He was dressed in a Marks and Spencer's green jumper, a matching green shirt and grey slacks and held the *Mail on Sunday* in his hand. His hair was greying at the temples and cut in a short back and sides.

I explained who I was and he immediately invited me in and we started chatting. Three of the children, all teenagers, were playing music in different bedrooms and one of them, a boy of about sixteen, was brought down and dispatched to make coffee.

We sat in the small lounge dominated by a black ash cabinet holding the television and video. A matching display unit was filled with videos, magazines and CDs.

'Jed Fulger,' said Harvey, when we'd exhausted Mersey beat and football and I got round to my reason for calling. 'He went to prison when he was barely nineteen. I've always said drummers were nutcases and he proved the point.' He suddenly looked embarrassed. 'Oh, I've just thought, you were a drummer, weren't you?'

'Don't worry, you're quite right. Most of us are.'

Fulger had been charged with grievous bodily harm after he had knifed another youth so badly that he lost the use of his right eye and needed two hundred stitches in his face and head. It came out in court that the Seaforth Slaves had been involved in a long-running dispute with a rival gang from Bootle which culminated in a pitched battle outside Lathom Hall in Seaforth.

The police had arrived quickly on the scene and most of the combatants fled when they saw them but Fulger carried on stabbing this boy regardless and he seriously injured four of the policemen who were trying to restrain him.

'As far as I know, he was put away for ever,' said

Harvey, 'and, to tell the truth, we were all a bit relieved. There was something about him that made you never quite sure he wouldn't turn on you. He never really fitted in with the rest of the group. They were all decent lads. He just happened to have a drum kit. Not everyone did in those days.'

'You've seen it in the paper about him, have you?'

'No, I've only read the back pages. What's he done?'

I told him as briefly as possible. 'Have you any idea where he or any of his family might be?'

'Not the slightest. Never heard of him from that day to this.' He shook his head. 'That's shocking. Let's hope they get him in time.'

'You've no idea what happened to his girlfriend. June Tarbuck, she was called.'

'Oh, I remember her. Jed was smitten with her, followed her around like a lost puppy. She didn't want to know, or rather, I'll put it another way, she didn't want to get serious. She was only a kid, seventeen at most, but he'd have died for her.'

Or killed for her, I thought.

'But you've not heard of her since Fulger left the group?'

'Not a thing. Never saw her again.'

Harvey could tell me no more so I took my leave. We promised to meet up for a drink and a chat about the old days but I knew I'd never call him. I might get nostalgic about the past but I prefer to live in the present; there's more new things likely to happen. Maria wasn't right about me all the time.

I rang Frankie but there'd been no phone calls and no news. Nearly two full days had passed since the finger arrived. Five days had elapsed between Mally Scrufford receiving the ears and Matt's body being found. But Matt was already dead by the time the ears arrived. Was Sammi also dead by now? Should the police be searching the docks?

I didn't want to think about it. Rescuing Sammi was the thing driving us on. That and finding Fulger, and I hoped that if we found one, the other wouldn't be far away.

I drove back to the flat and spent the rest of the day cogitating. Fulger had obviously been out of prison for a while so either he was living with somebody who was keeping him or he was drawing housing benefit. I couldn't see him working and I couldn't see him being still at the address he'd gone to when he was released. It would be too easy to trace him.

The obvious choice was his parents, if they were still alive. Otherwise, did he have any friends? I'd not be able to find out if he received visitors at Ashworth although the police would know.

Would June Tarbuck still be around? It seemed unlikely. She'd be married and probably a grandmother by now. He might try to trace her, however, so it would help to know where she was. But I didn't even know her married name. She could have been married more than once. Thirty years is a long time.

If Fulger's parents were dead, then the Housing Benefits people would have an address for him. I had a lot of dealings with the Benefits Office with my own flats so perhaps I could find out something there. But the office didn't open on a Sunday.

The rest of the day dragged. I watched the afternoon match on Sky but my mind was on the case. In the evening, I half listened to Joe Butler's country music show on Radio City. I turned in at ten. I wanted a good night's sleep for an early start.

I was outside the Housing Benefit office first thing Monday morning and at the front of the queue in the rush to the cubicles. The girl behind the desk recognised me and groaned. 'Not more trouble with your tenants, Mr Ace?'

We'd had a protracted altercation a few weeks ago over

a nurse who'd lived in one of my flats. She'd been claiming benefit, ostensibly unemployed, but really working for cash in three different nursing homes. The council found out and reclaimed the benefit. Unfortunately, the benefit had been paid to me so I had to repay it, but the nurse had left the month before and I'd no chance of finding her to recover the money. I lost the appeal after much arguing with the department.

'It's somebody called Fulger,' I said. 'Jed Fulger, short for Gerald.'

'What address?'

'He's applied for a flat in Percy Street. I want to check he's entitled to benefit before I take him on.'

'What's his current address?'

'He did tell me but I've forgotten. I think it's somewhere in Liverpool 17 or Liverpool 8.' They were the premier letting areas.

She tapped out a few keys on her computer and waited for the screen to come up with the information. In the next cubicle I heard raised voices. Some claimant was giving a girl a hard time. No wonder there were screens to protect the clerks from the public.

My girl looked up from her VDU. 'Everything seems to be in order,' she said.

'That's a relief, after the last trouble,' I smiled. 'Where's he living at the moment?'

'I'm sorry. We're not allowed to give out information.'

'He'll be leaving anyway when he comes to me, won't he? So it's not as though it's a secret.'

'I know but we can't divulge people's addresses without their permission.'

'It's just that I promised to take his tenancy agreement round and if I don't know where he lives . . .'

She shook her head firmly. In the films, Mel Gibson would have slipped her a £20 note and the information would have been his but I knew better than to try that.

It looked as though I was beaten and I was standing up

to leave when I got a lucky break. The guy in the interview cubicle next door, distressed about being refused his free state handout, tried to smash the security screen and attack the clerk. My girl jumped up and ran across to help her and press the panic button.

As she did so, she caught her arm against her monitor, which swivelled round, allowing me to read the screen. And there it was, Jed Fulger's address. The tenancy had started back in July. When she returned, as security men ran in to restore order, I quietly told her I understood her position and quickly left the building.

Fulger was supposedly living on Linnet Lane, Liverpool 17, coincidentally off South Albert Road. I'd actually driven past it on the night we visited the Stripes Club but I figured it was more likely to be an accommodation address, somewhere to have his housing benefit sent to, than his actual home.

I drove up and parked right outside. It was a double-fronted house, set back from the road, surrounded by trees and with several old cars flattening what would once have been a front lawn. The gable end needed pointing, there were a couple of fallen slates in the drive and the front door was wide open.

I counted ten bell pushes as I stepped into the hallway, which meant the house was probably divided into bedsits rather than flats. I knocked on the first door I came to, which was padlocked. Nobody answered so I walked down an unlit corridor to the back of the house and knocked on another door which had Flat Two scrawled on it in white paint. Still no answer. A third door was ajar and I pushed it open but it was a lavatory with a cracked plastic seat, stained bowl and a toilet-roll holder bereft of paper.

I walked up the wide staircase, aware of a musty odour of damp plaster mixed with the stench of tom cats. A bathroom led off the mezzanine floor and then, on the first floor proper, I was faced with four more doors. I knocked on the first one and at last someone answered.

'I'm looking for a Mr Fulger.'

'Never heard of him, mate.' He was about twenty, undernourished and unshaven. He wore a baseball cap back to front and was disinclined to continue the conversation. My foot stopped the door closing in my face.

'What the fuck . . .?'

'He's about fifty, fat, with tattoos on the back of his hands.'

'I said, pal, I've never heard of him. I don't know no fucker what lives here and I don't friggin' care, get it?' He tried, in vain, to shut the door.

'Who's your landlord?' I asked politely.

'What?'

'The landlord. Who do you pay your rent to?'

'He don't live here.'

'I didn't ask that, I said who is he?'

He wiped his mouth with the back of his hand. 'Why do you want to know?'

'I want to save you from getting hurt,' I said, 'and if you tell me his name, you won't.' I was a good six inches taller than him.

There was a second when he might have lunged at me but he thought better of it. 'Vincent Hall,' he said reluctantly. 'Now will you fuck off?'

I knew Vinny Hall, one of the city's great slum landlords. He lived in a large house off Ullett Road that he reputedly shared with at least three women at any one time.

I decided to pay him a visit.

Chapter Twenty-Five

On my way out, I sorted through a pile of letters, leaflets, junk mail and free newspapers scattered round the doorway. There was nothing addressed to Jed Fulger and Housing Benefit cheques were usually delivered on a Monday. The odds were, the payments were being sent direct to Vinny Hall.

Our paths have crossed over the years but our relationship has never developed beyond the superficial. I don't care for his business methods and we've never become friends. His flats are of a poor standard, he works various scams with council money and sleeps with many of his female tenants who can't afford his extortionate rents and reluctantly agree to pay in kind. Or maybe not so reluctantly, I don't know, but that's the sort of thing that gets landlords a bad name.

On the other hand, he was quite likeable to talk to and I wasn't averse to having a drink with him at the Landlord's Dinner. Like Tommy McKale, he was good company, an amusing raconteur and he'd never done me any harm.

I had a rough idea what particular fiddle he was working here. Someone, in this case Fulger, comes along wanting an address for the Housing Benefit people. Vinny lets him flat 11 for £60 a week. But in real life, there is no flat 11. The Housing send the money to Vinny every week and he splits it with Fulger, who is shacking up with a mate elsewhere. Who was his mate?

Vinny's house was a similar size to those in Linnet Lane, South Albert Road and most of the houses round

Sefton Park – grand Victorian mansions built originally for the wealthy shipowners at the turn of the century. Vinny occupied the whole of the ground floor and rented out the top rooms.

He looked surprised to see me. I'd never been there before but I was at the auction when he bought the place and it was common knowledge that he'd turned it into his personal residence and knocking shop.

'Come in, Johnny. Let me get you a beer.'

I didn't refuse. He led me into the large front room. A young girl in a dressing gown was on the couch reading a magazine.

'Go and get dressed, doll, I'll be up later,' he told her. 'One of the tenants,' he explained to me when she'd gone. 'Lives upstairs.'

'How many live down here with you?'

'Oh, it varies.' He beamed broadly. 'Usually I have a couple of lodgers. Some of these young girls leaving home for the first time get very lonely in their empty bedsits. Someone has to console them.'

Trust Vinny to turn serial seduction into a social service.

There was a tiny built-in kitchen in the corner of the room and he fetched a couple of bottles of the beer from the fridge. He opened them and handed one to me. Glasses, it seemed, were not on the menu.

'I need your help, Vinny,' I said, taking a slurp from the bottle.

'Oh yeah?'

'Fellow called Jed Fulger.'

'You're a bit late, old son, the Old Bill were round half an hour ago.'

I should have realised this. The police would be able to get all the information they wanted from the Housing Benefit people so it would be a simple matter for them to make straight for the landlord.

'What did you tell them?'

'Left a few days ago. No idea where he went, just disappeared. Happens all the time. You'd be amazed at how many people, for instance, send away for mail order gear to be delivered to places they no longer live at. They come back one night to collect it and when the bills come in they're long gone.'

I was amazed that so many companies fell for it but they did. I know because I'd seen the stuff in the hallways of my own places.

'But you do know, don't you, Vinny?'

'What are you saying, Johnny?' he said in tones of mock astonishment. 'That I would give false information to our boys in blue?' He liked his public persona as a bit of a scoundrel.

'I'm not the police, though, and I'm looking for Mr Fulger myself.'

'Owes you money, does he?'

'Vinny, you know why everybody wants Fulger, and if you didn't before, the police will have told you. I also know that, if you admit to knowing him, your little scam with the Benefits Office will be exposed and you'll be in deep shit.'

He said nothing.

'Now I couldn't give a fuck if you're robbing the council blind. If they're so stupid as to give the money away, that's their problem. But this is my friend's kid we're talking about. She's lost a finger already. How would her leg chopped off go along with your conscience?'

'Hang on a minute . . .'

'If you don't tell me, then you spending a few months in the slammer won't lose me too much sleep.'

He thought for a minute, then: 'How do I know you won't go to the police anyway, as soon as I tell you?'

'Because I want this bastard for myself.'

The tension went from him and he smiled. 'Ah, the Great Avenger, eh? So we're all the same under the skin for all your pious talk.'

I didn't like that but I couldn't deny it. I did want revenge on Jed Fulger, for Matt Scrufford, for Jenny Ogden, for Sammi Relphs and for me.

'I never said I was pious. I've got a personal interest in this thing, that's all.'

'Of course, you're supposing I know where Fulger is. What if he just comes round every so often for his cut?'

'I'd have to wait for him.'

'I might not know when he's coming.'

'You'd be getting yourself a new tenant till he showed up.' I was getting tired of the games. 'Look, Vinny, sooner or later, the police are going to be back. You're their only lead and they're not going to believe that shit you gave them. They'll take you down the station and they'll ask you how many of the gas appliances in your flats have safety certificates and how many of your beds are fireproof and did you know under the new Housing Act it's a criminal offence—'

'OK, OK. You win. So, what's it worth?'

'What!'

'I'm a grand overdue on my council taxes. It would be nice to get those bastards off my back.'

I was tempted to flatten him against his cocktail cabinet. 'I don't think you heard me right, Vinny. It's a little girl's life we're talking about.'

'OK. Worth a try, eh?' He smiled. 'No offence, Johnny. Yeah, I know where Fulger is. He's shacking up with a bird in Southport.'

'Not June Tarbuck?'

'I don't know who she is. And I don't have an address, just a phone number. I ring him and arrange to meet him with his cash.'

'Where do you meet him?'

'Usually at The Grapes in Formby.'

'I wonder why he gave you his number? Bit risky for him. He could have just rung you from a call box when he needed the cash.'

'To warn him if anything went wrong. Like now, for instance. Remember, it's a two-way deal. He could shop me as easily as I could shop him.'

'But you won't be ringing him, will you?' Then an idea struck me. 'Yes, why don't you ring him? Tell him the police have been round, the cover's blown and you've got the last lot of cash ready for him. You haven't paid him lately, have you?'

'No, it's been nearly a month. I owe him about £280.' Fulger had obviously been too busy stalking The Cruzads to collect his money but £280 would be a lot for someone in hiding or on the run and he'd not want to lose it.

I gave Vinny his instructions. 'Arrange to meet him tonight in The Grapes at eight. Turn up there with the cash. Make sure the law aren't following you. I'll be around. Once you've handed over the money, leave the rest to me.'

'I'm not signing this bloke's death warrant, am I, Johnny?'

'Would it bother you, Vinny?'

He drained the last of his lager. 'Not really. But it's a shame to let him keep that money. You couldn't get it back for me, could you, when you've finished with him? I mean, it won't be any use to him, will it?'

I smiled. 'Christ, Arthur Daley couldn't hold a candle to you. Yeah, fair enough, it's a deal.'

He checked a number in his wallet and went over to the phone. I watched while he dialled and memorised Fulger's number for future use. I'm good at remembering numbers. This one puzzled me, though, because it wasn't a Southport number but a Halsall one. Fulger must be living in one of the villages towards Ormskirk where it's all agricultural land and farms.

'Is that Mr Fulger? Vinny Hall here. Look, I'm afraid your tenancy has had to be terminated, Mr Fulger. If I can meet you this evening, I have £280 for you from our agreement and I'll explain the rest when I see you.'

He listened to Fulger's reply, then: 'Yes, they were but, of course, our business is confidential. I told them you'd left the premises last week without a forwarding address.' Another pause. 'Eight, yes. In the main bar.'

He replaced the phone and turned to me. 'He asked me if the police had been. Must have been expecting it.'

'He'd have seen yesterday's papers. He'll want to disappear as fast as possible.'

'But what about the kid?'

'That's what worries me, Vinny. He won't want to drag her along if he's on the run.'

'Won't he want her as a hostage?'

Who could tell? Fulger's motive seemed to be purely revenge. He'd not asked for a ransom so he didn't want money. As far as I could figure it, his only reason to stay free would be to finish his business with Frankie's daughter and maybe myself. How could anyone predict the mind of an obvious psycho anyway?'

'We'll have to play it by ear, Vinny. Once you've fingered him for me, you can disappear.'

'And you'll get my cash back?' he said anxiously.

'If everything goes to plan, I'll be round with it tomorrow.' He seemed satisfied with that. I didn't like to think of what might happen if everything didn't go to plan but Vinny's cash didn't even enter the equation.

My next stop was at Tommy McKale's gym, only a few blocks away.

'Twice in a week,' he greeted me. 'You must be a closet bodybuilder.' He escorted me up to his office, stopping to order two bottles of mineral water at the bar. 'Alcohol at lunchtime poisons your blood stream,' he said. 'Besides, like I told you on Thursday, there's a bigger mark-up on the mineral water.'

'I've found him,' I said.

The banter stopped. 'Good man. I thought you'd be round. I saw the paper this morning.'

He handed me today's *Daily Post*, which I'd not had

time to buy. The front page headline said ’Wanted – This Man’ with a description of Fulger and a picture that must have been taken at Ashworth Hospital, as Fulger was well in to his forties. He didn’t look overly crazy but he did look mean.

I glanced through the article and gleaned most of the salient points: ‘Released from hospital to pursue a crusade of hate . . . this man is dangerous . . . police advice not to approach him . . . little girl’s life in grave danger.’

I didn’t care for the ‘hospital’ bit. Made him sound like an invalid instead of a killer.

A girl brought the drinks in and Tommy handed me mine. ‘Do the police know you’ve found him?’

‘Not yet but I’d guess they’re not far behind.’

‘Where is he?’

‘I’m not sure exactly but I’d guess he’s holed out on a farm somewhere out at Halsall. He’d be able to hide the girl in the farm buildings and they wouldn’t be overlooked out in the sticks.’

‘And nobody would hear any screaming either.’

‘Precisely. Anyway, he’s fixed up a meeting tonight in The Grapes in Freshfield at eight o’clock with Vinny Hall, the landlord. Do you know him?’

Tommy chuckled. ‘I know Vinny. He’s got a load of property round Sefton Park, half of them brothels.’

‘I’m going to be in the bar quietly having a drink then, when they leave, follow Fulger home.’

‘And you’d like a bit of company in case he turns a bit unpleasant?’

‘Bit unpleasant isn’t the word,’ and I recounted some of Fulger’s exploits in the sixties.

‘You’ve already told me what he did to your mate’s son, Johnny. That’s enough for me. Don’t worry, we know how to handle people like that. We’ll go tooled up. Listen, won’t he recognise you in the pub?’

I thought for a minute. ‘You’re right. We think he’s

been stalking all of us in the group. I never thought of that.'

'So what you do is wait outside in the car. I know Vinny. I'll clock the guy he's talking too and have the boys waiting with the wheels outside. When you see us move off, you follow. We'll be in the Jag, TMK1, you know it, don't you?'

I said I did.

'Is there anyone else living with him?'

'Vinny reckons he's shacking up with a bird.'

'That's OK then. She won't be a problem.'

'We want the little girl alive, Tommy. I don't want to risk her getting hurt any more. And how will you get in the house?'

He patted my arm. 'Johnny, don't worry. These boys will get in through the roof if necessary, a slate at a time. Drink up, I need to get things moving.'

'I'd had no lunch but I wasn't hungry. I felt too nervous. It wasn't too late to ring the police but I still wanted to get Fulger on his own. I felt I had a score to settle.

One of the worst motives for getting involved in anything like this.

I drove back to the flat. I didn't want to ring Maria or Hilary, possibly so's not to worry them but mainly because I didn't want to put them in a position where they might feel they should inform the law.

Jim Burroughs was the last person I wanted to see at the moment and I left the answerphone on in case he rang me. I just hoped he didn't come to the radio station looking for me.

I took out an extra couple of sweaters and wore a pair of jogging pants beneath my jeans. For some reason, I thought it might give me added protection if Fulger came after me with a knife.

I took out a vegetable casserole I had in the freezer and heated it up. I might not have been too hungry still but I needed some nourishment. It could turn out to be a long night.

I found it hard work doing the show. For a start, it was hot in the studio with the two pairs of pants, then I had Ken coming in reminding me about playing cheerful records.

'We've had a couple of letters about that awful one you played the other night, that talking one, and someone who wanted to know where they could buy it.' He shook his head as if this confirmed that only sad people listened to my show.

He needn't have worried. I was working myself into a belligerent mood and this was reflected in the music. It was an hour of pure aggression: Meat Loaf, Bryan Adams, Ozzy Osbourne, Elvis's 'Hound Dog'.

Come five past seven, I was out of the station and in the car park before anyone could reach me. I remembered the night I'd opened the first Jiffy bag, with the fingernails, and it spurred me on as I set off towards Freshfield.

This was it. Only an hour to go and I'd have him at last. Only would I be too late to save little Sammi?

I wanted to let Frankie know what I was doing but didn't dare risk it. He might want to come along, which could jeopardise things, or he might decide to bring in the police. He'd be better at home.

If I'd known how it was going to turn out, I might have stayed in myself and watched *Coronation Street* instead.

Chapter Twenty-Six

I parked across the road from The Grapes, behind some other cars outside a late night Spar, where it wouldn't easily be seen. There were three entrances to the pub and I had two of them covered from my position. The third at the opposite side led to the car park.

It was still only seven thirty. At seven forty-five, Tommy McKale's Jag drew up and parked at the side of the pub opposite the Spar. I went over to him.

'There's another entrance on the other side, by the car park.'

'Don't worry, we'll sort it. Just wait for us to make a move then follow us. When we get to Fulger's place, I want you to keep well back and stay put in your car until I come and fetch you. You understand?'

I wasn't going to argue. I thought of Archie Bushell again. I was dealing with professionals here. The four men with him in the Jag looked the sort who'd take great pleasure in cutting off somebody's feet.

I went back to the car and Tommy walked into the pub with one of his men. I'd seen no sign of Vinny Hall. I put on some music and waited.

Eight o'clock came and went. A steady stream of shoppers walked past, going to the Spar and the off-licence further down.

I thought of the weekend when I'd sat over in The Grapes with Maria, on our way to Kaye and Alex's. They'd be at home now, just down the road, like everything was normal. Only I knew that tonight it wasn't.

I wondered where Maria was. And Hilary. I'd promised to ring her.

I looked up at what had once been Formby Ice Rink where I'd played with The Cruzads thirty years ago. Had Froggie and the Hoppers ever played here? That was where all this had begun, in the past, but now the past seemed to be merging with the present.

Jed Fulger had started this business. Now I was here to finish it.

The door of the pub opened and Tommy McKale came out. He ran to the Jag, jumped behind the wheel and pulled away. I started the engine and followed.

He stopped at the corner and his companion came from the car park and jumped in. The car started moving again.

Fulger must have left via the car park entrance and Tommy's man was tagging the car. I gently accelerated. My mobile phone rang. 'We're on track,' said Tommy's voice. 'He's on his own in that white Fiat Tipo three cars up. Stay behind me.'

'Where's Vinny?'

'Chatting up three little mysteries back in the boozer.'

Our convoy of cars turned right at the roundabout as if going back to Liverpool but took a left at the lights out into the country towards Halsall.

By now, the traffic had thinned out and only one car separated Tommy's Jag and the Tipo. I lagged behind. We were only doing forty.

After about three miles, Fulger's car turned off towards Haskayne. It was pitch black, no street lighting and few houses. We were surrounded by fields and footpaths. The Tipo suddenly lurched down one of the paths towards a lone farmhouse half a mile ahead.

Tommy stopped the Jag on the main road and came over as I pulled up behind him.

'We're going in,' he said. 'Stay there. I'll come for you.'

The five men started walking up the path towards the farmhouse. They all wore black jeans and sweaters and four of them had balaclavas on their heads.

I waited. I gave them ten minutes to reach the house and five minutes to overcome Fulger. The ten minutes passed. Nothing. Another five minutes. Nothing. And then, the sound of gunfire echoed through the night, followed by a horrendous scream.

I wasn't waiting any longer. I started the engine and roared down the track to the farmhouse, pulling up with a screech of tyres by the front door. I jumped out and ran to the door. It was locked. I stood back and kicked with the bottom of my heel, crashing it open.

In the hallway, one of McKale's men lay on the floor clutching his leg, which was bleeding profusely from a gunshot wound. He pointed to a door. 'Through the back.'

It was an old tongue-and-groove door. I pushed it open to reveal a large old-fashioned kitchen with a tiled floor and large slopstone with a water pump over it.

Sitting in a wooden rocking chair was a grey-haired little woman, moaning softly to herself. Another of McKale's men was crumpled against the wall, unconscious. A back door was open, leading out to the yard. I ran through it towards an outbuilding at the edge of a field.

As I came close, another of Tommy McKale's men emerged carrying what looked like a bundle of blankets in his arms.

'It's the kid,' he said thickly.

'Is she alive?'

'I'm not sure.'

'Oh Christ.' I turned back and went with him into the house. 'What's happened to Tommy?'

'Tommy and Denis have gone after your man.' He put the child down and I unwrapped the blanket from around her. Her face was deathly cold but I could feel a faint pulse.

'Where's the phone?' I barked at the woman who was still rocking in her chair.

She didn't answer but shook her head from side to side.

I ran outside to fetch my mobile from the car and dialled for an ambulance. 'Where the fuck are we?' I said.

'Somewhere near Haskayne,' said Tommy's man, 'but God knows what this place is called.'

There were some letters on the kitchen table. I checked the address. 'We're at Barbary Farm,' I told the operator, explaining that I had a sick, unconscious child here. 'And hurry, will you? It could be life or death.'

Then I rang Frankie. 'I've got Sammi,' I said. 'Don't worry, Frankie, she's going to be OK.' I cut short his babbling questions and told him we were out in the country somewhere near Halsall and that I'd sent for an ambulance. I hoped to God I was right about his daughter. She still hadn't moved. Maybe she was doped.

'Get down to the hospital at Southport, that's where they'll take her. I'll meet you there later if I can get away.'

I unwrapped the blanket again and took out Sammi's hand. There was a bloodstained stump where her little finger had been and angry bruises on her arms and legs. I was sickened.

'Look after her, will you?' I said to Tommy's man. 'I'm going to find Tommy and Denis.'

I placed the child gently on an old leather sofa and went out into the back. The McKale brothers were just coming back across the yard. Tommy was carrying an axe and wiping his hands on a cloth reddened with recent blood.

He grimaced when he saw me. 'Johnny, boy, was he trouble? The man is crazy.'

'Are you OK?'

'We're fine,' he said, 'aren't we, Denis?' His brother nodded. 'It's been a very satisfying night. You've seen the kid?'

'Yes. She's still breathing, just. I've phoned for an ambulance. Two of your men are hurt.'

'They'll live,' said Denis, as if shooting was an everyday hazard in his life.

'What about Fulger. Is he . . .?'

'He's in there.' Tommy McKale pointed to the outhouse. 'We've got him ready for you, Johnny.' He handed me the axe. 'He's all yours now,' and they disappeared into the kitchen.

Slowly I walked to the outhouse. What was I going to find?

I pulled the heavy oak door open and nearly fainted. Facing me at the opposite end of the building was Jed Fulger.

He was hanging from the wooden beam above a window by his outstretched hands where he had been nailed to the wood through his palms. Some of the small bones in his hand had been splintered and blood was still dripping from the wounds. Similar nails secured his legs to the bottom of the sill although they went through his jeans not his flesh.

He looked older than fifty. His hair was plastered to his skull with sweat and blood, his stomach protruded over the top of his jeans and his shirt was ripped along both arms.

He'd received some brutal blows to the face because several teeth were missing, his mouth was swollen, one eye was closed and his nose was broken. He was still conscious and half crying, half choking with pain but he managed a snarl as I approached him.

'You bastard!' he spat at me.

I moved closer to him. 'You killed my friend's son

who was a decent lad who'd done you no harm. You've mutilated a helpless little girl and would have killed another if she hadn't escaped.'

I couldn't believe it. He sneered. There was no show of remorse or guilt. He just sneered. I held the axe firmly.

'If there was any justice, you'd hang for this but there is no justice in this country any more.' I moved closer. 'How soon will it be before you're let out to kill again? Well, I'm going to make sure you don't.'

I lifted the axe. Who knows if I would have killed him had he not spoken. I don't, and I've thought about it a lot since. But he did speak and I didn't kill him.

'I loved her,' he said quietly. 'I loved her.'

I put the axe down. 'You loved who?'

'June. I loved her.'

'June Tarbuck?'

'She was the only girlfriend I ever had. Ever. She's the only girl I ever slept with.' His voice was rough with emotion and his injuries made his speech difficult. I was horrified to see tears forming in his eyes.

'He raped her, you know?'

'Who? Oggi?'

'No. Scrufford. In that van. She told me. She wouldn't lie to me. She told me she went with Ogden in the Peppermint Lounge. I could forgive her for that. I couldn't forgive him. She was drunk, she was with her mates. Fair game for you all, wasn't she?'

'Hang on, Frankie and I never touched her.'

'Does it matter? You didn't do much to stop it. Too busy enjoying your own little shags, weren't you?'

The word seemed obscene in the circumstances.

'But June was sober by the time Scrufford got her in that van. She told him she didn't want to go with him but he was having none of it.'

'Wait a minute. Mally didn't rape her. He told us she practically raped him. She let him drop everyone else off first. If she was frightened, she could have got out with any of us.'

'And how was she to know she'd be better off with any of you?'

I couldn't think of a reason.

'Just because she goes home with a bloke on his own doesn't give him the right to fuck her if she doesn't want it.'

'But it wasn't like that. Mally told us.'

'And do you always believe him? Is he the sort of person who always speaks the truth? Would you trust him?'

I thought of Sarah. And Maureen. And what Marilyn had said. And I knew Jed Fulger was right. I could never one hundred per cent trust Mally Scrufford's word.

He started crying properly now. 'When he raped her, he made her pregnant. We were going to get married and next thing, she was expecting his baby.'

'It could have been Oggi's?'

He gave a scornful laugh. 'Ogden came before he'd put it in. She told me. He'd never had a woman before. But Scrufford had. Twice he came inside my fiancée, twice, and put his fucking child inside her.' Tears were streaming down his face.

'She had an abortion but it went wrong. After that she could never have children. We could never have children. Malcolm Scrufford had a son but I could never have a son of my own and I wanted to make him suffer for it.'

I stood, transfixed by the horror of what he was telling me. I could never condone what he had done but, for the first time, I felt terribly sorry for Jed Fulger and the torment he had gone through.

'I was in this fight and I got put away for life. Every night I sat in that place of purgatory thinking of that bastard. And my June, all on her own, and one by one her friends getting married and having families. Oh yes, she stayed faithful to me, did June. Visited me at that place, never missed a week, all these years.'

I thought of the grey-haired woman in the kitchen. June Tarbuck.

I found my voice. 'And then they let you out and you looked for your revenge?'

'Do you blame me? Scrufford with kids everywhere and he couldn't give a shit about them and my June meant fuck all to him.' His voice rose to a scream. 'He never even cared.'

I spoke quietly. 'So you decided to take his children away?'

'I did. It was easy. The lad was outside the station. I asked him to give me a push with the car. It was in a side street nearby. It didn't take much to knock him senseless and get him here.'

'Why cut his ears off?'

'To make Scrufford suffer. Let him know what it feels like to hurt.'

'What about Oggi's daughter, the one whose hair you cut off?'

His expression darkened. 'She got away.'

'You didn't bring her here, did you?' I remembered Jenny said she'd been taken to a shop. If she'd been brought to this farm she'd probably be dead now.

'I found this empty shop. Easy enough to break in, all the others were boarded up. I was going to do it quick. I cut her hair off and went to post it. When I came back, she'd gone.'

'I can see how you feel you've got a grudge against Oggi and Mally, but why send me the nails and the hair? I never went with June and neither did Frankie, yet you cut off his little girl's finger.'

'You were all in it, weren't you? Run with the hares . . .'

'Why didn't you kill her?'

He thought for a moment. 'She looked so like June when she was little. So sweet. Even when I axed her she just looked at me and it was like it was June when she was ten. I couldn't harm her again. We'd been sweethearts since primary school, June and I. Neither of us had had anyone else, until that night. Scrufford ruined everything that night, ruined our lives for ever. Shouldn't he be punished for that?'

He was raving again. I felt drained. What a terrible tragedy. How did the saying go, 'as ye sow, so shall ye reap'?

'What are you going to do with me?'

I put the axe down. 'I'm sorry for what happened that night,' I said softly. 'I wish you no harm. You'll probably go back to the hospital.'

I turned away and walked slowly back to the house. Tommy and Denis were standing in the kitchen. June Tarbuck was still in her chair.

'Is he . . .?' Tommy inclined his head to the out-house.

'No. I decided the police can take him away.'

Tommy said nothing.

'How's Sammi?'

'Michael's with her. I think she's doped but she's still breathing.'

June Tarbuck rose to her feet and started to walk to the back door. She still hadn't spoken. Denis made to stop her but I held out my arm. 'Let her go. It might be their last chance to be together.' I tried to imagine her as the bright, bouffant-haired teenager in the miniskirt at the Peppermint Lounge but the grey-haired lady with the sloping shoulders, pink cardigan and pleated brown skirt seemed like another person.

She went out of the door. 'The ambulance is a long time,' said Tommy.

'Public sector cuts,' I said. 'Blame the Labour council.'

Suddenly, two shots rang out. We looked at one another then ran to the outbuilding but we knew what we'd find when we got there.

Chapter Twenty-Seven

The first shot had blasted most of Jed Fulger's chest away. His corpse hung by the nails in his hands. Lying on the floor was June Tarbuck. She'd put the barrel of the gun in her mouth before pulling the trigger so most of her head and brains were splattered against the stone wall behind her.

I turned away and vomited. Tommy McKale walked towards Fulger's body. 'It's a tidy end,' he said. He reached behind and extracted something from the back pocket of Fulger's jeans.

'Mustn't forget Vinny's money,' he laughed, and handed it to me.

'I'm not sure we should,' I said.

'Life is for the living,' said Tommy McKale. 'He's no use for it and, if you don't have it, you can bet it won't still be there when they bury him.'

One by one, the three of us returned to the kitchen. As we reached the door, we heard the ambulance siren.

'I think we'll be off,' said Tommy. 'I've always had a strange aversion to being in the same room as the law. Except, of course, at the Masonic dinners.'

I followed them to the door. 'I'll take the child.' I took Sammi from Michael and they left by the back door as the ambulance men rang the front bell. I saw the Jag disappear down the track as the paramedics came in.

'You'd better radio the police,' I said. 'This is the child that was kidnapped. I think they might want to be informed.'

I went back into the house and waited.

I didn't think Jim Burroughs was going to be too pleased.

By the time the police arrived it was gone eleven o'clock. Shortly afterwards, teams of doctors, forensics, reporters, cameramen, and TV people descended on Barbary Farm.

Floodlights were rigged up, stretchers, more ambulances and more police arrived, together with curious neighbours from distant farms.

Jim Burroughs, along with Sergeant Payton, guided me into a front room, shut the door firmly and said, 'Talk.'

We all sat down. I told him the gist of it, that I'd been having a drink in The Grapes when I spotted Fulger. I'd followed him in the car to the farm. Some men were waiting for him at the farm and beat him up. When they'd gone, I ventured inside, found the child in a corner and rang for the ambulance. Then I went outside and found Fulger nailed to the wall of the outbuilding. I returned to the house to find some pliers to release him when I heard gunshots and found the two bodies.'

'That sounds like a complete load of crap to me,' said Payton.

'And to me,' echoed Jim Burroughs.

I tended to agree but it had been the best I could think of in the short time available.

He stood up and cleared his throat. 'By the way, you might be interested to know that our boys raided a place called The Stripes Club last night. By all accounts, there was some very heavy stuff going on down there, whips and chains, that sort of thing.' He looked at me warily. 'You don't go in for all that business, do you?'

'You're joking, aren't you?'

He continued. 'You know, it appears they take videos of some of the punters . . .'

'Really?'

'And on one of them, who should have the starring

role but our old friend Colin Bennison . . .' I waited. 'Whipping the ass off some young kid. Not that you'd know anything about that, of course.'

'Shocking,' I said. 'What would his old mother have said if that ever got out?'

'There's more. On another video, he's in a pair of stocks being tortured by men dressed as pirates.'

'He always did like "Gilbert and Sullivan"—'

Sergeant Payton looked as though he'd like the opportunity to get me into the stocks himself.

'We confiscated a pile of cash books, too,' continued Jim. 'Quite a lucrative little set-up they had going there. The punters pay a fortune to get battered then pay again to stop people knowing they get battered.'

'Blackmail you mean?'

'Precisely.'

'So there's your motive for Bennison's suicide, then. After I'd talked to him at the theatre, he realised his exam fiddling days were numbered and he couldn't afford to pay the blackmailers so he topped himself rather than face the wrath of those monkeys at the Stripes Club.'

Jim Burroughs stroked his chin thoughtfully. 'Funny thing; on one video there was a couple the spitting image of you and Hilary.'

'I've got one of those faces that people think they know. I'm often mistaken for Pierce Brosnan.'

'And I'm often mistaken for Donald bloody Duck. Come off it, Johnny. I know you were there. And another thing, Matt Scrufford was also there, with Bennison. What was going on?'

I stood up myself. 'Jim, you've just solved a high profile crime for which you'll undoubtedly receive a commendation. Fulger's dead, Scrufford's dead and Bennison's dead. It's all tied up, neat and sweet. Worry about the details later. Right now, I'm tired and I want to go home.'

'I want you at the station at ten in the morning, to make a proper statement.'

'Make it two o'clock,' I said. 'I need a bit of sleep.'

I took a last look around the farmhouse and climbed into the car. It took me twenty minutes to negotiate a path through the mass of parked vehicles and milling people on the narrow track but I eventually got through and drove home.

At least I knew there'd be no more petrol bombs waiting for me.

I slept through to midday. It was like all the strains of the past two weeks had taken their toll and only a deep sleep could revitalise me.

When I woke, I took a long bath, full of Hilary's oils. I'd had no time to ring Hilary and now she'd probably be at work. Nurses, unlike librarians, couldn't be disturbed. I'd call her later and take her out somewhere on Saturday night.

I put on a suit and tie ready for my visit to the police station but first I walked down to The Diner for a late breakfast and a look at the paper.

I paid for a bacon sandwich and pot of tea and took a seat amonst the lunching office workers.

Sammi Relphs' safe release, naturally, was headlines in the *Post* with a full account of the tragic happenings in the farmhouse. Nothing had yet come out about The Cruzads and the revenge motive and I wasn't sure how much ever would now.

Jed Fulger would always be seen as a monster to the world at large but I knew a human side to the man. It hadn't made me lose any sleep over his death.

I finished my meal and drove to the police station for my meeting with Jim Burroughs. Kevin Payton wasn't with him.

'It's pretty certain she killed Fulger then shot herself,' he said. 'They were married, you know. Got married soon after he was put away.'

'No kids?' I asked innocently and he glared.

'If it wasn't for the fact that we want this thing tied up quickly, I'd have you for . . .' He stopped whilst he considered what he could charge me with. 'As it is, the official line is that there's no need to dig any more. We need all our resources for unsolved crimes.' He looked hard at me. 'On the other hand, there's a few things I'd personally like to know.'

'Come down the Masquerade on Saturday, Jim. I'll buy you a drink and we'll have a little chat.'

'When I got back home, I went for a walk round the Pier Head. I ended up in St Nicholas's Churchyard, overlooking the river. It was quiet and peaceful. Just the odd pigeon or two.

In a couple of hours I had the show to do. The evening was free. I knew I ought to ring Maria. And I ought to go and see Frankie, Mally and Oggi and tell them exactly what had happened last night at Barbary Farm. I owed them that. And Maureen, too. In fact, especially Maureen. Matt was her son.

And then the past could go back to where it belonged. To the past. I might keep in touch from time to time with Oggi, Frankie and Mally but I certainly couldn't see The Cruzads getting back together again.

Vinny Hall would be wanting his money but I reckoned he could sweat awhile. I'd be bound to see him in town one day.

I'd see the McKales on Saturday night. As far as I knew, their names hadn't come up at all, but I couldn't have done it without them. I owed them a favour.

There's a concert on at the Phil on Friday that I knew Maria would like to go to; the Royal Liverpool Philharmonic doing Vivaldi and some other stuff.

And on Saturday it's the Derby match at Anfield. I've managed to get a ticket and I'm quite hopeful for the Blues to at least force a draw.

I'd enjoyed being a detective, if you could call it that. And I guess you could, as I'd found the missing girl and the killer before the police had. I'd solved the Matt Scrufford Case for them. Maybe I should set up as a private eye. That would be enough to send Jim Burroughs into early retirement!

I stood up and checked my watch. So much to do but time enough for it all later. Right now, I fancied a sail on the river. I strolled back down to the landing stage in time to board the ferry across to Woodside. It was the *Mountwood* again. I always seem to get the *Mountwood.*

As the boat left the quayside, I stood on the top deck watching the Liver Building and the cathedrals fade in the distance. A herring gull flew over but I had no bread and it swirled away into the spray.

I closed my eyes and for a minute I was back on the *Royal Iris* again, banging the drums behind The Cruzads, as the girls in miniskirts and beehive hairdos jived to 'Twist and Shout' and the boat swayed on the choppy waves on its way up the Mersey.

Who'd want all that again?

A Coffin for Two

Quintin Jardine

[illegible]

[illegible]

[illegible]

A Coffin for Two

Quintin Jardine

After cracking their first case together as a private investigation team, Oz Blackstone and Primavera Philips find themselves simultaneously in love and in the money. And where better to lie back and contemplate life than the picturesque village of St Marti, on the rugged Costa Brava.

But is their new home quite so idyllic as it looks? Some very dark secrets begin to emerge as the inhabitants draw them into the intrigue which bubbles away beneath the surface, until suddenly, faced with a mysterious skeleton and an unauthenticated Dali masterpiece, Prim and Oz stumble across one of the century's most amazing stories . . .

'Entertaining . . . keeps you intrigued'
Carlisle News & Star

0 7472 5575 X

HEADLINE

The Jump

Martina Cole

Donna Brunos worships her husband and is devastated when he is jailed for eighteen years on a charge of armed robbery. Georgio swears he's been set up and – terrified he won't survive the rigours of Parkhurst – persuades Donna to help him escape.

Implementing the daring plan takes Donna into a twilight world she never believed existed – a world of brutal sex and casual violence. And the more she sees of the sordid underbelly of Georgio's business dealings, the more she comes to suspect that her beloved husband is not the innocent he claims to be . . .

'A big powerful read with a climax that will knock your socks off' *Today*

'Gritty realism . . . Martina Cole's star is in the ascendant' *Sunday Express*

'A major new talent' *Best*

'Gritty, atmospheric stuff!' *Today*

'You won't be able to put this one down!' *Company*

0 7472 4821 4

HEADLINE